Joker Poker

Joker Poker

Richard Helms

Writer's Showcase

San Jose New York Lincoln Shanghai

Joker Poker

Published by Writer's Showcase,
an imprint of iUniverse.com, Inc.

For information address:
iUniverse.com, Inc.
620 North 48th Street
Suite 201
Lincoln, NE 68504-3467
www.iuniverse.com

ISBN:0-595-08979-8

Dedication

For M. Warren Helms

1921–1999

Miss you, Dad

Acknowledgements

My deepest thanks to Raymond Chandler, Dashiell Hammett, Mickey Spillane, John D. MacDonald, Robert B. Parker, Elmore Leonard, Ross McDonald, and James Lee Burke for all pioneering and preserving this remarkable genre.

As always, I have to thank Alan Kaplan and his lovely wife Kate for their inexhaustible patience with first drafts, and their well-thought-out comments and suggestions. You will never know how much of this book is actually theirs.

My long-suffering spouse Elaine deserves a medal of some sort for putting up with my late hours, missed meals, and the long showers I take while working out some tricky plot point. She is a living saint, and while I don't deserve her, I'm not letting her go. Her editing skills have contributed immeasurably to the modest accomplishment in your hands.

Finally, I would like to thank Groff Conklin, one of the great pulp editors of the forties and fifties, who gave so many great authors their first chances, and who edited the very first grown-up book I ever read, *The Big Book of Science Fiction*. The stories in this collection stimulated a six-year-old boy's imagination, and challenged him to commit his own meager ideas to paper. I wish I could shake his hand.

One

It takes roughly twenty-five minutes for the human eye to adjust totally to darkness. During this period, pitch black is gradually detailed by odd shapes and shades of gray. Finally, what was formerly obscured by inky light is revealed completely, providing the dark adapted eye with an advantage denied any new individual who stumbles into the room.

I sat, with adjusted eyes, in a comfy chair situated in the middle of Stanley Porch's living room. Resting across my lap was my foot and a half-length of ebony dowel, the one I had gun-drilled and filled with lead. The chair, as far as I could tell in the blackness of that room, bore no distinguishing features, save for the fact that it was capable of supporting my economy sized frame without groaning or buckling. It didn't even belong in the room, as I had dragged it from another down the hall. I had no idea how long I would be forced to wait, and while I admired Porch's taste in Scandia design formal room furniture, I deferred to comfort for this particular watch.

The room had long since been committed to memory. I knew without the lights on that, at each corner, stood an exquisite piece of oriental pottery. There was no television, and in any case I had no need of distraction. Beneath my feet I could feel the thick pile through the soles of my Capezio jazz shoes, the ones I wore on these jobs because they had no discernible sole pattern. The carpet was a stylish forest green,

1

though in the now dusky light it looked as black as the sap lying across my thighs.

Porch, I knew, was dining at Paul Prudhomme's in the Quarter, as he did almost every Tuesday evening. He didn't know it, but I had observed him entering his personal code on his security system through high-powered binoculars. As the system had no eyes, dark adapted or otherwise, it neither knew nor cared who punched the seven numbers permitting entrance.

The back of my thighs had just begun to feel numb when I heard the rasp of a key in the front door. I hefted the billy and waited for Porch to walk in.

"What the hell," he muttered as the security system, already disarmed, failed to summon his attention. "I thought I set the son of a bitch…"

"You did," I replied quietly. Porch froze. "Don't turn on the light."

Porch's right hand had stopped halfway to the switch, and he stood suspended, perhaps a tad off balance, in space.

"Jesus," he whispered. "I didn't see you. What say I just leave and come back later…"

"Oh, for God's sake, Porch," I growled, "What do you think I am, some sort of chump? Just close the door and turn around slowly."

He pushed the door closed gingerly, and said, "Gallegher, that you?"

One thing you could say for Stanley Porch—behind those beady porcine features rested a first class mind, but no more common sense than God had given a billy goat.

"Just shut up and turn around," I ordered from the dark.

He rotated sluggishly to face me, though I knew his eyes would be groping futilely through the gloom. For Porch, I might as well be invisible, which suited me just fine.

"Leduc is disappointed," I said, reaching into my coat pocket for the maglite I kept there. "You were supposed to meet him Monday to make good on your marker. Do you have any idea how Mr. Leduc feels about eating alone?"

"I… I was out of town," he stammered. "Land deal, in East Texas."

I shook my head sadly, though he could not see it. I thumbed the switch on the maglite, and aimed it into his eyes. He reacted reflexively, raising his hand to ward off the intense beam.

"Please, Stanley," I said, "Don't bullshit me. This is not a good time to say anything stupid. You know the rules—you miss the pay day, and the vig is doubled. I'm here to collect. Mr. Leduc wants five grand. That's the interest on the money you borrowed. He wants the principle by Friday morning at ten." I paused, as he peered into the beam of light. "I'll gladly take a check, if you have the proper identification."

"Look, Gallegher," Porch pleaded, glancing around for someplace to sit. All of the seats were across the room. "I can pay the five tonight, but it's really gonna bind me up on this situation I'm working in Baton Rouge…"

"That's your problem. Write the check, Stanley." I was getting tired, and I had a set at Holliday's scheduled in an hour.

Stanley had about fifteen seconds to decide one way or the other, before I would be forced to make use of the club in my lap. I sincerely hoped he would make the smart move. Deep down, I don't like violence a bit, but I'd much rather inflict it than eat it. If Stanley didn't come across, Leduc could easily decide to take it out of my considerable hide.

Porch shuffled toward the dining room table, as I trained my maglite on him.

"I'll make it cash," he said. "Don't want to leave no paper trail, know what I mean?"

"Cash, check, whatever. Five grand," I said, trying to sound menacing. My ten percent would take another big chunk out of what I owed Leduc. "If you get too short, you can always hock some of the Tang dynasty stuff. Stay where I can see you, okay?"

"It's in my briefcase," he said, reaching for the valise on the floor next to the dining room table. I knew Porch well enough to figure that he wasn't dumb enough to try anything, so I let him place the case on the table and open it. I wasn't disappointed. He reached in, grabbed a sheaf of fresh bills, and held it up.

"I know who you are, Gallegher," he said. "Do you mind if I turn on the lights? This melodrama is boring the shit out of me."

The momentary quaver in his voice told me otherwise, as I reached over and snapped on a table lamp.

"Right, Stanley. You're the master of terrified boredom." In the sudden illumination, he squinted in my direction and smiled.

"Christ, you're a big one," he said. "Seems every time I see you you're two inches taller."

"Lifts," I replied. "Just put the money on the table."

"Sure, sure," he said, and dropped the bundle. "Want a drink? I'm gonna get some wine from the kitchen…"

I pulled my unwieldy mass from the recliner and stopped him.

"Just a minute, there's more."

"What the fuck…" he began, then he saw my eyes, and knew I meant business. "Look, man, you've got your money…"

"It's not enough," I told him. "This is my third visit. You keep holding out on Leduc, like he's gonna stand for it, and he keeps sending me out here to collect. That's not good for business. We have to make that right."

Porch had started for the kitchen, but now stood in the entrance to the living room. "How do you mean?"

"You know," I said glumly. I didn't like this part any more than he was going to. "We have to keep up appearances. Can't let word get out that Leduc allows people, even his old high school buddy, to welsh on him. We have to send a message."

He seemed to whiten three shades in two seconds, as I hefted the club in my right hand.

"I'm sorry, Stanley, but I'm going to have to break something."

"Christ, Gallegher…"

"Oh, come on, Stanley, you know how it works. Either you let me break something, or maybe next time Leduc might send someone else, someone not so refined and understanding. Next time you might get hurt real bad. Tell you what, though. I'll let you choose."

His eyes darted around wildly, as if searching for a route of escape. Let's face it, though, at six and a half and two-seventy, I make a rather decent roadblock.

"How in hell do I..." he started, and saw that it was useless to protest. "Jesus, can I at least take a drink first?"

"Whatever helps you through. Take my advice, though, and skip the wine. You need a belt of the hard stuff for this."

"Yeah," he said, nodding resignedly. "Don't suppose I can interest you in a snort..."

"Cut the crap," I told him impatiently. "You really want me to drink before we do this?"

"Guess not."

He opened the art deco bar in the corner and poured two inches of gin in a wide glass. It took him all of ten seconds to slam it down, and turn back to me.

"Look, I'd appreciate it if you'd make up your mind," I said. "I'm in kind of a hurry."

He had started to shake, and I could have sworn that his eyes were tearing up. Still, he managed to raise his left arm, fingers extended, indicating his choice.

"You sure, man?" I asked. "You might want that later."

"Just do it!" he half-squealed. "Get it over with!"

I had to give the little guy credit. He was taking his medicine like a man.

"Okay," I told him raising the billy. "You might want to close your eyes. It's easier that way."

His arm extended, he nodded, and his eyes squeezed shut tight. His shoulders shook with anticipatory sobs.

I took a short backswing, and swung the cudgel sharply down. There was a shattering crack. Shards of oriental Tang dynasty porcelain flew across the room. As a lover of antiquities, it broke my heart.

"Okay," I said, "You can open them now. Friday morning, Stanley, or next time I won't be breaking any goddamned vase, got it?"

He sat at the table, his head in his hands, surveying the wreckage I had wrought, and nodded grievously.

I let myself out, after resetting the alarm system.

Two

Take any of the major airlines into New Orleans. Grab a taxi at the terminal, and tell the hack driver to take you to the Marriot on Canal Street. Once you're there, hike down Rue de Chartre to Toulouse Street, in the heart of the French Quarter. Hang a right at Toulouse. Five or six doors down is a pub called Molly's, which used to serve the best fried oysters under ten dollars in town, before it was bought out and changed to booze only. Somewhere near Molly's is an alleyway you'd miss if you weren't looking for it. If you're lucky, you might catch a snippet of music coming from between two buildings. In the alley is the front door to Holliday's, two 'L's, like Billie, and that's where I live and work.

Better yet, don't come. Holliday's is one of the last unspoiled spots in the Vieux Carre. We don't serve fruity drinks in embossed glasses. There's only seating for thirty or so. If you ask to hear '*Saints*', I'm likely to wrap your ass into a pretzel. Otherwise, I spend my evenings on the raised platform Shorty the bartender has the gall to call a stage, jamming with Sockeye Sam, the nonagenarian piano player. Somewhere out front of the club is a sign that proclaims Sockeye as coming "straight from Preservation Hall". Sockeye himself says he did play that joint sometime in the sixties, just before coming to Holliday's six or seven owners and names ago, and so I suppose the sign is correct, sort of. I play a cornet.

Which is about all you can say about me. I never played at
Preservation Hall, or anywhere else for that matter. Holliday's is my
first and only gig, a midlife crisis kind of thing I fell into several years
ago after leaving behind a career as a college professor. More about
that later.

New Orleans, being situated next to a river of some note, is a steamy,
semitropical sort of place. Shorty is a cheap bastard who considers air
conditioning a plot by rich capitalist energy barons to separate hard-
working stiffs like him from their cash. The combination should have
served to drive customers away, but for some reason the regular crowd
showed up right on time, ten o'clock sharp, just as I was tuning up my
chops with a bottle of Dixie, thrown up into more Vieux Carre gutters
than any other brew.

From the corner of my eye, I noticed a flourish at the door, and
three fellows took the corner booth across from the bar. The middle
one, Justin Leduc, clearly called the shots. The other two, a couple of
thugs named Marcel and Rene, were Cajuns Leduc had hired to keep
the riffraff away. In a sense, Leduc had put me on the payroll for a
similar reason.

Shorty hates Leduc. Actually, everyone hates Leduc, but Shorty
has preserved for him a special black hellish place in his heart. Shorty
doesn't like to see Leduc within Holliday's four walls. The look he
gave me from across the bar was obvious.

Get it done and get him out.

I shambled across the floor and took a seat that gave Marcel and
Rene a clear shot at the front door. Leduc pulled a Monte Cristo from
his jacket pocket and snipped the end with one of those upscale stogie
tools the rich love so much. Neither Marcel nor Rene offered to light
the cigar. They were professionals, couldn't be bothered with tying up
their hands that way. Leduc understood, and lit it himself. His personal
safety was much more important than being pampered by these highly
paid watchdogs.

"So," Leduc began. He didn't say more. Didn't need to.

I reached into my jacket pocket, making Marcel's and Rene's eyebrows raise. Keeping my eyes on theirs, lest they decide to eat me for threatening their boss, I slid out the envelope Stanley Porch had given me.

Leduc opened it and, ignoring the fact that he was in a supposedly public place, took out the cash. He riffled the bills, and slowly counted them. I sat there, trying to figure out what animals the smoke from his Monte Cristo brought to mind.

"It's short," he announced finally.

"And Porch has one less Tang vase," I said. "He knows to have the rest by Friday morning."

"Should have busted his fuckin' hand," Leduc replied. "That pansy artsy-fartsy crap he collects could have been sold."

"Perhaps," I said. "Of course, the next time Porch needs one of his markers covered, he might remember a broken hand and go somewhere else. He'll be there Friday morning."

"Better be. Keep your cut?"

I nodded. It was a familiar, if disheartening ritual. I was also into Leduc, for almost fifteen grand.

This might be a good time to note that, among all my legion of faults, I am a gambling addict. I managed to skirt through nearly forty years before discovering this problem. It only became apparent when I landed in New Orleans and managed to run up an impressive debt in little more than three weeks. A friend introduced me to Leduc, who agreed to cover my gambling debts, for a friendly vigorish, and in return I could work off the debt doing collections for him.

The first job he sent me on was the worst. A fifty year old woman. Her husband had died, leaving her with an impressive estate and a marker for twelve thousand, payable to Leduc. She knew nothing about the debt, which her departed spouse had neglected to cover in the will.

So, in her grief, some jolly green Irish giant showed up on her doorstep in the person of myself, and demanded satisfaction.

I left an hour later, with a check. She wept openly as she handed it to me. It wasn't the money, she explained. It was the sudden revelation that her dead husband hadn't ever told her about his secret life. Her memory of him, she said, would now be tarnished by this deception. It wasn't my fault, she said, I was just doing my job. I thanked her, and let myself out, feeling about six inches tall. Pat Gallegher, Professional Bully.

Mom would be so proud.

"Yeah," I told Leduc as I nodded. "Keep my cut. How much do I owe you now?"

It was a stupid question. It implied that, at some point in an indeterminate future, I would actually pay it off. I knew better. The rate on this 'loan' wasn't as steep as Leduc charged all his customers, but it did compound almost by the minute, and the work I did for the slimy little weasel did scant more than cover the interest. It was his way of retaining my services, kind of the way Laban retained Jacob.

"Still a little more than twelve," Leduc said. "But don't worry, it's coming down. It's coming down."

He smiled, without affection, joy, or perhaps even the awareness of smiling, and with a single gesture all three rose from their seats.

"I'll call you," Leduc told me. "I may have some work for you this weekend. Maybe more, if Porch stiffs me on Friday."

I'd have invited him to stay around and listen to the show, but then I'd have had to deal with Shorty. Leduc pulled on his own jacket. Marcel and Rene kept their hands free, as always, to pull howitzers from under their jackets at the first sign of threat.

Twelve grand.

Jeez, that's more money than I make in tips all week.

Three

Leduc's visit had ruined my already dreadful evening, and I had a hard time dredging up the energy to do anything truly creative in the first set. I was slogging my way through, letting Sockeye Sam carry the load. We were doing something soulful and deceitful to '*Summertime*', when my chops gave out, and I signaled to Sockeye to break off and do a solo. Sockeye, who is quite nearly blind, picked up on it almost the second I put down the cornet, and was off on the most eloquent musical statement he could conjure with his ninety-year-old fingers.

I was languorously engaged in the process of clearing my spit valves, when my eyes wandered across the floor, to the very table where Leduc had been sitting an hour earlier. Now, the booth was occupied by Cully Tucker and a woman I had never met.

Cully Tucker is a fairly decent lawyer with a real self-esteem problem. He has been on a downwardly mobile spiral almost since he passed the bar. When I met him, shortly after moving to the Quarter, he was handing out business cards at funeral homes and emergency rooms. He's been my attorney ever since, not so much out of pity as because he remains to this day the only lawyer I know.

Fact is, Cully isn't half bad in the legal department. He's generally arrived within an hour whenever I've needed to be bailed out of jail, and his insight on wills and trusts has served me well on a couple of my moonlighting jobs.

Cully waved me over, and since I hadn't anything better to do, such as my job, I accepted the invitation. He introduced his partner as Clancey Vincouer. She was wearing a bit thin at the edges of her first facelift, though she still cut a handsome figure from ten feet out. Her blonde hair was perfectly arranged in a tasteful bob, and when she smiled her teeth bore testimony to the patient attention of an excellent dentist. She smelled like a million in crisp twenties, which led me to wonder what in hell she was doing in my little dive with the likes of Cully Tucker.

She offered her hand, which I took, noting the cool but confident grasp. This was not a woman to be ignored, but her furtive glances as she greeted me led me to believe that she was unaccustomed to the kind of club I call home.

"So, Cully," I asked, after giving Ms. Vincouer back her hand, "What's up?"

I asked this, you should understand, knowing full well what was up, and I didn't appreciate it one little bit. Cully Tucker was no slouch in the babe department, but Clancey Vincouer was so far out of his league that there was only one conceivable reason for bringing her to Holliday's. I suddenly felt very tired, as opposed the garden variety fatigue I'd felt before seeing him.

"Can we go upstairs?" Cully asked, his eyes leading mine toward the back stairs at the far side of the bar.

I sighed, shaking my head just to scare him. "Sure. Why not?"

The three of us took the back steps to my cozy quarters on the second floor. At one time in the Quarter's elusive past, the building which now housed Holliday's had been some kind of mill. The current owners had divided the second floor into two sections, half of which was now the bar, and half of which now housed the offices of a fishing concern. The floors, as is typical of old mills, were made of heart pine, highly polished and waxed. The wall between my quarters and the fish offices was thick, well insulated, and now covered with a floor-to-ceiling bookcase, complete with a library ladder attached to runners at the top.

As she walked into the twelve foot high room, Clancey stopped and stared at the bookcase, which was crammed with hundreds, perhaps thousands, of volumes I had collected over the course of three decades. It was a common reaction. Who, after all, might expect an intellectual horn bum, especially in a dump like Holliday's?

Besides the bookcase, the room was comfortably furnished with a couch, recliner, and a couple of tables. A Murphy bed stood folded up against the far wall, across from the bookcase. For once I was glad I had indulged in a bit of housecleaning. I offered Clancey Vincouer the recliner.

"Okay," I said, nodding to Cully. "What can I do for you?"

"It's about your, uh, sideline," he said.

"French pastry cooking?" I asked. "Racing pigeons? Animal husbandry? Exactly which sideline do you mean, Cully?"

He was beginning to redden a bit in the ears. He could discuss my most closely held secret with a woman I had never met, but he couldn't mention it to me. He was deep in Indian territory, and he knew it.

"You know," he urged hesitantly. "The favor thing."

I nodded, and directed my gaze toward Clancey, who in any case presented a much more rewarding view.

"Mr. Tucker, of course, is referring to my sideline doing favors for friends, and friends of friends..." I turned back to Cully, my eyes shooting poisoned daggers into his left ventricle. "... the sideline he would never talk about outside this room, because he knows how much I want it kept private. Would that be the sideline, sir?"

Cully nodded, appropriately cowed. "Yeah, Gallegher, that's the one."

"I'm so relieved," I announced, in a voice that I hoped clearly conveyed that I was not at all relieved. "What about it?"

Cully cleared his throat. "It's like this, Gallegher. Ms. Vincouer is a client of mine, and she came to me several days ago with a problem."

"Actually," Clancey interrupted, "Cully is more than just my attorney. We knew each other in college."

"Not possible," I countered. "Cully is incapable of carrying on a relationship for more than six months without cheating, alienating, or killing the other person."

"Perhaps," she said coolly, earning another sizable chunk of my respect, "but I haven't been in constant contact with him. I did have dinner with Cully about a month ago, to discuss some matters in my will, and he happened to mention you and your various occupations."

I walked over to the wheezing refrigerator, shooting Cully another fatal glance on the way, and pulled out a Dixie. I offered one to each of them, but they both declined. It wasn't important. I can drink alone.

"And?" I asked.

"This is rather difficult," she said.

"I can relate. What can I do for you, Ms. Vincouer?"

"I've lost someone."

"Careless," I offered, taking a long pull on the Dixie. "No one significant, I hope."

She glanced at Cully, with that unmistakable look that says *What kind of flake have you hooked me up with?*

"Look, Gallegher," Cully said, "This is kind of sensitive. Ms. Vincouer has been seeing a young man, not her husband. He's disappeared."

I stared at him, without responding. I didn't even blink.

"His name is Sammy Cain."

I did blink this time, only because my eyes had dried out.

"I have a picture," Cully said, reaching into his coat pocket. "It's pretty recent."

He handed the picture to me across the couch. I peered at his hand as if he held some kind of flesh-eating bacteria, but at last my curiosity got the better of me, and I took the photo.

Sammy Cain wasn't half bad looking, for the manly, outdoorsy type. His eyes, a cobalt blue, gleamed from obscenely high cheekbones framed by a reddish-brown beard. His nose, just a tad large for his face, served only to emphasize his masculinity. This was a man's man, a killer of large and ferocious beasts. He looked as if making him disappear would take some doing.

"No offense, Ms. Vincouer," I said, placing the picture on the burl walnut coffee table, "but is it possible that this character just got tired and moved on?"

"Pat…" Cully started, moving in to defend his unlikely friend, but Clancey waved him off.

"No," she said. "It's a fair question. Sammy and I were supposed to meet for lunch this past Monday. My husband was out of town on business. Sammy didn't show up, so I drove to his apartment. I have a key, so I let myself in. He wasn't there, either, but his luggage was still in his closet, as were most of his clothes. I… I waited for several hours. He never came home. I left a note, but he hasn't called since, and I've left several messages. Two days ago I went back to the apartment. I found everything exactly the way I had left it. My note was still on the refrigerator."

"Okay," I said. "I can see why you didn't call the police, given the nature of your relationship. On the other hand, the phone book is full of private detectives. Why not glom onto one of them? I'm sure Cully knows a couple…"

"We've already covered that," Cully said. "But you don't know everything, yet."

"I think…" Clancey said, but stopped to choke back a sob. "I think my husband had Sammy killed."

Four

And suddenly it all fell together.

Let's say, for the sake of argument, that you have suffered some significant loss, such as money, or a painting or, as in the case of the unfortunate Ms. Clancey Vincouer, a studly boy toy. Let us also suppose, in our fantasy, that this lost object has some illicit qualities that motivate you to keep it a secret from your spouse, the police, or the local newshounds. Or, we can surmise that you believe it was stolen, kidnapped, or disposed of by a loved one whom, in the course of doing so, engaged in a felonious act. Again, you are motivated to keep this a secret.

A private detective would, by law, have to inform the police if he or she uncovered a felony. It says so in the Hardy Boys Detectives' Handbook, and it's worth the private cop's license to ignore this caveat.

In such a case, it would be to your advantage to know a large, mean looking gentleman whom, as it happens, doesn't mind engaging in an occasional act of violence. It also wouldn't hurt if that gentleman knew a thing or two about finding things. It would help if he wasn't licensed, and therefore not honor-bound to report any deeds he discovers that violate the community standard.

I am such a gentleman, and I come pretty cheap in the bargain.

In other times, and other places, there were terms for what I do. In feudal England, it was *knight-errant*. In feudal Japan, it was *ronin*. Here, in the latter half of the twentieth century, the popular term is muscle. It's not as romantic, but I can live with that. I'm not in it for kicks.

A trained psychiatrist could, perhaps, explain why I purposely throw myself in harm's way as I do. Yin and yang, anima and animus, the interconnectedness of all things. Maybe I just feel intensely guilty about shaking down other gambling addicts, and need to do something to assuage my conscience.

Maybe I'm just hyperactive.

In any case I was, for better or worse, exactly the gentleman Clancey Vincouer was seeking at this moment. It kind of pissed me off.

"Perhaps you had better tell me more," I said quietly.

She stared out the window for a moment, gathering her thoughts, and then launched into her story.

"My husband is Lester Vincouer," she said. "He owns a canning firm, inherited it, in a way, from his father. Lester took control of the company when he was only twenty-four. It may have been worth a couple hundred thousand at the time, nothing to make the Fortune 500. Over the next twenty years, Lester built it into a fifteen million dollar a year corporation. He took the company public about five years ago, which pumped over twenty million into the capital fund. Lester used this to expand into Texas and Oklahoma, and to begin diversifying into other businesses. For, oh, the last ten years, he has been consumed with work. I married Lester when we were both in college. I knew at the time that he had some money coming, but that didn't matter. I was in love with him—maybe his image, actually. He came across as self-confident, in control, masterly, all the qualities that were sure to set a southern debutante's heart aflutter."

She turned to face me. "I haven't felt that flutter in almost a decade. Not from Lester. About six months ago, on a gambling trip to Biloxi, I happened to sit at the same roulette table as Sammy Cain. My luck took a decidedly lousy turn, and I ran through a couple of thousand in chips in less than an hour. I didn't care. It was Lester's money, after all, and I figured he owed me something. Sammy didn't know this, though. He offered me a couple of hundred dollar chips of his own to play. I knew at the time he was trying to pick me up, but I didn't give a damn about that either. Don't get me wrong, Mr. Gallegher, I'm not a loose woman. Sammy is my first affair. I didn't mind it when he flirted with me, though. It felt rather nice.

"Anyway, as it happened, my luck turned, and I doubled the two hundred in fifteen minutes. We both played a bit longer, and then, I suppose out of appreciation, I offered to buy him dinner."

"And one thing led to another…" I surmised.

"Not at all," she answered, a little stunned that I would suggest such a thing. "Sammy was a perfect gentleman. We had dinner, talked about our respective lives, and that was that. He told me that he also lived in the New Orleans area, in Kenner, and that he worked for an airfreight company at the airport. He said he spent all his time tracking missing packages, that he was deskbound, and he took the trip to Biloxi to clear his head for a few days."

"You told him all about yourself?" I asked.

"Of course, including that I was married and had been for almost a quarter century. He laughed at that, saying that he hadn't been around much more than a quarter century. It was a joke. I discovered later that he's in his mid-thirties."

"Did he say which company he works for?" I asked.

"No. Just that he was with an airfreight firm. He never gave me a work number. If I wanted to call him, though, he said, I could reach him at his home. He gave me his telephone number, and we said goodnight."

"What happened next?"

"I didn't know what to do. I found myself thinking about him a lot over the next couple of weeks. Lester was deep into the building of a new cannery in Baton Rouge, so I had a lot of time on my hands.

Finally, out of desperation I suppose, I gathered up my nerve and called him one evening."

"He was home?"

"Oh, yes. He invited me out for a drink. I didn't accept, at least not right away. Instead, we agreed to meet for lunch the next day. We went to a quiet place in Metairie, an Italian restaurant he suggested. It was quaint, and the food was good, and the wine... Well, I had a bit too much of the wine—a lambrusco, as I recall. As the lunch progressed, my head became lighter and lighter, and before I knew it I was having ... thoughts."

"Ah," I mused, "Love in a lambrusco bottle."

She appeared hurt. "I don't think so. Not love. I'm no spring chicken, Mr. Gallegher. I know the difference. It was lust, simply put. I probably knew, even before I called, what would happen. I wanted it. I wanted to be taken, passionately and without reservation, by a man that made my heart flutter. If you're going to be rude, I'm not certain we should continue this conversation."

"Suits me," I said, tossing the Dixie bottle into the trash. I used to keep a recycle bin, but I got tired of the hassle. "I haven't decided whether to help you, yet. Your story is interesting, maybe even a little arousing. On the other hand, I have a job, and while these little favors I do tend to keep the arteries from clogging up, they also take time from my triple-tonguing exercises."

This reference apparently startled her, and she stared at me stonily.

"It's a horn thing," I explained, "What you do need to understand, though, is that whatever it is you want me to do, I don't have to do it. I gave up that 'have to' thing years ago when I dropped out of polite society and became a creature of the night. Now, with that all understood, is it safe to assume that lunch led to a recumbent assignation?"

"I beg your pardon?" she said, blushing.

"You slept with him sometime between the cannolis and cocktail hour?"

She nodded. "Yes. It just… happened. It was like a switch went off in my head, and I said, 'Yeah, why not?'. It was like Sammy saw me make the decision, and fifteen minutes later we were in his apartment. It was wonderful. I hope I'm not embarrassing you…"

"Fat chance," I assured her.

"…but Lester was, once, a long time ago, really aggressive, you know, in bed. It was like he couldn't get enough, and he always had a new idea. It was, I don't know, exhilarating. He hasn't been like that in a long time, though. Sammy brought all that back…"

I broke in, "If you'll permit me. You went home that evening, your toes all curly, but still a bit ashamed of what you had done. For the first time in your life, you had cheated on your husband. You vowed never to do it again, told yourself that you'd call Sammy and explain that it had all been so wonderful, but it was over, and thanks for making you feel so much like a woman again. However, several days later, you began to feel the ache, and the desire to recapture that exhilaration was more than you could bear. So you called Sammy, not to break it off, but to suggest another tryst, which he granted. As time went on, the rendezvous became more frequent, the guilt less painful, and you even started to get a little brazen about it all. You were owed, after all. Lester, the great provider, had neglected his most connubial of obligations, and you had the right to seek that satisfaction elsewhere. Am I close?"

Her mouth had dropped open as I had laid her life out before her. "That's very close to it."

I tapped the framed degree on the wall between the bookcase and Murphy bed, the one proclaiming my Ph.D. in psychology from Loyola. "I am not without experience in these matters. I only have one question."

"Yes?"

"How did you keep it all from Lester? Presuming, I suppose, that it wasn't Lester who arranged for Sammy's disappearance?"

The color rose on her throat, to merge with the flush around her ears. "I... I have this friend, Meg Coley. About two months into the... the affair, I began to panic. What would happen if Lester became suspicious? How could I explain going out so many times a week? Meg was visiting one day, and the subject just... came up. It was as if the whole mess just bubbled over and I told her everything. She was so understanding. She even said she wondered why I hadn't done it a long time ago. She told me I needed a cover story. So, we decided to tell Lester, if he ever asked, that I was going out with Meg. We agreed that I would call Meg whenever I was supposed to meet Sammy, and she wouldn't answer the telephone that evening. That way, if Lester were to become suspicious, and tried to call, he wouldn't reach her and put her in the position of having to make some silly excuse for why I wasn't there. It was sordid, of course, and sneaky, but it enabled me to see Sammy whenever I wanted.

"Then about two weeks ago, Sammy and I were... together, and he mentioned that he thought he might have been followed earlier that day. It had rattled him. Sammy said he had been shopping for a present for me. There was this man, a big man with a beard, and Sammy had seen him in several of the stores at the Mall. It seemed that wherever Sammy went, there was the man. He said it was unnerving.

"That was the last time we met. We were supposed to get together later that week, but, as I've explained, he never showed up."

"And," I added, "you believe that your husband found out about your affair, and had Sammy followed. You also believe that, when Sammy disappeared, your husband was responsible."

She leaned forward, cupping her forehead with her hand. "I... don't... know," she nearly sobbed. "I've been a nervous wreck for days. I miss Sammy, and I can't imagine why he's been away, and his apartment hasn't been touched. What am I to think?"

I sighed, and said, "Perhaps that some other woman's husband found out about him, and that other woman's husband is responsible?"

She glared at me, her eyes glistening but fiery, and hissed, "You are a filthy man!"

"And, in a former life, I would have said that you are a vain, selfish, immature woman-child. You expect that the fire of your early marriage could burn bright forever, that somehow you would escape the encroachment of middle age and the natural development of personality. At a time in your life when you should be consolidating your wisdom and sagacity, you are instead out strumpeting about with a man ten years your junior." She started to protest, but I cut her off. "I know, I know. You are in love, or at least some distant relative of it. Has it occurred to you, dear, that you met when Sammy tried to pick you up? Are you so narcissistic as to believe that you were the first woman he ever attempted to seduce? We should consider the possibility that Sammy Cain, as tender and generous as he may seem to you, has been knocking off bored rich housewives all over the delta."

She was becoming truly furious all over again, so I held up my hand. "As I said, that was a former life. You seem to believe that your husband, who up until three weeks ago was too wrapped up in his business to give you the time of day, has regained sufficient interest in your goings-on to interfere, perhaps violently, in your affair. Fine. That's enough for me. You want someone to either confirm that Sammy is alive without asking Lester a sackful of embarrassing questions, or to find out what Lester did without the obligation of informing the police should it turn out to have been nefarious. Fine. I can live with that. As it happens, I am lusting after a complete mint set of Bix Beiderbeck seventy-eights I discovered in a local antique shop, which the owner insists will set me back almost a grand. I don't have a grand right now, but I do have you. I think we can make a deal."

Which is exactly what we did.

Five

There have been, perhaps, only five or six people this century endowed with talent clearly on loan from God, and Limbaugh ain't one of them.

Bix Beiderbeck, the left handed cornetist, on the other hand, came damn close in the first two decades. Even on scratchy old seventy-eights, the genius came through in crystal clarity.

Thanks to a young woman in Baton Rouge who had been careless enough to allow herself to be photographed in and out of fascinating costumes and gymnastic postures, I had been able to acquire a top of the line stereo system, complete with a Denon surround sound amplifier capable of duplicating the acoustics of Carlsbad Caverns, if needed. My compact disk system, a programmable affair, held over ten disks at a time, and the Bose speaker system I had secreted about my humble quarters produced remarkably little harmonic distortion. All things considered, given a choice of my system or actually being there, I'd take the electronics.

Among its short list of failings, however, was the fact that my turntable, despite wow and flutter ratings that defied measurement, did not have a setting for seventy-eight RPM. So, I sat in my overstuffed recliner, my size fourteens dangling out the second floor window over Holliday's, sucking down a Dixie and listening to the Bixster on an old

RCA monaural record player I'd bought second hand at a flea market in Slidell for fifteen bucks.

And it didn't sound half bad.

Beiderbeck, I am told, never took a lesson in his life. He just picked up the cornet one day, blew into it, and conjured heaven from the instrument, like Mozart. Because of his lack of tutelage, he apparently learned the wrong valve technique. They say that's what made his music so unique. I tend to side with those who claim he was divinely inspired.

I was looking for a little inspiration of my own that greasy afternoon, as my feet slowly steeped in the hundred percent humidity just outside the window. Clancey Vincouer's little problem presented some interesting possibilities. While even I would like to think that people find happiness by the strangest twists of fate, the chance meeting of Clancey and Sammy Cain ate at me voraciously. It was too opportune, too chancy for my blood. True, Sammy might have just been sharking about for rich little twists in need of some masculine attention, and Clancey happened along at just the right moment. In fact, that was my primary theory.

On the other hand, there was also the possibility that their meeting was no accident. Who knows how many matronly gamblers Cain scouted before choosing to hit on Clancey Vincouer, or how long he might have watched her from the relative safety of the dollar slots? Was his appearance at her roulette table as spontaneous as it sounded, or was it the chase at the end of the stalk?

I had to hand it to old Sammy, though. His technique was nothing less than pure class. Most of the babehounds make a move right away, fully aware that with the right blend of ingratiation and gallantry, they can have their marks off their feet within an hour of meeting. Sammy, on the other hand, had taken the chance that Clancey wouldn't call. He had wined and dined, nibbled at the bait, and then refused to strike. He was either as innocent as Clancey portrayed him, or he was one shiny piece of work.

Which left me with the task of finding him.

I was surprised that Clancey knew so little about him. In the age of infamous viral contagion, casually exchanging body fluids was something more than a slight risk. Yet, all she apparently knew about Cain, other than the obvious physical traits, was that he worked for an air freight firm at the airport.

The morning after Cully Tucker brought Clancey to see me, I had tried to follow up that lead. Posing as an adjuster for the Fidelity Life and Casualty Insurance Company, a ruse I had employed successfully many times before, I had called every air freight firm in the book. My cover story was simple. Sammy Cain had filed an accident report following a rear-end fender bender in Mississippi, and I, representing the other guy, had some questions regarding his medical bills. Nobody ever questions an insurance guy, for fear he might get their name and try to write them a shitload of term life.

Nobody, though, had ever heard of Sammy Cain. Several of the people I called were sympathetic, though. They all said they had been rear-ended before, and hoped that I was able to help poor Sammy, whoever he was.

After running through all the airfreight lines at the big airport, I started in at some of the smaller fixed base operators in surrounding parishes. Nothing.

Whoever Sammy Cain was, he for sure wasn't what he had told Clancey Vincouer.

So I sat, tinny waves of Beiderbeck caressing my temporal lobes, and considered my next move. I supposed I could toss Sammy's apartment, using Clancey's key. It was a start at least. That's how it works, no matter what the TV detectives say. You ask a question here and a question there, throw a little furniture around, muss up the landscape, and see what turns up. Sometimes you score, mostly you don't. Maybe, along the way, you get someone's attention, and piss them off enough to try to stop you. That's always informative.

So far, though, all I had was Sammy's one big lie to Clancey. It was time to find out just who Cain was.

So, I went to church.

Actually, I hardly ever go to church, anymore, despite the fact that I was the width of a red hair away from ordination years ago. In the midst of a prayer in my final semester at the seminary, I realized that I was sending, but not receiving, leading me to believe that I was largely talking to myself. I couldn't shake the impression, and doubting my ability to lead a congregation with my newfound agnosticism, I turned instead to a more introspective science.

It is a widely known but little appreciated fact that the Church of Latter Day Saints maintains one of the most comprehensive genealogical libraries in the world. It is their contention that they have some sort of power of reverse salvation. If they can convert one amongst us to the Mormon faith, they can then also consider converted all that individual's predecessors. Of course, in order to convert the departed, you have to know who they are, so the Mormons have collected an amazing compilation of family histories, current and past census records, birth and death certificates, marriage licenses, and immigration records. Using this method, they hope to fill heaven with Latter Day Saints, in a retroactive sort of way.

It's a technique I've also heard was used rather successfully by the Democratic party in Chicago.

In any case, I hoped to cull from this vast repository of names some shred of information about the shadowy Sammy Cain.

The curator of the Mormon Genealogical Library in New Orleans was an elderly man of remarkable jocularity named Quentin Wardell. I had used the library on many occasions. Quentin saw me come in the door, and immediately rose to take my hand.

"Patrick!" he greeted, in that voice he uses with everyone, but which makes you feel that your visit is the high point of his day, "Welcome back! Can I offer you something to drink?"

Actually, I could have used a Dixie, after the muggy drive over in my antediluvian Pinto Runabout, but the church sort of frowned on alcohol use in the library, so I declined.

Like most buildings in New Orleans, the one housing the Mormon Library was six days older than baseball. If I chose to lean back, I would have found a remarkable domed ceiling illuminated by numerous stained glass scenes depicting great moments in the Mormon Church. The walls were fined oiled wood with recessed panels, and the carpet thick and lush. The smell was musty and bookish, with a brisk tang of tanned leather.

Quentin sat next to me at his desk, which he had turned so that it never separated him from his guests.

"So, Patrick," he opened, "what will it be today?"

I fished in my pocket for the scrap of paper on which I had made my sparse notes to that point in my search. "Sammy Cain," I said, handing him the paper on which I had written his name and current address. "I suppose it's actually Samuel, but I don't have a middle name. No birth date, either, but I'm told he's in his middle thirties, so I figure he was born somewhere in the early to mid-sixties."

"Ah," Quentin said, nodding with delight, "a challenge. Well, let's see what we can do…"

An inexperienced visitor might have expected Quentin to first consult some sort of card file or register, and then select one of the thousands of leather volumes lining the walls, maybe blow some dust off of it, and then start perusing index after index for some mention of Cain.

Of course, the Mormon Church, like everyone else in the free world, long ago gave up paper for megabytes, and Quentin merely turned to his computer and grabbed the mouse to begin his search. It was nowhere near as romantic, but I was grateful for its rapidity.

"Why don't we first check the 1970 census records," he suggested. "It is an unusual spelling of the name, you understand. Most people of this name entered the country from England, where it was spelled with an 'e' at the end. However, the 'Cain' version of the name was typical in the southern portion of the country where, I'm sad to say, education was never at a premium until well into this century. And, here we are..."

It was that quick. In a little over a minute, Quentin had selected a list of over two hundred names.

"These are all the families named Cain that listed children in the 1970 census. Now, if we cross-compare it to a similar list from the 1960 census..."

It took a couple more minutes, but he was able to drop maybe a quarter of the original list.

"All right," he chortled, rubbing his hands together, "Now, to narrow it a little further..."

He selected the Tax Records files in the main menu, and ordered a search for children in the families on the list with the first name Samuel. The computer made no change in sound as it searched, but when it did produce a list, it was only ten names long.

"You didn't mention why you need this," Quentin noted. "Another favor, Patrick?"

Quentin had helped me so many times that I had finally taken him into my confidence.

"This guy's gone missing," I told him. "Someone wants me to find him."

"Dear, dear," Quentin clucked. "You become involved in the nastiest of businesses. I might be able to narrow this a little further if you know where Mr. Cain was born."

"Sorry, Q," I answered. "At this point, you know as much as I do." Which was, of course, not entirely true. Hopefully, Quentin did not know that Sammy had been playing Tunatown Trolley with Clancey Vincouer.

"Let me print it out for you," he offered, and hit the appropriate keys. Over the hum of the laser printer, he added, "By the way, you might be interested that I've been able to find a link between your great-great-great-grandfather and family Coursey of Dublin, Ireland."

"Coursey?"

"Oh, yes, a very noble family, originally de Courci, included a governor of Ireland under one of the Henrys, and several early members of the House of Burgesses in Virginia. Wouldn't mind adding them to the fold, you know…"

His hint wasn't wasted on me. "Sorry, Q, but I'm not quite ready to convert."

"Oh, well," Quentin sighed. "Will you at least come back and tell me the story when you find this Mr. Cain? I do look forward to hearing of your little adventures."

"Count on it," I told him. "As a matter of fact, I have one I haven't told you about yet. No names, you understand…"

He crossed his heart. "Soul of discretion."

"Okay," I said. "I got a really sweet stereo system out of this one. See, there was this woman in Baton Rouge…"

Six

My Nixon-era Pinto groaned as I swerved off Lakeshore Drive in Lake Terrace onto the long, tree-lined driveway to Clancey Vincouer's home. Land values along Lake Pontchartrain had taken on a life of their own over the last couple of decades, and communities like Lakeshores East and West, Lake Vista, Lake Terrace and even Citrus down the pike had become the playgrounds of the *nouveau riche*. Acreage formerly left to vermin and salt marsh had been reclaimed, filled in, fertilized, graded, subdivided, and sold as premium homesites to people with more money than horse sense, on which they built opulent homes of no apparent utility other than status.

I knew, even before the manse loomed in front of me, what it would look like. There were hundreds like it scattered across the delta—reproductions of antebellum 'planter's cottages' built to shelter three or four generations of a plantation family, along with separate quarters for the slave help. The real versions still passed from father to son in some areas, but according to real estate records in the court clerk's office Vincouer had bought his at an estate auction almost fifteen years ago, and it had only been six years old then.

It was the house I dearly hoped I would never live in. Don't get me wrong. There was nothing architecturally unsound about the old palace; neither was it particularly esthetically displeasing. Still, I had given over the last five years of my life to a sort of ascetic self-denial, owning little more than my records, books, and horn. I could live for weeks on Clancey Vincouer's covered front porch and never piss in the same place twice. What Clancey and Lester, just the two of them, needed with a home the size of the Pentagon was beyond me, and probably always would be.

I parked the Pinto, turned it off, and left it chugging in the turnaround situated at the base of the front porch. I had called ahead to let Clancey know I was coming, and to guarantee that I wouldn't be caught there by Lester. If he did knock off Sammy Cain, I sure didn't want him to catch me with his old lady.

The front porch was sixty feet long and fifteen feet deep, with closely spaced cypress boards on the deck and a tongue-in-groove ceiling. The Vincouers had added four or five modern electric ceiling fans to keep the skeeters down. Running the length of the porch was a railing just made for putting your feet up and watching the darkies going about their chores, with carefully turned balusters painted in the obligatory plantation white.

The front door was a real piece of work, undreamt of when North fought South. It was two doors, actually, hand rubbed walnut and oak with a polished brass knocker on each door. I figured one was for show and the other for go, but for the life of me I couldn't figure out which was which. I took my chances and rang the doorbell.

I was gratified to discover that it didn't play Winchester chimes. From somewhere deep inside the big house came a hollow *ding-dong*, rich mellifluous tones that clearly had no electronic origin. Through the translucent etched glass at the sides of the doors I saw a shadow appear from the back of the house and grow larger as it approached the front. There was a rasping sound of locks being sprung, and the door on the left swung open with barely a whispered hiss. I had guessed wrong. I was sure it was going to be the right.

"Mr. Gallegher," Clancey Vincouer greeted. "Won't you come in?"

"Butler has the day off?" I asked as I crossed the portal to enter a foyer almost as large as my digs over Holliday's.

"No butler," she said, smiling. "I manage on my own, thank you. We do have a maid." She added the last almost as an afterthought, like I really cared whether she did her own housework.

"Can I get you anything? Iced tea? A beer?"

Ah, she had hit my happy button.

"Beer's fine," I told her.

"Please follow me to the sunroom," she said, and led me down a long glossy heart-pine hallway, the walls filled with original oil portraits of stiff, unhappy people long dead and buried.

Clancey was dressed for lounging, in a loose, silky pantsuit printed with a royal blue paisley design. Her unfettered breasts bounced the flimsy fabric like rollicking puppies, but I got the distinct impression that she had no erotic conquests planned for the hefty Irish hired man. It was just a way she had of saying 'This is my house, and we play by my rules'. I could dig it. I was even a little proud of her, as when she strode between me and the sunroom windows, the silhouette of her mature but still well-kept form projected against the silk made it clear that, when she had gotten her face lifted, she had resisted the urge to do the whole package. Nature abhors a fifty-year-old woman with twenty year old tits.

She opened a faux marble art deco freestanding bar, and from the mirror-lined innards extracted a single wineglass. From the bottom of the bar, which cleverly housed a refrigerator, she pulled a bottle of Amstel. My heart skipped a beat, in anticipation that the rest of me was about to be spoiled.

"Glass?" she asked.

"Don't bother," I replied. "I won't be holding it that long."

She handed me the Amstel, poured herself a glass of white zinfandel, and in almost the same motion waved for me to take a seat by the french doors leading out to the patio.

As I sat, I saw that what had been intended to represent the house slaves' quarters had been transformed into a nifty little cabana for the olympic-sized pool just beyond the patio. Glistening shafts of light reflecting from the water darted through the french doors and played tag among the fox hunt prints above the antique mantel in the sunroom.

Despite my aversion to its excessive size, I had to admit that the house and grounds were expertly assembled and meticulously kept. Clancey waited for me to turn my attention back to the matter at hand.

"Your investigation," she opened.

"Yes," I said, reaching into my inside jacket pocket for the report I had prepared on the inkjet printer in Shorty's office. "Actually, it didn't take long to identify Sammy Cain. After I narrowed the list of possible people to a dozen, roughly, I accessed a compact disk program I bought by mail about a year ago, listing almost everyone in the country by last known address, with certain other historical data."

I stopped as a distinctly human movement outside the french doors flitted across my peripheral vision. One of the doors in the slaves' cabana had opened, and an admirably proportioned woman in her thirties was arranging her beach towel on a chaise by the diving board. She was tall, by most standards, maybe five-ten, with thick wavy red hair and legs that stretched from earth to heaven. Her generous feminine features protested being contained by the scant bikini she had painted on for her swim. When she turned toward the house, I could see her face, vaguely reminiscent of a lissome Botticelli's Venus, before she dove into the pool, leaving scarcely a ripple.

Clancey Vincouer calmly sipped her wine, aware of my distraction. I glanced back at her sheepishly, as if I had been caught peeping into the girls' locker room.

"Ah, your daughter?" I ventured without thinking. The sudden frigidity of her gaze reminded me that she and Lester had never had children. Mrs. Gallegher's clumsy boy had done it again.

"A friend," she replied, coolly. She did not want to elaborate. "What did you find?"

I cleared my throat. "Mrs. Vincouer, the reason I came by today... Well, I found some information you might want to know. I thought you should hear this before I continue the search. The Sammy Cain you were involved with was born Samuel Francis Cain, in Rolla, Missouri. His parents were Kent and Frances Cain. Dad was a mine services supervisor. Mom was an accountant. Sammy grew up in an upper middle class neighborhood in North Rolla..." I stopped.

"Yes?" she urged, her eyes and posture betraying her fascination.

"I... spoke with Frances Cain this morning. It seems that Kent Cain, Sammy's father, died about five years ago. It was sudden, an aneurysm. According to Sammy's mother, well, she thinks it was really a broken heart. Kent Cain, it seems, adored Sammy. He was the only child, and from the start Mr. Cain had big plans for him. For a while, it looked like Sammy would fulfill all their dreams. He was the first string quarterback on the high school football team, and until the eleventh grade he was an honor student. Then, in his junior year, the grades started falling. He began to act erratically. There were telephone calls in the middle of the night, all hours. Sammy took to leaving the house early in the evening, and not returning until four or five in the morning, if at all.

"Then, about halfway through his senior year, he was arrested for stealing a car with a couple of other guys in his school. It was his first offense, and because he was still a minor it was handled in Juvenile Court, nothing more than a year's probation. Kent Cain figured Sammy had learned his lesson, that he'd been scared straight.

"The problems continued, though. Sammy graduated from high school, by the skin of his teeth, and dropped out of college less than a semester in. He kept getting into trouble—a little con here, some petty theft there."

I stopped and tried to divine what was happening behind her eyes. Her face was flat, neither angry nor dismayed. She appeared more shocked than anything else.

"Shall I continue, Mrs. Vincouer?"

This brought her out of it, with a tiny start.

"Yes," she replied, her voice husky, "Please."

I took a moment to review the paper in my hands.

"Sammy moved from place to place—Lexington and Louisville in Kentucky, Cincinnati, Las Vegas, San Francisco, Tahoe. He wrote his mother and father constantly, telling them where he was, what he was doing. She read some of the letters to me over the telephone. He told them he was selling insurance, working as a buyer for Macys, doing a ski instructor gig. I checked. None of it was true. He told you he was working for an airfreight firm in New Orleans, at the airport. He wasn't and isn't. It's all lies, Mrs. Vincouer. Fact is, I had a hard time pinning Sammy Cain to an honest, tax-paying job anytime in the last fifteen years. His credit rating... well, he doesn't have one. No credit cards, no mortgages, no car payments, no installment loans. Sammy Cain is a real person, but he hasn't left enough of a paper trail to wipe your butt with... sorry, ma'am."

"That's all right," she countered, accenting it with an imperious wave of her hand. "Quite all right. How does he... get along?" she asked. "What does he actually do for a living?"

"This and that," I answered. "There are lots of little arrests, probation sorts of things. It seems that whenever he gets convicted, he simply flits across the state lines. The crimes, mostly bunco stuff or assaults, or fraud, aren't big enough for the P.O.'s to put a detective on his trail, so he seems to move pretty freely. Lately, though, his career has taken a decidedly nasty turn."

I drew a breath, and drove right through this part. "In Las Vegas, he was accused of ripping off a fifty year old woman on a gambling holiday, took her for almost twenty grand, a sort of 'loan' meant to pay off a marker debt. The day after he got the check, she couldn't find him. In Tahoe, he soaped off a widow in her fifties for almost three months, starting as a handyman. It didn't take long for him to get real handy in the bedroom, but he came up missing along with several choice pieces of the widow's jewelry. In Galveston, he promised to marry a woman in her forties, and lived with her for almost five months while he supposedly was looking for a job. He finally convinced her he had found work, as a securities salesman. He got up in the morning, went to work, and came home in the evening like a regular joe. One day, he came home and told his intended about this sure-fire, can't miss bond deal, guaranteed to make them both rich. Said he got the information inside, so she should keep it secret. Told her it was a foreign government investment, and that he had to fly to Sierra Leone to close it. He took off with almost thirty grand of her money, and she hasn't seen him since."

I folded the paper and replaced in in my pocket.

"Mrs. Vincouer, Sammy Cain has a black soul, right to the core. He's a major league shakedown artist. If he hadn't disappeared, he'd have eventually set you up for an expensive lesson in *laissez-faire* economics. With all due respect, ma'am, if Lester did find out about Sammy and left him sucking delta silt, he probably did you a major favor. You were being set up for a first class dicking."

Her eyes lit up at that one, the first sign of life I had seen in minutes. Her face contorted, and a rapid flush rose above the vee neck of her silk pantsuit. Her hands shook as she narrowed her eyes and hissed at me.

"You… are… a… *filthy* man!"

That was the second time she had said that to me. I've been called worse, and by better than her. It sort of rolled off my back.

"Compared to Sammy Cain, ma'am, I've got a heart of solid gold, as big as the head of a baby, to quote Tennessee Williams. You asked me to find Sammy Cain. You can't hit what you can't see."

"Where is he?" she demanded shrilly.

I stared at her.

"You said it. I hired you to find Sammy. Where is he?"

I shook my head. The sad part was, she really meant it. Despite the fact that I had clearly nailed Sammy to the wall as the scumbag he was, she still wanted to find him.

"I don't know," I told her. "He could be anywhere. Maybe he thought you were catching on to him, and he took off to hunt elsewhere. Maybe you're right, and Lester got rid of him. Maybe he's got his fingers in more than one pie, and someone else had him eliminated. I don't know where he is."

She drained the glass of wine, the way guys in the desert suck down a canteen of water.

"You haven't finished the job," she said at last, a stray lock of hair falling across her forehead.

I had to admit it. She had me.

"No," I agreed, trying to maintain eye contact. "That's the other reason I came here. As far as I'm concerned, I've done my job. I may not have delivered Sammy Cain to your doorstep, but maybe I went one better." I picked up the paper from the glass tabletop in front of me. "I brought you the real Sammy Cain, not the slick image he showed you. If I were you, I'd take this sheet of paper, burn it, and give Lester the hottest night of his life when he gets home. Then get up the next morning and thank providence that you didn't piss all this away for some asswipe like Cain."

She started to protest, but I quieted her by raising my hand.

"On the other hand, " I continued, "if you want me to continue the hunt, you need to be aware of a couple of things. Sammy Cain is the kind of douchebag I dream about squashing. I've got the smell of him in my nostrils, and if you turn me loose after him I'm not going to stop until I find him. I don't care who I piss off, and I don't give a damn from this point on whether you want me to stop or not. Don't bother calling me off. I'm not just working for you from here on in. I'm also working for a woman in Vegas, and another in Tahoe, and a third in Galveston. That's just the way I am, and if Cully Tucker didn't tell you about that when he was reading you my resume, well, that's not my fault. So, Mrs. Vincouer, what do you say? Cut your losses now, or go for the big enchilada?"

"I don't know about you," said someone behind me, "but I'm intrigued by the enchilada."

I whirled around, and Venus stood there in the doorway, her hair slicked back with pool water, the smell of chlorine suddenly permeating the sunroom. I had missed it by at least an inch. She was five-eleven easy in bare feet, and her eyes were the color of spring foliage. She had pulled on one of those short-short armless terry pool robes, and cinched it tight around her impossibly trim waist. She was hypnotic, almost chemically attractive, and somewhere south of the Levis button Big Jim and the Twins were getting ready to rumble.

I stopped myself, with a silent but salient reminder that this sloppy, lumbering son of Eire didn't have a chance. Still, the beauty in the doorway extended her hand.

"Meg Coley," she said, "I'm Clancey's beard, as I'm sure she already told you."

"Pat Gallegher," I replied, taking her hand. It was cool, the way fine jade is, no matter what the room temperature. Her impeccable nails dragged along my palm as we separated, or was that my imagination? I searched for some elaboration, some way of explaining my role in this curious five character parlor mystery, but nothing adequate came to mind. I just never gave much thought to who or what I am, and at that exact moment I wasn't feeling all that creative. Reluctantly, I turned back to face Clancey Vincouer.

"Ms. Coley is obviously a romantic," I argued. "But she doesn't know the whole story…"

"Call me Meg," Ms. Coley purred behind me. *Purred*, damn it!

I ignored her, and continued. "I can't be any more serious than I am now, Mrs. Vincouer. This is the last chance you have to drop this search. Sammy Cain isn't worth finding, but unless you give up now, I will find him. Dead or alive."

Clancey stood and crossed the room to the bar again. She filled her wine glass, and gestured to Meg Coley, who nodded. Clancey poured some wine into another glass for her friend. Something else happened between them in that moment and it shot through me like x-rays. There was a secret pact formed, based on a hidden agenda, a shared confidence that didn't include me. Meg Coley wasn't just telling Clancey Vincouer that she wanted a glass of wine. She was agreeing to a damn sight more than was ever trampled out of a grape.

I didn't have a choice, I realized. I had been bought, and now I was expected to deliver.

I let myself out, and drove back down the tree-covered drive without looking back at the palatial main house. All the way to Lakeshore Drive, I tried to figure out where to look next for Sammy Cain.

Seven

I had to admit it, Meg Coley had struck a nerve, one of the rawer, less protected ones close to the surface. I had gone a long while without a taste of the ol' boy-girl thing. It had been almost a year and a half since Claire Sturges had died not six feet away from me, messily, in her own living room.

Adam Kincaid, a deranged, cancer-ridden psycho from my deep past, had reappeared to even the score with me before he succumbed to his illness. Claire and I had been a sort of on-again-off-again item for months, ever since I had done her a favor finding Baxter Flagg's killer. It had been innocent at first, lots of dinners and movies to keep each other company, but with time the conversations became more intimate, the hours later, and finally one night I just didn't bother going home.

Kincaid found out about Claire, and used her to get to me. It was a gory scene when the police arrived. Kincaid was pulped up on the sidewalk six stories beneath Claire's apartment patio, and Claire was lying open-eyed and cooling on her living room floor, with one of Kincaid's forty-fives in her chest. I was sitting against the wall, sobbing because my damnable luck had held one more time while hers was running out.

Some days, life really sucks.

It was during my recovery from that little Greek tragedy that I came across an old high school annual with a cryptic note written by Joanna

Strong. She had inscribed "Thanks for everything, including things I would have to tell you about in person," next to her picture. Somehow, I had never bothered to find out what she meant by that, but that moment seemed as good as any to track her down and ask.

It took me the better part of a month to find her, doing it the hard way, driving from town to town picking up the snippets of her life she had dropped in the course of three marriages and divorces. I finally found her in upstate New York, mired in a marriage of convenience to a banker she saw maybe once a month.

As it happened, she hadn't a clue what she had meant by the note, and chalked it up to some girlish crisis long forgotten. She did remember me, though, and welcomed me into her home as a refreshing breeze from her relatively uncluttered, infinitely less complicated past.

And, oh boy, was that sweet. There was no pretense, no embarrassed fumbling. We just fell together to salve each other's wounds. We'd screw some, cry some, and screw some more, without any attempt to convince ourselves it was anything more than mind-numbing escapism. It was empty as Al Capone's vault, but it did the trick. We parted after a week, both much happier. I still grieved for Claire all the way back to the Quarter, but I felt a ton better about me.

It had been several months, and I still heard from Joanna from time to time. She was the last, though, and when Meg Coley purred at me, I nearly went through the roof.

Searching for Sammy Cain couldn't occupy all my time. I did, after all, have my day job, even if it was at night. Just as the Budweiser clock over Shorty's bar struck nine, I climbed onto the platform next to Sockeye Sam's piano and the two of us launched right into a spicy rendition of "*Spain*". Sockeye claims not to care about the newer stuff, but he was into it this evening. When it came time for him to break into his solo, I lowered the Conn band cornet and scanned the room. To my surprise, Stanley Porch had taken a seat near the bar, where he sat sweating profusely while trying to look nonchalant, sucking on a Michelob.

Well, I figured, *let him sweat*. I had work to do, and if Porch was in such a state he had to come to my home for a change, he could damn well wait until the end of the first set.

It made me steamy, Porch coming to Holliday's. I try to keep my private life and my indentureship to Leduc separated. Shorty likes it that way, even if Leduc doesn't give a damn, and I have to keep peace with Shorty. Still, very few people know about my contract with Leduc. Fewer know that their friendly neighborhood enforcer toots his horn at a local bar. I prefer this arrangement. It's simple, and I don't have to devote a lot of attention to which hat I'm wearing at any given moment.

Ignoring Porch's passionate gestures, I launched into something long and indulgent based loosely on Harburg and Lane's "*Look to the Rainbow*". It was easy. I could remember my Dad singing that song to me when I was little, rocking me gently each night, after my Mom died. Even as I launched into the chorus, I could smell that piquant combination of Old Spice and old sweat, as he cradled my skinny little Irish body in his arms and rocked me back and forth. I could remember looking up into his dark, lost eyes, and the wetness that gathered there more frequently the longer his wife lay under the cemetery loam.

Like most the sweet things in life, though, it had to come to an end. That song always exhausted me, even as it used to put me to sleep in my Dad's lap, and I set the horn down to rest my weary chops. I ignored the irony that I had chosen the one tune guaranteed to expedite this loathsome encounter with the Porchster, and shambled off the ersatz stage to his table. I stopped, first, on the way, to grab a cold Dixie from Shorty. He knew I was coming. He had it out on the counter, uncapped, waiting for me. It was a ritual between us, born and nurtured through the long years I had slaved here.

At least, I think the beer was for me.

I drew up a chair and sat facing Porch. His cheeks were more florid than usual, his brow literally drenched with flopsweat.

"Gallegher," he began, "You gotta help me."

Any number of witty replies flashed across my tongue, but I settled for the sublime.

"Why?"

That got him. He'd probably expected me to turn him down outright, and he was full up to here with counter arguments. This question, as it happened, had completely evaded him.

"Huh?" he asked.

"Why do I have to help you, Stanley?"

"Well…" he started, hoping that by framing an answer, one would come to him. It didn't. He settled back in his chair and stared sullenly at the drink he'd been nursing for almost a quarter hour. "I'm in big trouble."

I nodded. Porch is a wheeler-dealer. He competes in the arena of words and ideas. He's made a lot of money a little at a time, hustling people into spending cash they need for crap they don't. His weakness, though, and that of most the hustlers and barkers I run into, was that he couldn't handle colliding with a silent, unmoving object. He waited for several seconds for me to add something verbal to the nod, and then shook his head.

"Man, I can't do it," he said at last. "I've tried everything, and I can't come up with the cash. You gotta…" he stopped as I gave him my mean warning look, the one that makes brave men's blood run cold.

"I'm sorry," he corrected, accurately. "I was wondering… I mean, is there any way you could talk Leduc into giving me an extension?"

I drained the Dixie in one huge, intimidating gulp, and stared at the porcine little shit. I lowered my voice to a sinister hiss, straight out of some *film noir.*

"You have to be joking," I whispered. "Leduc doesn't give extensions. He *takes* them."

To accentuate the point, I made snipping motions with my fingers. Porch's eyes went wide, probably straining from the pressure of his balls hiding right behind them. I was getting to him. I'm ashamed to admit it now, but it was sort of fun.

"Aw, come on, Gallegher," he pled, in a strained, whiny falsetto. "Isn't there something you can do?"

"I just work for the man," I said. "He calls, I come. He says go, I'm there. He says hurt, I break things. He likes that arrangement. I'm not sure he'd take kindly to me telling him how to run his business."

I let him stew on this one for a minute, while I retrieved a fresh Dixie from behind the bar.

"Maybe…" I said, as I sat back at Porch's table, letting the last syllable hang there, like the light seeping through a condemned man's hood on the scaffold. "No, forget it. It wouldn't work."

I had him. He bit, hard, and the hook dug, deep. He leaned forward, his eyes searching for any shred of hope.

"Wait," he urged. "Don't be so quick. What is it?"

"Aw, you wouldn't like it."

"*What*?" he almost squealed.

"Then again," I mused, reeling him in a bit, "it couldn't hurt to try. What do you owe Leduc again?"

"Fifteen thousand, and change."

"You have the change?"

He nodded. "I can get it by morning, when the bank opens. It's more than my ATM daily limit, or I could get it tonight."

"Morning will be fine," I said distantly. "Wait here."

I crossed Holliday's to the stairway leading to my loft, taking care not to forget my beer, and used the phone in my apartment to page Grover.

Grover is a pimp. There is no way you could look at him and not know that he is a pimp. He has little beady pimp eyes, and slicked back pimp hair, and these long, skinny pimp fingers decked out with shiny gold pimp jewelry. If you were walking down Bourbon Street and saw him from fifty yards across the street, you'd be hard pressed not to say to yourself, 'Now, doesn't he look like a pimp'.

In addition to his other habits, he is also an accomplished sneak thief, pickpocket, con man, and a hell of a fence. He's the kind of guy who could steal your radio and leave the music playing.

Grover called back within five minutes. He knew it was me, by my number. He knows all the numbers on this side of town.

"Yo, Gallegher," he greeted. "Don't tell me you looking for a twist, man."

"No way, Grove," I said. "What do you think you can get for a fresh Lexus?"

"Which model?" he asked, and I could almost hear him consulting the Blue Book he keeps in his head.

"The big one. Leather interior, all the bells and whistles."

"Maybe twenty grand."

"Interested in making a quick turnaround of a quarter?" He knew I was referring to twenty five hundred.

"I don't know," he said, warily.

"All legal," I added. "Not a thing dirty in it. I have this guy, see, who needs fifteen big ones right now. If I can talk him into it, would you be able to put that together tonight? You can turn the car around before dawn and still have time to make the rounds of your girls."

"I can steal it for free," he said.

"Come on," I urged. "This is a business deal. All on the up and up. I got him hooked. He just needs to be pulled into the boat."

There was a long silence.

"Where you, man?" he finally asked.

"At the club. Are you interested?"

"You said a quarter. I give this 'guy' you got fifteen, and I turn the car around for twenty, that five grand."

He was bullshitting me, and I knew it. He would get twenty five, easy, for the Lexus, and he was still trying to stiff me.

"Finder's fee," I countered. "I found the guy, and the car."

You could almost hear the gears turning.

"I give you two," he said. It was his way. He had to believe that he was going to get a little ahead on the deal, or he wouldn't bargain. What the hell, though? It was found money no matter how much it was.

"Okay, but only because I'm in a hurry, and we have such a long business history."

I heard a snort from his end of the phone, his somewhat uncharacteristic way of laughing.

"Yeah, whatever. Okay, Gallegher, I be there in fifteen minutes."

I hung up the phone and returned to the table. Stanley was working himself up into a real lather, like he thought I was recruiting him for a bank job or something.

"Well?" he asked.

"Where's your car, man?"

He paled, a bit, but managed to stammer, "It's... it's in a pay lot, over across Canal."

"Is your title in it?"

He nodded. Stanley was a slimeball among slimeballs, but he was also smart, and he could see the handwriting on the wall.

"I have this guy," I started, "He's interested in buying your car. He'll only deal through me, and he can only come up with fourteen grand. I'm sure you can get the other grand," then I added, "and change."

So I lied. Shit rolls downhill. I have to make a living, too, don't I?

"Yeah, I can do that," Porch said reluctantly, "but that car, man, it sold for over thirty..."

"Hey, you know how it goes," I argued, "Damn things lose half their value the minute you drive them off the lot. That's why I always buy used. How else are you going to sell that car by eight in the morning, if I don't get it done for you?"

He looked suspicious, but it was just the avarice in him.

"Don't worry about it," I chided him. "You take the money you were able to raise for Leduc, take out the grand and change, and use the rest for a down payment for a new car. And stay away from the baccarat tables until it's paid off."

Porch glanced around the room, as if he were searching for some kind of financial escape hatch.

"Look, we don't have a lot of time," I pressed. "My guy, he's going to be here any minute. What I need is for you to get the title out of your car, and bring it here. Just sign the sales line. Don't worry about the notary, my guy has one on his payroll. You bring the title, I'll have the cash, you can pay off Leduc tomorrow, and you don't have to worry about some fellow bigger and meaner than me showing up at your house this weekend. It's easy, it's quick, just like that."

He looked genuinely pained.

"You came to me for help," I said, leaning back in my chair. "You don't want it...?" I shrugged.

"No," he replied, defeated. "It's a deal. Fourteen thousand?"

"Firm," I said.

And, to cement the deal, I thrust out my hammy right paw. Porch flinched for an instant, then his own hand disappeared into it.

"Okay," I told him. "Go get that title."

Fifteen minutes later, I came down the stairs from my palatial digs over the bar, with one hundred forty crisp new franklins in an envelope, and ten in my pocket. Porch's title stayed in my apartment with Grover, who was already on the telephone lining up the sale, which would net me another twenty bills.

I handed him the money, and he grabbed at it like the golden teat. I didn't let go, though. He tugged once or twice, then looked up, exasperated.

"What gives?" he whined.

"Just this," I said, again selecting my most menacing persona. "I just saved your fat little ass, Porch. If I hadn't done you the favor you asked, you'd have been in intensive care this time tomorrow night. You owe me. Someday, I'm going to collect on that debt. Understand?"

"Yeah, sure," he agreed, still concentrating more on the envelope.

"No, I don't think you do," I argued, still clutching the money. "Someday, I might call you, and say to come, just like Leduc does to me. When I do, you'd better come, right then, without asking a lot of bullshit questions. You may have satisfied Leduc, but now I'm holding your note."

His eyes had left the envelope now, and were focused on my own. I conjured up something vile, filthy, and despicable from the coal-black nether regions of my soul, and filled my eyes with it. That was when I saw it. He was terrified. It would be months before he would be able to even think of me without a sudden need to rush to the bathroom. It had to be that way. It was the only way I could depend on him to be there if I needed him.

"Yeah, okay," he said, as if he couldn't wait to put several miles between us. "I understand. It's a deal. You call, I'll come. You got it."

I released the envelope, which disappeared into Porch's jacket pocket almost faster than I could see it move.

"Good." I said. "Now, the best thing you can do is get out of here before my guy shows up. If he sees you, he might want his money back."

I could have sworn I saw smoke as he dashed out of the bar.

Eight

"Forgive me, Father, for I have sinned," I said, as my nose wrinkled at the intrusion of ages-old dust and cheap incense. The confessional was dark, dank, and cool compared to the steam bath outside the church. It was already mid-autumn, but the Vieux Carre keeps its own calendar, the whimsies of which take no man's desires into account.

"How long since your last confession?" asked the wheezy voice on the other side of the ornate wooden grate. If I squinted just enough, I could make out the silhouette of Alphonse D'Agostino—Dag to his friends—lounging on his end of the box.

"Four months, but I've been out of town a lot."

"The Holy Church can be found everywhere, son."

"I know, Father. I'll try to remember. Since my last confession, I've killed a man. Well, two, but one was an accident."

Dag coughed lightly. He'd heard this particular one before. Still, I was pretty sure it fell outside the bounds of his typical confession.

"Was your life in danger at the time?"

Well, now, was it? Barry Saunders had me in his sights, my hand stuck in the freezing ice water of the beer cooler at Holliday's. He had already told me he intended my death to look like a robbery-related shooting. Yeah, my life had been in danger. It had been nothing but dumb luck that I remembered the pistol Shorty kept under the cash register.

"Yes. If I hadn't killed him, he would have killed me."

"It is a grave thing to take another person's life, son, but in the interest of self-defense, it is not a sin."

"I made a lot of money by killing him. It wasn't the reason I killed him, but I did profit."

"One shouldn't profit by the self-inflicted death of others, but it happens. I'm sure you will do the right thing with the money."

I weighed his words. Dag had a way of putting the squeeze on you without actually coming out and saying it.

"I, um, I cheated a man who came to me for help."

There was a long pause, while Dag tried to figure this one out.

"Did you help him?" he said at last.

"His immediate problem is resolved. He faced physical harm if I didn't help him, and now he doesn't…" At least, that's what I hoped. I didn't actually know whether Porch had delivered the money to Leduc. For all I knew, he had driven straight to Harrah's and blown it at baccarat. If so, he was now beyond my help.

"You made money by helping him?"

"It's what I do, Dag… Father," I corrected. I realized I was sounding a little irritated. Dag, like Quentin Wardell, knew all about my sideline.

"Yes, that seems the case. Well, you did keep your agreement to help him. If you made money in the process, and if he is out of danger, then I've heard nothing so far that sounds like more than a business arrangement. If it were a sin to help people, then every psychiatrist in town would be here."

On my side of the confessional, I smiled. Dag had an interesting take on the world. Then I cleared my throat for one he couldn't shake off.

"I slept with another man's wife."

"That's a biggie," Dag said, almost immediately.

"I'm not going to make an excuse about it, like saying she didn't really love him or anything. It just happened, that's all. It's over. I don't think I'll be seeing her again." Then, for emphasis, I added, "Ever."

"That's good. Temptation can be a difficult thing to overcome."

Boy did I know. And Dag did, too. Father Alphonse was an alcoholic, like a lot of priests. It's like some kind of sublimation for the other things they swear off when they take up the cassock. They listen to people spew out the filth and effluvia of their lives all day long, and then have no one to turn to when their own secret fears assault them in the blue-black hours of the night. Sometimes, their closest friend comes in a bottle. Dag was like that, and I couldn't count on both hands the times I'd delivered him back to the church in the bag before he joined AA.

He gave me absolution, and I did my penance. Then I wended my way to the back of the church, where Dag kept his office. He was sitting at his desk, forehead cradled in one hand while the other was busy writing figures on a legal pad. I knocked on the door.

"Pat," Dag said after looking up, "please, come on in. Have a seat."

I did, and waited for him to finish.

"Blasted bills," he growled as he put down the pencil. "I'm going to have to deliver a real barnburner of a sermon this week. Maybe then the parishioners will dig a little deeper for the collection. What can I do for you?"

I fished an envelope out of my pants pocket and dropped it on the desk in front of him. He took it and looked inside, emitting a long low whistle.

"This money..." he started.

"It isn't the money I cheated the guy out of, and it isn't the money I got after killing the other guy," I told him. "In case you were wondering."

"Fair enough," Dag said, and stowed the envelope in his desk drawer. "As it happens, I just this morning received a bill for the plumbing repairs in the soup kitchen. The church owes you its thanks."

I leaned forward, my hands resting on his desk. "I'll take a favor."

Dag knew better than to question my motives. After the time we had spent together, he could be certain I wouldn't take advantage of the situation.

"Name it."

I settled back in the leather-upholstered wing chair. It was the kind of chair made for a guy my size. Folks of my length and width do not prefer Scandia designs.

"I'm looking for a fellow, he's Catholic. He's not a nice guy, but I'm hoping he hasn't lost all his religion. You can take the boy out of the church, but... " I winked at him.

Dag nodded, sagely. "The early training does tend to insinuate itself, no matter how far you stray. You want me to check with the other parish priests to find out if he's in their congregations?"

"Yeah," I said. "You guys have a better network than AT&T."

"I won't violate the sanctity of the confessional, and neither will the others..."

"And I wouldn't ask you to. All I want to know is whether he's attending somewhere. Maybe I'll get lucky. Maybe he's teaching a Sunday School class."

Dag fingered the money, as he stared at me, as if he could just make out my soul somewhere behind my eyes. I didn't mind. He was entitled to his fantasies.

"I'll see what I can do," he said finally. He picked up the money. "You didn't have to do this."

"Now that we've established our mutual lack of obligation, I have work to do," I told him, and started to rise.

"Wait," Dag urged. "I... I'm not sure I've ever thanked you for, well, for keeping me out of trouble all those times."

"Save it. It's not a good idea for parishioners to stumble across the shepherd stinko in the Vieux Carre gutters. I considered it a public service. I figure I've sucked up enough of your absolutions over the years to make up for it."

"Perhaps. The Church lost a good one in you, Pat."

"But the music world gained a giant." I smiled and stood, extending my hand. "Hang in there, Dag. Get the plumbing fixed."

We said our goodbyes, and I strolled out of the church, pausing for just a moment to genuflect. I wasn't even sure why. It wasn't as if I actually bought into all the pomp and circumstance. Maybe it was something even deeper and more profound than faith, something like force of habit.

When I thought about it, I hadn't given the issue of Heaven and Hell a lot of consideration, at least not in the last several years. There had been a time, perhaps, when such concepts were important. It would have been comforting to believe that Claire Sturges, who had died because I was just a fraction of second too slow, had awakened to find herself in some paradise of golden paths and celestial choirs. I only wished I could dredge up some faith in the idea.

I had seen far too much death, though. I remembered how, as a college professor, I had lectured confidently about the near-death experience, as some sort of abstract construct devised by the mind to cope with ultimate finality. When a man I barely knew and cared less for died in my arms early on the sweetest Sunday morn since the first one, death became a hell of a lot less abstract. I recall gazing into his eyes, looking for some sort of revelation, some sort of reassuring epiphany. All I got in return was the same sort of glassy, vacant stare one finds in a seafood market. I was not comforted, and it was no picnic for the other guy.

My mother, before she died, tried her damnedest to deny the corruption of the tomb. She believed, against reason, in ashes to ashes and dust to dust. Somehow, she could not bring herself to consider putrefaction and decay. I, on the other hand, found myself with a more realistic perspective on the whole checking-out thing. Some days, I thought it was that perspective that kept me alive when all about me seemed to be biting the big one. Other days, I just didn't give a damn. It was just a matter of time before that black mood came over me just before someone decided to draw a bead on my fat fanny. In the meantime, I found my solace in doing little things that mattered, like finding Sammy Cain, and getting Dag's plumbing fixed with my ill-gotten gains. Yin and yang, anima and animus, the quartering of the world into active and passive principles, call it what you will. I just figured if this was my day to get dirt shoveled in my face, my myriad sins were balanced by my largesse. It might not count for diddly in the ethereal sphere, but at least my conscience wouldn't bother me as my vision faded.

Besides, I could deduct the donation on my tax return.

Nine

The crowded room was filling with cigarette smoke as I stood and took my place on the slightly raised dais, in front of the cheap directional microphone. I licked my lips lightly, and surveyed the assembled mass of people staring back expectantly. If there was ever a time for performance anxiety, this was it. I was a pro, however, and I had stood in this spot many times. I reached out, gingerly grasped the shaft of the microphone stand, and leaned over to being my face close to the mike.

"Hi, my name is Pat," I greeted them, "And I'm a gambling addict."

The gathered masses, as if forming a Greek chorus, sonorously replied, "Hi, Pat."

Geez, it was little more than the liturgy I'd been taught in seminary—greeting followed by practiced response. How tough could this be?

"I like blackjack," I continued. "Like it a lot. Like it so much I dropped over fifteen grand on it over the course of a few weeks. I, uh, decided that, no matter how much I liked it, I wasn't going to be one of the all-time great players. So I decided to quit. That's why I'm here. I have a problem with my gambling behavior, and it took control of my life."

Okay, so much for Step One.

There was a smattering of polite applause from the group. Three years ago, you could have counted the members of the local Gamblers'

Anonymous on the fingers of both hands. Since then, though, Harrah's and the Flamingo have moved over the border from Mississippi, and the numbers of the flock have just flourished like kudzu.

Actually, I hadn't gotten within field goal range of a casino in months. I don't even own a deck of playing cards. In the global sense, my recovery was going great guns. They say you have to dance with the one what brung you, though, and for me that was GA. I was in sorry shape when I attended my first meeting, all raw nerves, fear of destitution, driven largely by caffeine. Leduc had already started to put the squeeze on me, and I was afraid of becoming some sort of underworld flunkie. Now, though, I was the picture of self assurance.

Being an underworld flunkie, I had discovered, had certain benefits. While I was still in debt up to my eyeballs, I had reached a level of stasis, in which I wasn't necessarily catching up, but I also wasn't slipping back. While that might look pathological to the casual observer, I found it disturbingly comforting.

Besides, I thought as I droned on through the next two Steps, I had bigger problems at the moment. Specifically, I had gone almost a week without making the slightest progress in my search for Sammy Cain. After my discussion with Clancey Vincouer at stately Wayne Manor, I had hit the proverbial wall. It seemed as if Cain had merged with the ozone. There was nothing from Dag, though he assured me that he had made his inquiries. I had set up a daily stakeout near Cain's apartment, hoping that he might show up to clean his bathroom or check the expiration date on his milk. No dice.

Maybe Clancey was right. Maybe ol' Lester had done in Sammy. Maybe Sammy was already swept out into the Gulf, moldering in the silt a mile below the surface, never to be found.

Or, it could be that he had once again done the exit stage right routine, and was setting up shop in St. Louis, or Miami, or Mexico City. If that were the case, I would find him in time. In the interim, I spent my days sitting in the Pinto reading the collected works of John D.

MacDonald, and playing the occasional game of electronic chess. My nights were spent, as always, on stage at Holliday's.

I finished my testimony, again to smattering applause, and stepped down. As another poor soul made his way to the dais, I strode to the back of the hall and grabbed some iced tea and a couple of gaggy, stale oatmeal cookies. The fluorescent overhead light cast a stark luminescence over the seated members. Suddenly, I didn't want to be here anymore. Like a parishioner who has been given absolution and received the host, I was aware of the urge to leave as quickly as possible, return to my secular life, and resume my naughty ways.

Besides, it was time to go to work.

Hours later, I had given up standing, and was seated on a tall bar stool. It had been a good night, both creatively and in terms of tips. It was a little after two in the morning, barely lunchtime for me, and I was working my way through a lumbering improvisation on Paul Desmond's charts of the theme from *M*A*S*H*. I had been on stage for almost forty-five minutes, and my jaw was beginning to get tight. It was time to take a break. I meandered my way back to the theme, and Sockeye and I wrapped up the set.

Shorty was waiting for me at the bar with my obligatory Dixie.

"There's someone here asking for you," he said, pointing toward one of the dark corners of the bar.

"Hope it's Sammy Cain," I murmured, taking the Dixie. I glanced over, and my heart skipped a beat.

As I lived and breathed, there was Clancey Vincouer's dear friend and alibi, Meg Coley. She sat there, all carmine tresses and trim calves, in a green form fitting skirt and white blouse open just a little too much for my blood pressure. She noticed me noticing her, and waved covertly, as if she feared causing a stampede from the bar in her direction.

I navigated my way between the tables, and sat across from her without saying a word.

She made the gambit. "So, how's it going with the whole enchilada?"

"You can't put a schedule to genius," I noted. "He'll show up sooner or later."

"Boy , you're a big one," she observed. "Bet you're mean, too."

"You'd lose. I am large, but with the heart of a poet."

"A poet, hmm? You mean, like Shelley, or Oscar Wilde?"

Her meaning was not lost on me, but I decided not to take the bait. "Wilde wasn't a poet. He was a playwright. I'm more like Yeats."

There was an instant, just a glimmer, of surprise. "Well-read, too. I'm impressed."

"Thank you. Now you can go back and tell Clancey I'm not squandering her money."

"Don't be ridiculous. Do you really think I'm here to spy for Clancey Vincouer?"

Directness seemed the best approach, if only to help me ignore her hand, which had come to rest halfway up my thigh. "Yes," I said, "I do."

"Then *you'd* lose," she simmered. "That would make us even. Aren't you a real cynic, though."

"Let's say I have a healthy distrust for serendipity. This bar isn't exactly on the Hot Spots tourist maps. You're not likely to just stumble into this place. So, since you're here, and since Clancey Vincouer has been here, I can only surmise that she sent you."

"My god, you *are* a cynic. I have to admit, though, that I did ask Clancey some questions about you. You know what I'd like to see?"

I was reluctant to ask. She dug those perfect nails into my thigh.

"I want to see your big, wide…" I braced myself. "…bookcase."

"My, uh, bookcase?"

"Yes," she said coyly, "What did you think? Clancey told me about this bookcase that took up one whole wall. I'm fascinated by books. You can look at a person's books and tell almost everything there is to know about him."

There were so many options, so I settled for my own version of coy and charming. "Now why on earth would you want to know everything there is to know about me?"

She pouted—*pouted*—and I even believe I caught the momentary batting of eyelashes. Whatever her game was, she was very, very good at it.

"You have to admit, you are an unusual specimen."

"Specimen?"

"We live in boring times, don't we?" she said. "Our heroes are investment bankers and the occasional athlete. The romance is leaking from our modern world. Then, I hear about you. Here you are, a man who places his life on the line for the most meager of pay, and you call it a favor!"

Damn Cully Tucker. Just how much had he told Clancey Vincouer about me?

"It's hardly like that. It's not like I set up shop and hung out a shingle. What was it John Lennon said? *'Life is what happens while you're making plans for life'*. Well, that's sort of what happened to me."

"Still, it's fascinating."

Okay, let's get a couple of things straight right here and now. I have been on the unlucky end of a gun more times than I care to recall over the last several years. Mostly through the intervention of ungodly good fortune, I have survived to tell this tale, but it helped that I wasn't stupid. I know a setup when I walk blindly into one. Meg Coley, delicious as she appeared on the surface, had more on her mind than a simple perusal of the Gallegher Library. Whether that ulterior motive was as simple as a jolly romp and toss, or darker and more sinister, could not be divined as we sat in the dusk of the back corner at Holliday's. If it were the former, the worst I could say about myself the next morning would be that I had been selfishly and wantonly used, and I'd be eternally grateful for the privilege. As for the latter possibility—well, as I mentioned earlier, one of the ways I find out what I need to know is by walking through open doors and hoping there's nothing deadly on the other side.

It helps keep the reflexes keen.

"Well, come on then," I said, and led her to the narrow back stairway. Moments later, we stood in my humble abode.

"What beautiful floors!" she exclaimed.

"A benefit of the renovation by the fish company next door, " I told her. "And here's the bookcase."

I motioned toward the far wall.

She didn't say a word, but rather walked straight to the left side of the case and started perusing the titles.

I don't use any particular cataloging system. A volume on laminar flow rates might live just next door to a collection of eighteenth century love sonnets. I tended to know where a particular title was located, but a stranger might stroll for hours looking for, say, the collected works of Jack London. While she browsed, I grabbed a Jax from the refrigerator, and settled into my comfy green lounge chair. I was in no rush. If I didn't get downstairs before the next set, Sockeye Sam would start without me. Shorty didn't make me punch a clock.

She surfed from shelf to shelf for almost a quarter hour, occasionally pulling a tome from the stacks and flipping through it with lithe, lively fingers as I sat jealously across the room sucking down a brew. My delusion that her interest was a thinly disguised attempt at seduction was vanishing like smoke.

As she skimmed a first edition copy of Maugham's *Catalina* , her attention was caught by my framed diploma on the wall running perpendicular to the bookcase. Still carrying the book, she crossed the floor to gaze at it.

"A doctorate?" she asked, with the usual mixture of curiosity and surprise.

"Piled Higher and Deeper," I replied. "My personal testament to the ability to withstand five years of education above and beyond the call of duty."

"What in?"

"Psychology. Clinical."

She returned to the stacks and replaced the Maugham novel in precisely the spot from whence it had been taken. I appreciated her consideration, even if I didn't plan to read that particular book within the next decade.

"You're a psychologist?" she asked, as she took a seat on my threadbare sofa near the window. She stretched languorously, pulling her legs up to tuck underneath her flanks, as if she intended to stay there awhile. I couldn't take my gaze from her eyes, the color of fine jade.

"Was," I corrected. "My license expired years ago. I haven't seen a clinical client since the Reagan administration. I taught for a while."

"College?"

"A university in the northeast, which I believe would prefer I not associate my name with its own."

"Why did you leave?"

I failed to suppress the heavy sigh that almost always accompanied the answer to this question.

"There was a difference of opinion," I told her, "between a young lady—one of my students—and me regarding what I had told her she would have to do to get an 'A' in my Abnormal Psych class. There was a series of hearings, leading right up to the Christmas holiday break. Somehow, during the break, I got fed up with the process, and I just didn't come back in January. It is my impression that the school was relieved. That was the end of my teaching career."

Her stare never wavered. People tended to take one approach or another to this story. Either they sympathized with me for my tragic misfortune and unjust accusation, or they excused themselves quietly, disinterested in spending any further time with a person who might do such a thing.

Meg Coley shook her head, and waved her hand nonchalantly.

"It happens," she said.

That was a new one. Still, I managed to reply, "To the best of us. Can I get you a beer?"

"Do you have wine?" she asked.

As it happened, I did. I kept a nicely appointed rack in my tiny kitchen.

"White, red, or blush?"

"Surprise me."

I disappeared briefly into the galley, and retrieved a chilled bottle of Gewürztraminer from the refrigerator. After opening it and presenting her with a glass, I returned to my recliner.

"So," I said, "Tell me all about Sammy Cain."

She sipped her wine as she lounged across the sofa, then said, "I don't know much about him, other than what Clancey told me. We met once, when he picked her up at my apartment in the Garden District."

"You don't live in Lake Terrace?"

"Oh, God no!" she exclaimed. "Unless you can afford a plantation, why live out there? Let's face it, if you aren't here in the Quarter, or in the District, this can be a mighty depressing town. I just visit Clancey out there, use her pool. It's a good thing she told me you were coming the other day—I don't always wear a swimsuit."

I tried to ignore the comment, at least for the moment, but the image was far too intrusive to put away entirely.

"What was your impression of Cain, the time he picked Clancey up?"

"Oh, come on, honey," she said, chuckling slightly, "I could figure him out from twenty yards. He's a ladykiller. All superficial charm and disarming manners. There isn't a genuine bone in his entire body. He's as phony as a Chinese Pharo deck. On the other hand, he's a great dresser, and he obviously knows how to treat a lady."

"Until he fleeces her," I noted.

"Until then. Even then, I'll bet, a lot of them continue to carry fond memories of the bastard. I've met a lot like him in my time. They come, and they go, and they're good for a fun rollick while they're around, but you know it'll never last."

"Did Clancey know that?"

She stretched just enough to make her nearly diaphanous blouse pull tight against her generous bosom. I tried to concentrate.

"The wine is delicious, sir. May I have more?"

"Why not?" I said, and lumbered across the room to replenish her glass. "One refill, coming up."

"Oh, no," she argued, reaching up to steady my hand as I poured. "You must never say '*refill*'. That would imply that the lady is such a lush that she has emptied her glass. You have to say '*freshen*'."

Her glass was three-quarters full, so I twisted the bottle gently to keep it from dripping, with a tiny thrill as her fingernails dragged across the back of my hand.

"I'll try to remember," I said, after setting the bottle down. On impulse, I sat at the far end of the sofa rather than returning to my chair. She didn't scream or run from the room, which I took as a small victory, so I stayed there.

"So, did Clancey know it wouldn't last with Cain?"

"I don't know," she said, after cooking the notion for several seconds. "I know she's never had an affair before. She told me that much. I also told her it would end in tears, but she wouldn't listen. She was blinded by him, you know. He was all hair and muscle and dick... oh, I'm sorry."

I swept at the air with my hand.

"No foul. I know the word. I've even seen one or two in my time. She was blinded by him..."

"It was what he did. He knows how to impress people. It's his skill. I know that kind of person very well."

"Because you're one of them?"

I had expected her to recoil in anger, or slap me across the puss, or maybe just toss the wine in my face, but she didn't. It was as if, somehow, I had entered into her confidence, and she realized that I was onto her. She smiled slyly, and I knew I was being seduced. Having glommed onto her secret, she didn't mind using it on me openly.

"Are you being a psychiatrist now, Mr. Gallegher?"

"I was a psychologist. Psychiatrists are M.D.s. Some habits are hard to break, like confronting someone who's trying to get under your skin."

"To avoid countertransference."

It was my turn to smile.

"Okay, so you've had some classes. Yes, to avoid countertransference."

"And you think I'm trying to get under your skin?"

I settled my Jax bottle on the end table, and said, "It's hard to tell who's trying to get under whose skin around here. You don't live on the Vincouer estate, but you visit frequently to work on the seamless tan. You know what Sammy Cain is, but you also agree to play the beard for Clancey so that she can continue bedding the rat. If you refused, you might lose all the bennies associated with being Clancey's closest, dearest, bosom buddy. In her gratitude, she gives you things, and you like things. For all I know, she really did send you here tonight to check up on me. Maybe she's waiting at home for your report, perhaps with some expensive bauble of a gift socked away as a thank-you. In many ways, you're as cold and calculating as Sammy Cain. You're peas in a pod, trading on your beauty and superficial charm in return for a shot at the easy life."

She sipped at her wine. "Beats working."

I emptied the Jax and nodded. "Yeah, I guess it does at that. Of course, even as I know I'm being conned, the question keeps coming back. Just where in hell is Sammy Cain?"

She placed her wine glass softly on the coffee table, ensuring that there was a coaster underneath it. Then she leaned over and, without ceremony, pressed her lips against mine. I could feel the waxy gooeyness of her lipstick as it rubbed against my mouth. Instinctively, I reached out and pulled her to me. It had been a long time. It was good to feel this again.

She pulled back slightly, to draw a breath, and murmured, "Who gives a damn where Cain is?"

I felt dizzy as I fell into her emerald eyes, and I pulled her back toward me, reveling in the aura of expensive cologne that wafted across my nostrils.

"Right," I said, just before diving in. "Who gives a damn?"

Ten

I was lying in bed, in the dark, the melange of blues and zydeco and rock and jazz from the Quarter drifting through my open window, as the room took on a bluish tint from the neon sign in the voodoo shop across Toulouse Street. My nose was filled with the scent of hibiscus and sandalwood from the woman whose slightly matted tresses flowed across my barrel chest.

Women after sex are at their most mysterious, like cats lounging in a ray of sunlight. Their breathing, so scattered and catchy only moments before, becomes measured, almost hypnotically rhythmic. The warmth that emanates from their bodies carries their own musky aroma of satisfaction, and not a one smells exactly like any of the others. They have shared a centuries-old secret, and the fruits of their experience and fears, and for a moment you join with the current of their lives, where you live with every man who has gone there before you, and you thank them so intensely for what she learned in their embrace.

It is a time when you, and she, are most vulnerable, physically and emotionally, naked to the pursuit of advantage.

Lying in the dark, in that half-slumbering, postcoital nothingness, my sentience drifted in and out of reality with her respiration. It was a time for profundity and discovery, an opportunity to tap into the great collective unconscious and cull, if only momentarily, great forgotten truths.

And all I could do was think about the way she smelled.

It had happened suddenly, almost frenetically, as we plunged into each other on the couch. The games were over, the coy pretense put aside, as our mouths pressed against each other and we explored each others' reserves. She asked if I had a bed, or were we going to be animals and take each other on the floor. I pulled down the Murphy as she yanked her blouse from the waist of her skirt. Before she could unbutton it I was across the room again, and our hands sought and played and rejoiced in the findings.

And we were in bed. There was no knowing how or when it happened. I simply became aware that we were on the mattress, our skin tingling slightly from the coolness of the sheets, and she was the most desirable woman I had seen in my adult life, all warmth and hard edges flowing into soft womanliness. Her slender, tanned arms and the full length of her meter of legs wrapped about me as I responded so readily to her.

Our explosions had been cataclysmic, as she and I grappled for the ecstatic peak of our union, and just as quickly as we stopped shuddering we fell exhaustedly across each other, huffing and gasping.

And now her head rested on my chest, her hair cascading across my torso as certainly as in some torrid love novel, and her breath swept across me like some tropical zephyr, accented every several moments by a murmur that was almost like a contented purr.

The notion launched itself stealthily, from this sort of intrapsychic Oort cloud situated about the outer reaches of my mind, where all my self-doubts and insecurities live and party.

You are not worthy, it whispered, at first seemingly as part of her languorous wheeze, the way an enemy camouflages itself to escape detection until the moment you are its own. *You do not deserve this.*

The hell I didn't. I was tired of giving into my self-image as a loser. I had been running from life for as long as I could remember, and while I knew that this was not true love, neither could it be said that I had no right to enjoy it. This woman snoozing sanguinely in my arms was no more and no less than a predator, and I was not so foolish as to believe that she could be domesticated. For all I knew, her seduction of this sweet son of Eire was simply a small part of a larger plot that would lead to my downfall, and my submission to her undoubtable charms was my own fatal flaw.

Well, like with Sammy Cain, who gave a damn? Did I have so much in this hardscrabble life to lose? If so, then why did I go to such great lengths to wager it on adventures of pity, and toxic crusades?

In ancient times, in the civilizations of mezzo-America, it was not uncommon for a man to be singled out and chosen for delivery to the gods as a token of devotion and worship. The man, who knew his fate as surely as he welcomed it, was lavished on and provided with all the civilization had to offer. He was lionized, icons with his likeness were erected in the squares. All the finest luxuries of the civilization were his for the asking. He could eat the finest food, and sleep with the most beautiful and exotic maidens, right up to the morning he was strapped to the altar to have his still-beating heart excised from his chest, to be shown to him as his vision faltered and dimmed, with the smile still frozen on his face.

If I were being primed for the deliverance to the altar by the jolly lass whose naked skin rested on my own in the dark steamy room over Holliday's who really gave a damn? It would have to be a quick and nimble priest who could strap me down, and even if he did I might allow it for the opportunity to have romped with the red-headed hoyden who lay with me.

She stirred slightly, and may have even moaned a bit, as she rolled off my chest and settled her head on the next-door pillow.

"Damn," she murmured.

"Damn?" I whispered back.

"*God*damn," she cooed. "I had hoped you would be nice, but I never thought... I think I pulled something."

"I know you did."

"I mean, like a muscle. I'll give you exactly a thousand more times to get this thing right."

"Well," I sighed, "that's all fine and good, but what will we do tomorrow night?"

She giggled, in a way that led me to believe that she seldom did or had in quite a long time.

"My, aren't you ambitious?"

I reached across her for a glass of water on the bedside table. "Just wishful thinking. There is a problem, though."

"Nothing that can't be worked out, I hope."

"I have to go back downstairs," I told her. "We've been up here for over an hour, and I'm still at work. Do you have to go?"

"Baby," she said, after kissing me lightly, "I don't have to do a damned thing I don't want to."

I returned the kiss, and started to roll out of the Murphy bed. As I searched for my shirt and jeans, I asked, "What's your favorite song?"

She shinnied upright and wrapped the sheet around her nakedness. I was a little saddened by it.

"Old standard or rock and roll?" she asked.

I pulled my sport shirt over my head. "Pick one."

"Something by Sinatra, I think. One of the old things, the days with Nelson Riddle. *Nice and Easy.*"

"*You Make Me Feel So Young?* "

"Are we going to talk in song titles, love?"

"It's a thought." I started to pull on my pants, wishing that there was some way to look dashing in the process. Richard Brautigan wrote, decades ago, about women when they dress in the morning, and how their bodies slowly disappear and come out quite nicely all in clothes, and how there's a virginal quality to it. Somehow, I had no such illusions about how this slightly paunchy horn player came off struggling into a pair of forty-two-long Levis.

"Then, by all means, steer clear of *The Lady is a Tramp*."

For a moment, I got the distinct impression that, as I had been lying in the dark wrestling with my own inadequacies, she had been engaging in a spot of self-deprecation herself. Here was a woman with a history, one I was none too certain I wanted to know.

"How about *A Nightingale Sang in Berkely Square*?"

"I love it," she sighed. "It carries absolutely no intrinsic emotional baggage."

I finished with the socks, and started to put on my sneakers. Suddenly, like Brautigan's woman, I had my clothes on, and the beginning was over.

"The floor is beautiful, but it transmits sound like a drum. You can hear every note I play downstairs. If you don't want to go, I'll play *Nightingale* for you."

"And if I want to go?"

"Then I'll play it and hope you want to come back."

I was surprised at myself. I was almost glib.

"I have to go," I said, as I crossed the polished heart pine and sat on the edge of the bed. "Sockeye's already played one set without me. I'm going to owe him one." Almost as an afterthought, I said, "We close the bar at four."

She pulled my pillow over and propped it up against her own, and fell back on them.

"Wake me up at four," she said.

We had breakfast about one the next afternoon at Cafe du Monde, sweet greasy beignets dusted with ten-x powdered sugar and strong chicory coffee. I would have killed for a Dixie, but I thought it might be a bit much for a first date so early in the day. The cold front that had blown through during the night, sending lush breezes across my bed through the screened window, had left the air cleanly laundered and springtime sweet, and I could swear I could see for miles across the Big

Muddy as we walked to breakfast. The grass on the hillside on the river side of the cafe was just recovering from the blistering heat of the hell we call summer in this Bacchanal by the Sea, and was showing off its Sunday colors, looking much like a crayon drawing mixing blues and greens in the sterling sunlight.

We hadn't spoken much on the walk over. After I had finished my set, I had crept up the back steps to my quarters over the bar, hoping she would still be there and half-dreading that she might not.

I found Meg snoozing dreamily, naked across the bed, lying on top of the sheets. The breeze off the river was flowing in through the window, making the ends of her hair dance in the light from across the street. I remember undressing quietly before nuzzling in beside her. She awoke with a bit of a jump, little more than an exaggerated twitch, and scanned the room with some alarm before she realized where she was and who else was there.

The next hour disappeared in a frenzied entanglement of arms and legs and low guttural moans and gasps, until we both fell apart covered with a fine lover's sheen and contented smiles on our faces. This time we covered ourselves with a sheet before drifting off to sleep.

I awoke first, around noon. The music from the Quarter had been replaced by the sounds of the Vieux Carre replenishing itself, as beer trucks and delivery wagons made their rounds of the restaurants and bars. There was, borne on the currents of air flowing in my window, the stale smell of beer evaporating in the midday sun, the effluvia of the previous night's party on Bourbon Street.

I sat in bed and watched Meg sleep, until she roused herself several minutes later, perhaps cued by some unconscious awareness of being watched. She stretched and rolled over to cuddle with me. It felt good, better than I could remember in too long.

We showered, and walked to breakfast, where I now found myself wrestling with all the detritus of powdered sugar that dotted my windbreaker jacket and jeans. It smeared as I swiped at it, leaving little sugar comets wherever my hand dragged.

Meg was polite, and stifled her amusement as I struggled. Somehow, she had managed to eat every speck of her beignets without dusting herself with it, save for the remainder she licked from her fingers.

"I listened to you last night," she said. "As I was falling asleep, you were playing downstairs. It was soothing. You play very well."

"It's an acquired talent," I told her. "I'm still learning."

She leaned forward, her face framed in the steam rising from her coffee.

"You were terrific. I'm still tingling."

"I'm still learning about that, too. Want to take a walk?"

She nodded, and we rose to leave. The Cafe du Monde is one of the hottest venues on the tourist maps, and the tables outside under the roof are among the most prized. As soon as we stood, it seemed, there were two more people in our seats. I cautiously reached out and grasped Meg's hand, just strongly enough to make it look like I cared, but not so forcefully as to scare her. She squeezed back, as she slipped her sunglasses on with her free hand.

We walked back toward the Aquarium, on a concrete walkway by the Mississippi. Out on the brown water, a moldy ancient tug shouldered a barge loaded with railway cars past us toward the Gulf. God knew what was in the cars, or where they were going. It was a common enough sight on the river. The tug tooted its horn twice just as it chugged past us, midway across the water. Meg jumped again, reminding me of how she had started when I came to bed after work. She was high strung, but trying to be relaxed about our being together.

"Clancey told me you were going to be a priest, once."

"How'd she find out?"

"Your mutual friend, Mr. Tucker, told her. It's true, then?"

"It's true," I said. "It was a long time ago."

"What happened?"

"A little of this, a little of that. It didn't work out."

She shook her head. "From priest to psychology professor. Some transition."

"And from there to horn player in an New Orleans dive. I seem to be slipping farther and farther from grace."

She slid her arm around my generous middle as a gust of autumnal air whisked about us.

"Oh, you're graceful enough. What will you do with Sammy Cain when you find him?"

I rolled the question around a couple of times. "My first impulse is to take him off at the neck for being so elusive and such a slimeball. That's not what I was hired to do, though. There are others around for that sort of thing. I suppose I'll just tell Clancey and move on."

"You're not so tough, Gallegher."

"Never claimed to be. Things happen, and you get caught up in them, and before you know it you're someone else, doing something you never imagined. It happens to a lot of people. And while we're on the subject, just what is it you do for a living, Ms. Coley?"

She shrugged, and led me to a shade tree just off the concrete path. She sat, and I sort of lumbered my way down beside her, the way camels do when their riders dismount.

"I work part-time, when I'm called, in banking. It's not exactly regular work. I spend a lot of time with friends. My parents left me a considerable trust fund. I don't have to do much."

"It was generous of them."

"Perhaps," she said, gazing out over the river, toward the twin bridges. "On the other hand, never having to worry where my next meal is coming from, maybe I don't accomplish all I could. I'm thirty-one years old, I was married exactly once, for exactly five months, when I was nineteen, and I've never held a job for more than a year. That's my life story. No seminaries, universities, or night clubs. No great adventures, or slain dragons. I've just happened, like creation."

"Well," I ventured, leaning over to kiss her, "I'm glad you happened to me."

She accepted a peck, then pulled back.

"Pat, no promises. No pledges, no declarations, no commitments. I'm glad I happened to you, too, and I really, really enjoyed that. Don't count on me though. I'm not that constant. Like Sammy Cain, I could up and disappear anytime, if only because I want to. That goes along with being independently wealthy, and with being me. If I decide to go, I won't take you with me. I won't take anything. You'll just wake up one day and I won't be there and you'll never know what became of ol' Meg. If you can deal with that, you and I can have a lot of fun."

I leaned back against the tree. "You forget I know how to find people."

She giggled. "Yeah, I know how well you've done with Cain. Do me a favor, though. If I go, don't try to find me. I won't want you to do that. If I go, it will be because I don't want to be found."

I grabbed at a blade of grass, and rolled it between my fingers, weighing her request.

"You said it," I replied at last. "No promises."

"No," she said. "Not a one."

I tossed the grass into the breeze, and it flew several yards before its own gravity brought it to rest.

"Boy, can I pick 'em," I mused.

"Don't be a fool," she said, "I picked you. Now let's go back to your room."

It was a long, delicious afternoon.

Eleven

I took Meg to eat at Irene's that evening. I had the veal scaloppini, and she toyed with shrimp cakes. We drank a fine valpolicella, and stared exhaustedly at each other over the checkered tablecloths, with barely the strength to talk. All around us, photographs of famous people who had dined there stared down approvingly. At least, I think they all approved. They were all smiling. As I finished a cannoli, I set down my fork, and leaned in close, careful to avoid immolation by the table candle.

"You," I whispered, "are going to put me in a hospital."

"Can't do that," she said. "Clancey would never forgive me if I made her private eye an invalid. She'd never let me come to her house again and sunbathe nekkid."

I winced at the image. Arousal was becoming almost exquisitely painful. I decided to change the subject.

"Would you like to do something tonight? That is, of a social nature?"

"Damn!" she exclaimed, almost under her breath. "What are you, some kind of machine? I'm going to have to go home and sleep some-time, you know."

"I was talking about, I don't know, a club or something. A movie."

She tried, with absolutely no success, to stifle a yawn. "I don't think so, love. You should get some sleep, too. You still have to work tonight."

"I'm afraid there's nothing for it. If I go to sleep, I'll be out for the duration. As long as I stay awake, I can function. Besides, I play better tired. Let me see you home? I keep my car in a garage just behind this restaurant."

"Don't bother," she said, with a dismissing wave of her hand. "It's out of your way, and I'm grown up. I swear I won't question your chivalry. Walk me to a cab?"

I paid the bill, with Meg protesting all the time that next dinner would be on her. We left Irene's, and strolled down Bourbon Street toward Canal. It was early evening, and kooks and creeps were out in abundance. Near the corner of Toulouse I spied Grover shilling a gaggle of college kids, promising them all kinds of perfumed delights. He should have been throwing in free penicillin.

There was a cab waiting at Chartre, and I held Meg's door open for her as she slid in. She blew me a kiss, and then she was gone.

It was a nice night, full of the promise of autumn, with the crisp, tingling bite of cool in the air. It was no kind of night to think of Sammy Cain, so I trundled my way down Toulouse, past Molly's, and stepped into my own dark environs at Holliday's.

Shorty was waiting for me.

"Where've you been?" he asked. "That woman's been calling for you for almost three hours."

"What woman?"

He picked up a note he had written on an old bar receipt, and handed it to me. It was from Clancey Vincouer. According to Shorty's eighth grade scrawl, she had called on the hour since five o'clock. I checked my watch. It was five minutes to eight. Given her pattern, she would be ringing again in a few minutes.

"When she calls, transfer it up to my room," I said, and hurried up the stairs.

I had barely changed clothes before the phone beeped.

"Mr. Gallegher," Clancey began. "I need you to come."

Her voice was full of anxiety and despair. I tried to calm her down. "What's wrong?"

"It's Sammy, Mr. Gallegher. He's moved out of his apartment."

"That's not possible," I told her. "I've been watching the place during the days, and some nights. It would have taken quite a while to move all his stuff out without me noticing either the movers or the moving trash. Why do you think he's gone?"

She seemed to sob, just a bit, but continued gamely. "I went over to his apartment tonight. I was going to leave another note for him to call me if he came back. There was nothing there."

"Nothing? At all?"

"It was stripped to the walls. The furniture, the clothes, his television. Everything. I asked the woman at the front office, but she said she didn't know he had left. She was angry, she said he owes her money."

"Where are you?" I asked.

"I'm calling from my car, in front of the apartment. Please, can you come? Maybe you can find something out for me."

I assured her that I was on my way, and hung up. I had two hours before I was supposed to go onstage downstairs, so I grabbed my Saints cap, threw on my windbreaker, and dashed out to get my car.

Ms. Vincouer was right. The apartment had been gutted to the walls. I felt like scourging myself as I walked from room to room, surveying the utter and complete emptiness of the place. I had sat outside just two days before, reading a Raymond Chandler novel, and never saw a thing. It didn't take an Einstein to figure out that whoever had cleared this depressing hovel had done so while I was romping with the leggy red-head. My Catholic upbringing flooded back in a torrent, full of repri-mands regarding the wages of sin.

"This was done in the last two days," I said. "I've been busy, and didn't get by here today or last night. How did you find out about it?"

She wrung her hands nervously, as if worried that I was accusing her of something nefarious.

"I... I wanted to come by and leave Sammy a note, to ask him to call me when... if he came back. I used my key, let myself inside. This means he's alive, though, right?"

I stifled the impulse to turn her head around once or twice. She had just been royally dicked by this compost heap of a man, and her first response was relief that he wasn't dead. On the other hand, I had to come to grips with the fact that a large part of my frustration was directed at myself, for falling down on the job.

"That's one of the possibilities."

"What else is there?"

I pieced the scenario together in my head as I gazed around the room.

"Okay, let's say you were right when you came to me, and that your husband found out about you and Golden Boy here, and that Lester decided to punch his one way ticket on the off-planet shuttle. I know he was an athlete in college and all that, but is he a violent man?"

She considered it for a second, then shook her head. "No, not really. Sometimes he loses his temper at tennis or golf and throws a tantrum, but he's never hit anyone or destroyed anything. No, not violent, I suppose."

"So he wouldn't likely try to do in Cain by himself, right?"

"Probably not. But he could find someone to do it, couldn't he?"

Damn right he could. New Orleans is an interesting study in social boundaries. Drive down Rampart Street, and on one side you'll encounter the ancient splendor of the French Quarter, on the other side the squalor of the projects. The parish fathers have made great efforts to clean up the city's image, but the plain and simple fact is that the Big Sleazy is, hands down, one of the most dangerous burgs in the country. Take a walk down Canal Street after nine o'clock some night, and tell me you don't feel the cold hand of death clutching at your chest every time you pass a cluster of surly young toughs gathered on the sidewalk. In a city where thousands of people take the measure of their lives in the number of condoms stuffed with crank or eight-ball or rock they have in their pocket, it's easy to buy practically anything with little more than spare change, and that includes someone else's untimely quietus. Some of the protohumans spawned in the polluted pools of the projects will stop your beating heart just for the 'action'. Stay within the invisible barriers formed by Rampart, Esplanade, and the river, and you can walk about securely, without the frequently intrusive fantasy of frigid steel slipping between your ribs as sinewy fingers snake about your wallet pocket. Stray outside, and you're prime to make headlines in your hometown newspaper.

This was different, though. If Sammy Cain hadn't cleared out himself for brighter pastures and newer pigeons, then whoever had taken him out had gone to the extra effort to erase his existence. That could only mean one thing.

"If he's been killed, it was a professional job, and an expensive one at that. This obliteration of every shred of Sammy Cain indicates a desire to not only eliminate, but annihilate him. Presuming that Lester is behind this—and understand, I'm not at all sure I buy that—then this is as much a message to you as it is retribution against Cain."

"I don't understand."

"I think you do. This is mob shit. Anyone could bribe some psychopathic little shit to kill Cain with little more than a buck and a promise. This took organization, though, the kind that only the families can muster readily. The fact that they waited until I wasn't around means they knew I was watching, which also means Lester knows you hired me. They're posting notice, Ms. Vincouer, and it says 'Back Off'. Sounds like good advice to me."

"Lester is trying to scare me into being faithful?"

"I wouldn't put it past him. Maybe this is just frills, though, a goodie thrown in as a favor to be repaid later. Stripping the world of all of Sammy Cain's trappings is a terror tactic, one that Lester might be asked to make good someday."

"Or maybe Sammy came back and moved to another city."

"Maybe he did," I said, sadly. This woman was having a hard time getting off the linear thought track. "Look, I know a good deal about this stuff. If your husband killed Sammy Cain, and if he used some greaseball connections to do it, this is bigger than you or me. This is something you don't want to test. Best thing you can do is forget it, and make Lester very very happy. This is a dark side of life you could go years hoping you don't run into again."

"And if he's alive?"

"Then you're better rid of him. He's bad news, Ms. Vincouer, like cancer or AIDS. If he's alive, I'll find him, and I'll let you know where he is. Maybe I'll jerk a knot in his ass first, or show him what happens to the little head when you let it do the thinking for the big one."

"You wouldn't," she argued, a bolt of anger in her voice. "I didn't hire you to hurt him."

"What do you think I do, Ms. Vincouer?" I asked petulantly. "You think Cully Tucker knows me because I go around finding lost dogs and cats? What I do is because I'm big and scary and intimidating, and sometimes I have to put serious pain on some poor jerk whose worst crime is running his finances a little close to the bone. I need a lawyer on my side, because what I do is just to the left side of legal. This guy Cain yanks my chain, and when I think about him I really want to yank back. You're not paying for advice, but this is free. Forget him. Let him fade away, dead or not. If he's sucking river mud, you'll never see him again. If he's not, he sure as shit doesn't want to see you. You had your midlife crisis fling. It's over. Let it go."

She scanned the room where Cain had lived and breathed, and eased out something resembling a fatigued sigh.

"You'll call me when you find him," she said, and turned away. Without glancing back, she walked out the door.

I still had an hour to kill before I went on at Holliday's, so I called Cully Tucker and asked him to meet me at Molly's. There was a time, maybe half a decade ago, when Molly's was a quaint Irish pub, and it served a damned decent fried oyster platter with slaw and toast and a schooner of suds for less than seven bucks. Those days are long gone, now. The overhead got to them, or the pub changed owners, or maybe the Health Department closed the kitchen, but now Molly's was just another open bar with video games and pool tables and a long polished wooden bar. In the back were a couple of desolate booths for people who didn't want the bartender butting in every thirty seconds. Cully and I took one of the booths.

I sipped at the frothy head of a mug of Heineken, and settled back in the booth. The cushions had been discarded long ago, and I was stopped by bare wood carved with a generation of bar graffiti.

"Just what is it with Clancey Vincouer, Cully?" I asked.

He took a sip of his beer. "She's in love, Pat. She can't see shit for all the hormones. Remember how you were with Claire?"

"I wasn't in love with Claire," I corrected. "We had a nice arrangement. It worked for us."

"Yeah, right. That's why, every time you saw her up to the day she died, you got this marshmallow look on your face and couldn't play blues for shit."

Cully could talk to me this way. I didn't necessarily like it, but I allowed it. When the police had busted into Claire's apartment, with her splattered all over the living room rug and a dead cancer patient on the sidewalk five stories below, I had been curled up against the wall, sobbing softly and mumbling incoherently. At the police station I dropped my dime on Cully. He convinced the detectives that I had acted to protect Claire—badly, as it happened—and to defend myself. No charges were pressed.

"Clancey's like that, Pat. She knows there's nothing permanent about Sammy Cain. She probably knew the day he picked her up that it would end in tears. She didn't care. All she knew was that one look from that pumped up gigolo made her all gooshy inside, the way she felt back in college every time Lester spiked the football in the end zone. She doesn't want to give that up, man. It reminds her of when she was young, when she wasn't more than halfway to the grave. That's potent stuff, my man."

Like I didn't know. Ever since Meg Coley had shown up at Holliday's, I had become aware of my own sense of mortality put on hold. Hang around the Reaper long enough, and he begins to grow on you, a kind of really quiet and somber sidekick. I had recently become aware of my own morose and morbid fascination with what happened on the other side of the veil, perhaps in anticipation of my own death. Like Clancey Vincouer, I was far enough past halftime that I had more memories than ambitions.

When Meg ripped her shirttails out, though, it was like I was eighteen again in the front seat of my Ford Maverick, about to do the juicy watusi for the first time with Sally Mierscynski. The future was rich and broad and voluptuous, and I was going to live forever.

In Meg's eyes, the color of fresh spring rye grass, as she grimaced in pleasure astride me, was a secret promise of immortality. They said, *'Don't worry about the fuckups and the tragedies that brought you to this crucial moment in your life. You can still have it all, and you can be eternally young in my adoring eyes'*.

Even if that was only what I wanted to see in them, it was a heady and intoxicating potential. Here was a chance, once and for all, to grasp at something that wasn't mired in corruption and decay and missed opportunities and pledges unkept. It was addictive, and I didn't blame Clancey Vincouer one bit for trying to preserve it. There were moments, I'm sure, when I would have traded my last five breaths for another second with Claire.

Cully had changed the subject. He was describing a case he had watched in court that day. It was highly likely that he hadn't actually had a case there, but had just dropped by to sit in the back pew and eat his salami sandwich while he picked up some pointers on trial procedure. I never said he was a good lawyer, just that he worked hard at it.

"Hey," he said, as he finished the story, "You hear about Boom Boom?"

Harvey 'Boom Boom' Scolari was one of my brethren in the enforcement business, working for the Anolli family. *'Family'*, of course, was a bit ambitious a term for them, as they consisted primarily of Claude and Francisco Anolli and their baby sister Angelica. Of the three, Angelica was the real brains, and the most vicious. She managed Claude and ChiChi the way Sigfried and Roy manage their white tigers. It was a small operation, and the other spaghetti families in the city tolerated them because they stuck to loansharking, some small-time gambling, and the occasional shakedown.

"No, what about him?"

"Boom Boom got blown up, but good. Seems he was taking a cut off the skim from one of the poker houses the Anollis operate. Angelica had a protection deal going with Lucho Braga's outfit, sort of subbing out the police payoffs on the house. So one night one of Lucho's soldiers decides he wants to play a friendly game, and he drops in on the Anolli house. He's no chump, he can see how much money is on the table, and he knows what Angelica is supposed to skim for Lucho. So he reports this to Lucho, who checks it out. You don't fuck with Lucho, you know, I don't care if he is almost eighty and his pecker's half eaten away with the cancer. So Lucho sends a different guy each night to the Anolli poker house for about a week and a half, and every time he gets the skim, it's short.

"Lucho figures the Anollis are trying to rip him off, so he visits Angelica one day about a week ago. One thing leads to another, and ChiChi makes the comment that Boom Boom has a new Caddy he's been showing off all over town, a real pimpmobile he's touting around like it was his first-born son. ChiChi and Claude pick up Boom Boom and bring him to Angelica, and she interrogates him for a couple of hours about his finances. This much we know for sure.

"So, two days ago, somebody walks up to Boom Boom while he's sitting outside the poker house in his bright shiny new bourgeois-mobile, sticks a .22 automatic behind his ear, and empties the clip. Like that's not enough, they dump two or three gallons of gas on the car and toss a match. When the flames got to that thirty gallon gas tank, Boom Boom went up like a roman candle, not that he knew any-thing about it. Damn car burned down to the asphalt before the fire trucks even got there. The fuckin' wheels melted half a foot into the street. To do a decent burial, they're gonna have to plant him *and* the car together. I'm not sure you could tell where one ended and the other began. Some assholes just don't learn. All the dago families talk about *omerta* and honor and all that shit, but when push comes to shove the bottom line is don't fuck with their women or their money. That's all that really matters."

He sat back and let it sink in. I couldn't tell whether he was looking for my reaction, or just wanted me to get some kind of message.

"Not to worry," I said. "It's not like this is some kind of career choice I've made here. This thing with Leduc is temporary."

Cully leaned forward. "Listen to me, Pat, mick to mick. There is no such thing as 'temporary' with these dudes. Let them get their hooks in you and you owe your soul to the company store."

"What are you trying to say, here?"

"Just a warning, that's all. Boom Boom may or may not have been skimming, but he sure as shit never knew what hit him in the front seat of that DeVille. If they want your ass, Pat, you won't see them coming."

"Tell me something," I asked. "Let's say you wanted to get rid of someone. How would you go about it?"

He drained the beer, and gestured to the waitress for another. "What're you saying, man?"

"I was wondering what kind of hoops you have to jump through to—you know—get rid of someone."

"You planning some kind of whack, Pat? Because as your attorney, I have two pieces of advice. One, don't tell me about it. Two, don't even think about it. There are places you can go that I can't get you back from, and that's one of them."

"It's not me," I told him. "This Sammy Cain character, his apartment was stripped in the last forty-eight hours. Clancey's hoping he's just on the run, but she's still scared her husband might have had Cain erased. So, I'm wondering what kind of juice you have to carry in this town to make a guy totally disappear, like he's one of those Soviet un-persons."

"It takes a lot."

"Who would you go to? Lucho Braga?"

Cully thought it over, while the waitress dropped off the new mug of Heineken. "He could get it done. What you're talking about takes some time and some manpower. Just stripping the apartment had to take four guys a couple of hours. You're looking at a good upper five-figure job."

"What if Braga, or whoever, just did the whack for cash, and did the rest as a favor?"

"You mean, like the Godfather. '*Someday I'm gonna ask for a favor in return*'. That kind of thing?"

"That's what I had in mind."

"Sure, then. That could happen. I don't think Lester would do it, but it could happen."

"Why not Lester?"

"He's not stupid, Pat. He's vain and he's self-absorbed, and he thinks of little except his canning empire, but he's no jackass. He knows that once you owe the families you never really get out of debt. He'd want the whole thing paid out, lock stock and barrel. Signed, sealed, and delivered, freight on board."

"So somewhere in Lester's finances, given that he's behind the vanishing of Sammy Cain, there should be a conspicuously missing hundred grand."

"Not necessarily. Maybe I shouldn't be telling you this, man, but I feel sort of bad about ratting you out to Clancey in the first place. Maybe it'll even the ledger. Clancey told me that Lester has been depositing into an offshore account for years. Calls it his 'retirement fund'. God only knows how much he's salted away, and if he drew from that then there's no way to trace him through his books."

"You say the move alone would take four people. What's the possibility they'd be stupid enough to talk to someone about it?"

"They aren't in the moving business waiting for an assistant professorship to open up at Tulane, Pat."

"Which of the families owns moving companies?"

"How in hell would I know? Lucho Braga, for sure. Beyond that, you got me."

"Keeps coming back to Braga, doesn't it?"

Cully set down the mug in mid-quaff, and pointed at me with his index finger. "Don't even think about it. You think Lester hired Braga to feed Cain the black pill? Fine. Tell Clancey you think Cain's dead and let it rest. She'll grieve, she'll feel like shit, but nobody else will get hurt. You try to dig into this thing, and you're gonna end up like Boom Boom."

I glanced at my watch.

"I have to get to work," I told him. "Want to come over and sit through a set?"

He waved at the air with his hand. "Naw, I have to run over to the jail, visit a couple of guys getting arraigned tomorrow. I picked them up as a public defender, with the parish picking up the tab. Gotta talk them into pleading and throwing themselves on the mercy of the court."

"Whatever happened to innocent until proven guilty?" I asked as I slipped on my jacket to leave.

He didn't answer, but as I walked out of Molly's, he was still sitting in the booth laughing at my funny joke.

Twelve

The night wore on slowly. Tips were lousy, the crowd was off because of a jazz festival in town, and my head was in completely the wrong place for work. Half of it was wandering the alleys and dark streets of the Sleazy searching for any trace of Sammy Cain. This favor had become bigger than a set of mint Beiderbeck platters justified, and it was beginning to get on my nerves. I was becoming anxious to dust off Clancey Vincouer and her histrionic middle-aged desperation, maybe spend a couple more nights playing spin the pickle with Meg Coley, maybe even catch a couple of Saints games.

What I didn't want to do was get mixed up with the Sicilian brotherhoods in this town. Working for Leduc was one thing, but there was little appealing about squaring off against people who would kill you *and* torch your car.

My father once found out I was hanging out with this Greek kid who lived on our block. He was overjoyed.

"You can't lose with the Greeks," he had told me, as he slapped me on the back. *"Once you're in with them, the sky's the limit. There's nothing they won't do for you."*

Their fellows from across the Mediterranean, on the other hand, seemed to get it all backwards. Once they do something for you, they want you to return the favor forever.

It was for this reason that I always gave the Anollis and the Bragas a wide berth. I knew that Leduc was tied in somehow with Braga, and that he did business with the Anollis, but I took great pains to know as little about that as possible. Who needs the aggravation?

I took a break around one in the morning, and I started to call Meg, but decided it was too late. She had been pretty whipped out when I sent her home, probably more from her own effort than mine, and I decided to let her sleep. I was getting groggy myself. It had been a busy couple of days.

Shorty decided to give it up at three. The already sparse crowd had dwindled to next to nothing, and he wasn't about to burn lights for people who weren't buying. I was grateful for the opportunity to knock off early.

I helped him lock up the bar, and trudged upstairs to grab some winks. With Sammy Cain's apartment cleared out, there was nothing to stake out the next day, so I figured I'd sleep in and start a new search angle in the afternoon.

I had no sooner gotten to sleep before there was insistent pounding on my door. I slipped into a pair of shorts and opened the door just enough to recognize Marcel's sharp Cajun features.

"For Christ sake," I said. "I was almost sound asleep. What the hell is this, the Reader's Digest Sweepstakes? Go away."

I started to slam the door, but Rene's size fifteen blocked it. I opened the door again, and glared at them.

"This is ridiculous. I'm not going out tonight, got it?"

Marcel shook his head slowly. Rene stood stock still, his foot still wedged in my doorjamb. Neither said a word. People from their planet seem to communicate telepathically.

"You guys want a beer?" I asked, as I turned to walk back to my bed.

They followed me inside, but stopped just this side of the door. They stood there again, hands held loosely at their sides, trigger fingers just itching for action. I was reasonably certain that Leduc had given them directions to bring me in alive, contrary as that was to their genetic programming, so I took my time getting dressed. Let's face it, when the goony Cajun brothers come calling, you go with them, even if you have been up for over forty hours.

I grabbed my Saints jacket from the walnut coat stand next to the door as they led me out. Marcel led the way down the back stairs to the street, with Rene just behind me in case I decided to try something desperate, like dash back upstairs to bed.

Leduc's Lincoln Town Car, one of the real ones made before they started looking like a Mercedes, was at the curb in front of Molly's. We sat in the back seat, Cajun-Mick-Cajun style. I turned to Marcel.

"Read any good books lately?" I asked. He stared straight ahead, either ignoring the question, or trying to figure out what a book was.

"Don't you just hate it?" I observed, "The designated hitter rule? Seems to me that if they give it to the American League, then the Nationals should get it too."

They stared ahead. I might as well have been talking to myself.

"You know," I told Rene, "I've always liked you best. I don't know, I guess it's just your crazy, spontaneous, devil-may-care nature."

No response. I turned to Marcel. "Of course, you have your nice features, too. Quiet, sensitive, I bet you just cried like a baby at *Titanic*."

If he did, Marcel wasn't proud about it, as he kept his gaze riveted directly toward the Lincoln hood ornament.

It was time to try Rene again. "You know, I'm willing to bet I could take you in a fair fight."

This time, Rene turned his head the absolute minimum required to catch my eyes, and he smiled. It was like looking at one of those great white sharks at Seaworld, and I couldn't tell which amused him more, the notion that I could take him, or that he might ever be suckered into a fair fight. It didn't matter, as I turned to Marcel.

"See, you owe me five dollars. I told you I could make him smile first."

I was growing tired of the game, and had awakened just enough for irritation at being rousted, so I settled back and closed my eyes. They couldn't keep me from snoozing on the ride over to Leduc's place.

I lost track of time, but presently the car stopped, and I felt myself rise almost a half foot as the quarter ton of Cajuns in the backseat stepped out the side doors. They didn't look inclined to let me stay, so I slithered across the fine Corinthian leather, and took my presumed place between them.

Leduc was waiting for us in his living room. He was sitting in front of a fireplace the size of Atlanta, with the most realistic gas logs I had ever seen inside. He was dressed, as always, as if getting ready to leave for the Cotillion. As we entered the room, Marcel and Rene stopped and took their customary places on either side of the door, just in case some small foreign army should try to invade.

"Come on in, Pat," Leduc said, "Take a seat."

I shambled across the ankle high pile carpet, and plopped down across him in the first available substantial seat. It's not a good idea to damage furniture belonging to someone who holds your note for fifteen grand.

"I have an opportunity for you," he said. "I've been very pleased with the work you've done. Stanley Porch paid all his debt, right on time. Your cut brought your debt to me down by almost a grand. How would you like to retire it completely?"

"Who do I have to kill?" I asked, regretting it immediately as I realized that the concept was not at all outlandish.

I was relieved when Leduc said, "Don't be foolish. I don't kill. Dead men don't pay up, and they don't come to me when they need more money. No this is something special. I've acquired a certain wagering enterprise..."

A bookie joint, I surmised.

"...that's doing very well. The profit margin has been much better than I anticipated. Like most businesses, however, we have our share of bad debts. There's a man I want you to visit. He likes to bet on sporting events, and he's not good at it. He owes me a lot of money. Would you like to know how much?"

My mouth was dry, not so much because this slimy little Arcadian bastard scared me, but at the prospect of cutting loose from him.

"Sure, how much?"

"Two hundred large."

I was always good at math. It didn't take me a breath to calculate my cut in a collection that size. I would not only pay off Leduc, there might even be some left over for retirement.

"What's the catch?" I asked.

"Catch?"

"Yeah, why me? Up until now you've only used me for the nickel and dime stuff, ten here and ten there."

Leduc shrugged his shoulders, and said, "You don't want it..."

"No, no, don't get me wrong. I'm just curious."

Leduc took a drag off the Macanudo cigar he was holding, and let the smoke drift around his head like an aura.

"Fact is, Pat, you've more or less served your purpose. I took you on when the business was building. My enterprises have grown substantially, and you just don't fit in with the plans. You're a smart dude, but you're no wiseguy, you know what I mean? On the other hand, I can't just let you off the hook for the money you owe me. That's not good business. I know you'd have a hard time scrabbling up the cash on your own, and it wouldn't do to send some muscle out to shake down some of my muscle. So, I figure, why not give you a big job? You go to this guy's house, you convince him to make good on his debt to me, you pay off all your debt, back vig and all, and settle the score? Hey, man, it speaks to me."

"I'd be grateful," I said.

"I was hoping you would say that. Now this guy I want you to visit lives out in Lake Terrace. He's a pretty big dude, but you're bigger so I wouldn't worry about that. I've already asked him twice to come across, and he keeps putting me off, you know 'I'll have it next week', or 'Give me a little more time'. I'm tired of that, because I know he has the stuff. He's just holding out on me. So, if you would be so kind as to convince him to part with the two hundred, I'll get off his back, and you can go back to your life. Sound like a deal?"

"Yeah," I said, nodding. "It sounds like a good deal. Who is this guy?"

Leduc fished a card out of his jacket pocket, and handed it to me across the coffee table. I stuck it in my Saints jacket without looking at it.

"You still going to meetings, Pat?" he asked.

"Several times a week."

"That's good," Leduc said. "Real good. It's good for business when a bad gambler can't quit the games, but I wouldn't like to see you in trouble again. I like you, man. You're not like most of the guys work for me. I can tell you got some class. I hope, after you pay off, we can stay friends."

"That would be nice," I said, with a forced congeniality that I hoped did not betray my sincere desire never to see this piece of bayou vermin again as long as I lived.

"Good," he said. "Good." And he took another drag from the cigar.

I could see that the conversation was drawing to a close. Leduc, despite his attempt at conviviality, was way too focused to sit around and shoot the shit with the hired help. I stood and thanked him for his kindness, and excused myself.

Marcel and Rene walked me back out to the car.

"That's okay, guys, you can take off now," I told them, as I stepped into the backseat. "Why don't you go for a swim or something? I promise I won't tell your boss."

They waited silently and patiently while the driver took me out the gates of Leduc's home, probably trembling with fear that I might escape the limo and attempt to burglarize the place.

This being Leduc's car, I presumed that it would be fully appointed. On a hunch, I tapped the button to open the bar, and found a couple of nicely chilled Amstels. I had never seen Leduc drink a beer. He was a champagne man, thought it helped his image as a raconteur. The beers, I rationalized, had been intended for me. I opened one with a silver church key hanging in the bar, and took a long sip. It was smooth, just cold enough to take off the bite, but not so much that it killed the hops.

As we hit the I-10, I fished through my jacket for the card Leduc had given me. It was hard to read in the passing glare of the overhead mercury vapor lights, so I reached up to switch on the overhead lamp.

"Oh, hell," I wheezed as I read the card. It said:

Lester Vincouer
4706 Lakeshore Drive
Lake Terrace

I believe I have mentioned that I don't like coincidences. Some things, like running into a friend in a faraway place, can occasionally be dismissed as just the end consequence of being among the billions crowding a rapidly shrinking planet. On the other hand, when you are asked to put the muscle on the husband of a woman for whom you are already working, the permutations become almost incalculable. Little words like 'setup' start to insinuate themselves unbidden into consciousness, leaving the short hairs prickly and attentive.

This was going to take some doing. Even if carefully planned and expertly executed, this particular assignment still had about a thousand ways to blow up in my face. With all this in mind, I took the only reasonable action available to me.

I fell into bed as soon as the driver dropped me off, and I slept until two the next afternoon.

Thirteen

I awoke to the sound of delivery trucks and cheerful workaday banter out on Toulouse Street. Sometime during my slumber a storm had blown through, sweeping all the crap out of the air and leaving behind a greasy, overhumid feel to my sheets and skin. I had slept through the meteorological fireworks, so my window had been left open. My first thought was that I should be more careful—the humidity would play hell with my books. My second thought was of how good it felt to just lie there, drinking in the fresh air, the total relaxation, and the smell of fresh cinnamon buns and coffee.

Cinnamon buns and coffee?

I sat upright, just as Meg Coley walked out of my kitchenette, wearing a smile and a bright green ribbon holding her cerise hair back to flow down over her luscious shoulders.

"Oh, hell," she said as she saw I was awake. "I wanted to surprise you—while you were asleep, that is."

"This is surprise enough," I said. "How in hell did you get in here?"

"Shorty, that cute bartender downstairs, let me in. I told him I was bringing you breakfast. Now that you're awake, would you like a cinnamon bun?"

Oh, well, let's see. On the one hand there was this terrifically gorgeous two yards of naked redhead standing next to my bed, and on the other hand I had access to what smelled suspiciously like very fresh, very warm pastries.

It was time for a tiebreaker.

"What kind of coffee?" I asked.

"Arabica, with just a hint of Irish cream."

Damn. The redhead would just have to wait.

We ate on the couch, she curled up on one end in what had to be a consummately practiced pose designed to allure without being down-right raunchy, and me trying not to look way past forty and way over my optimum weight.

"Good," I managed as I reached for the coffee cup. "This was a great idea."

She placed her coffee cup back on the table, and said, "It was the least I could do. Clancey called me last night. She told me what happened, Sammy Cain moving out and all."

"If that's what happened," I reminded her.

"I feel just horrible, monopolizing your time over the last couple of days. If it hadn't been for me, you might have been there when he cleaned the place out."

"I don't regret the tradeoff," I told her. "I'm still not certain it was Cain who emptied the apartment. It's the most likely explanation, but just because the place was gutted doesn't mean Cain did it."

She took another sip of coffee. "I don't understand."

"I had a talk with Cully Tucker last night, just after I left Clancey. With the right amount of money, it wouldn't be so hard to wipe some-one off the face of the earth, just eradicate all traces that they ever existed. If that's so, it isn't such a large logical jump back to Lester and all his money."

"Someone would go to all that effort?"

"Someone like Lester might. From what Clancey told me, this cat doesn't like to lose. What's your take on him?"

For a moment, she seemed alarmed. It wasn't much, but she clearly didn't like me digging into her about Vincouer.

"Me?"

"Sure," I said, trying to ignore her reaction. "I've never met Lester. You're so tight with Clancey, I figured you've had a chance to form some opinions about him."

She hugged herself suddenly, as if chilled. I wanted to pull her to me, help keep her warm, but the vibes were all wrong. I was sure she wouldn't take it well. Her discomfort had nothing to do with the ambient temperature. She was tapping into some frigid place deep in her soul, a place where I wasn't exactly welcome.

"I don't like him," she said. "He's mean. You're right. He doesn't like to lose. He never did. Clancey told me once about a date they had in college. He was the first string quarterback at LSU, years ago, before I was born, would you believe it? He had a bad day, couldn't make the passes drop where he wanted them, got sacked a number of times. He was furious, disgusted with himself, and with his teammates. He picked up Clancey, with his throwing hand all wrapped up and taped. He told her he had punched a hole in his dorm room wall, right though the plaster and the lath."

"He's violent."

She nodded. "Not long ago, I arrived at the house. I didn't expect him to be there. Clancey gave me a key, so I let myself in. It's okay, she had told me I could. So I walked around back, to the cabana, and started to get undressed. I heard this god awful racket, a dog howling. I looked out the back window of the cabana, and saw Lester beating one of the golden retrievers. He was hitting the dog with a stick, as big around as two of your fingers. I never knew why. I didn't want to know. I couldn't stay there. I left and went back home."

I started to say something, but she interrupted.

"You're going to find this out anyway. It's the way you are. You have that look, like you're relentless, and you want to know everything. I trust you, though, and I know you won't take this the wrong way, because you understand how I am. I … I slept with Lester."

It was hard. Fifteen years of clinical practice asserted itself, and I put on *my 'you can't shock me'* face, ignoring the fact that all the air had suddenly been sucked out of the room.

"Okay," I said, hoping it didn't come out as a wheeze.

"It was over a year ago. Clancey doesn't know. It was only a few times, and the first time was almost a rape. He came home while I was sunning by the pool. I told you I don't always wear a swimsuit there, especially if I'm not expecting anyone. Lester was supposed to be in Texas, on business. I suppose he came home early."

"What happened?" I asked, not really wanting to know.

"He must have seen me from his room. Clancey was out shopping. He walked out of the sunroom. He was naked, himself. He told me not to worry, it was okay. He dove into the pool, and swam a couple of laps, ending up at the side of the pool where I was lying. I was on a deck chair, didn't even have a towel. He pulled himself out of the pool, and I could tell he was, um, aroused."

"Aroused," I echoed.

"Hard. He had an erection. He seemed to enjoy showing it off. He walked over and sat on the end of the deck chaise, and he pushed my legs apart, as if he owned me and had every right to. There was never any attempt to justify it. He just… did it right there on the chair. I was stunned. I didn't know what to think."

"And," I noted, "You didn't want to kill the golden goose."

Her eyes became like onyx, and her mouth tightened in anger. "That's cruel."

"It's what you do, dear."

"That doesn't make it any less cruel. I know what I am, Pat. And you may be right. Maybe I did let it happen for fear of losing my little taste of the good life. Maybe allowing myself to be violated was the price to pay. It doesn't help to throw it up in my face."

"I'm sorry."

She neither accepted or rejected my apology. She went on with her story. There were two other times, both when Clancey was away, once at Meg's home.

"I finally told him I couldn't do it anymore," she said. "Clancey is my friend, I said. It wasn't right to do this to her. But that wasn't really it. Lester is hard and cold and cruel. He's small, and dark. He's a petty man who peaked at twenty and spent the rest of his life trying to compensate for feeling cheated."

"It's easy to see how he felt," I said. "You're on top of the world, a college quarterback, big man on campus. Suddenly, you're out in the world, the crowds stop cheering, and you're whole life is canning fish. Maybe you get rich off it, but it's still canning fish. The fun's over."

"That's the way he sees it," she said. "But he still wants to win. It shows in his business deals, in the way he took me by the pool. He's getting a reputation in the business world. Not many of the people he's dealt with have come out ahead. It's like he's playing some kind of big game where every deal he makes is a point scored."

"And he gambles," I ventured.

"God, yes. He fancies himself a sports expert. Since the canneries took off, he has the money, I suppose. Clancey doesn't seem to think there's a problem. Yes, he gambles."

"And loses a lot?"

"I wouldn't know. Why do you ask?"

I lied. "Just wondering. I'm sorry about what he did to you. You're right. I know what you are, and I understand why you do things. Considering the mess I've made of my life over the last decade, I can't say much. I don't care if you slept with him."

I reached out to her, and pulled her to me. The chill was past. Her body felt amiable and receptive. She had said she could trust me. I was not so certain of her. For the moment, it didn't matter.

"Now, how exactly had you planned to surprise mc?" I asked.

She showed me.

I was surprised.

The sunbeam that had graced the sofa earlier had worked its way across the room and now fell on the bookshelf, leaving behind the growing chill of late afternoon. We weren't quite asleep, and in fact hadn't even dozed. It was just a lazy hour after the furious passion, and neither of us had any place to go.

"I have a favor to ask," I said quietly.

She didn't answer, exactly, except for murmuring contentedly and snuggling a little closer.

"I need to know when Lester is home."

Her eyes opened, and seemed to search mine for some explanation.

"I can't explain. It might have something to do with Sammy Cain. I don't know."

So I lied. So sue me.

"He's home now," she told me, almost reverently. "He came home last night. He should be there for several days. There's a trip to Baton Rouge next week."

"Clancey told you this?"

"Yes."

"I need another favor."

She waited, without asking. She was a cool one, this jolly lass.

"I need you to get Clancey out of the house. Take in a movie, or go shopping, it doesn't matter. You just need to get her away."

Her face reflected the hundred and one questions she wanted to ask. I had learned, though, that this woman knew when she shouldn't know something, if only for her own protection. She was big into self-preservation.

"For how long?" she asked.

"A couple of hours. Maybe three."

There was a long pause, while she deliberated the question. Without a doubt, she was weighing the possible consequences for herself. Clearly, I wasn't asking so that I could have ol' Lester out for a friendly round of golf. Just as clearly, I planned to do something that would confuse the issue of being hired by different parties to find Clancey Vincouer's paramour, and put the muscle on her husband for almost a quarter million. One problem didn't necessarily have to impact on the other, if I played it right. I couldn't do it alone, however. She didn't know any of this, and her internal argument took a few moments to resolve.

She pulled back the sheets, and padded across the room to the telephone.

The conversation was brief, something about a 'shopper's alert', and an invitation to dinner.

"Tonight," she said as she cruised back between the sheets. "I'm picking her up at seven-thirty. That doesn't leave us much time."

I have been assured by the best private investigators that you can go anywhere in America if you simply carry a clipboard and a brief-case. I had both as I climbed the front steps to the Vincouers' ranging front porch.

At first, I had considered taking the sneak thief approach, and just appearing in Vincouer's living room, unannounced and unwanted. People like Vincouer are of a kind, full of the assurance of invulnera-bility. They go about their every day eating in the right restaurants, wearing the right suits, using the right toothpaste and deodorants, and convincing themselves that they can't be touched. They say to them-selves, *I'm in charge, I am the master of my ship of life, and I'm going to live forever, and God help any poor son of a bitch who fucks with me.*

And then, of course, I step in and fuck with them, and most are worse for the experience. It wears on them, the thought that their elab-orate protective shells can be penetrated so easily, and their peaceful security destroyed with such facility. The first time I invade is usually a shock. The second time is worse, because the poor bastard has had time to think about it. They all pay by the third, because by then they know that if they don't, someone even worse will take up the job, and in their blissful complacency they can't conceive of anyone worse.

It's hell on me, too. I reminded myself of this as I rang the doorbell, and plastered a fake canvasser smile on my face.

And waited.

And waited.

Nobody came to the door. I checked my watch. Meg had told me she would pick up Clancey at seven-thirty. It was just past eight. She had assured me that Lester would be home.

I rang again. Nobody answered.

It was time to revert to Plan B. I stepped around the back of the house, to the sunroom area and stowed the clipboard and briefcase by the fence. Maybe Vincouer was taking a dip in the pool.

The water was clear and bright and flat. Nobody had been in the pool for hours. The lights were off in the cabana, but there was some light in the house.

I had slipped on rubber gloves just before walking up the drive, so I didn't worry about leaving prints. I could see the security panel at the end of the hallway, at the front door, through the windows of the sunroom. The lights were all green, so either Lester was careless, or he was home.

Some months earlier a friend of Shorty's had sold me a set of lockpicks, but I didn't like to use them. Unlike the way it's done in the movies, picking a lock is a pretty labor-intensive process involving a hook, a punch, and both hands. Lots of light helps, too, and even then it might take some time. It isn't very quiet, and any cop can tell by the scratches when a door lock's been jimmied. The best burglars still get caught from time to time, and an amateur like me is sure to get pinched sooner or later.

One fellow I'd met in the bar, a guy who sold security systems, had told me it was better to leave the doors unlocked and the security system armed. His reasoning was that the thief was coming in, lock or no lock. At least with the door unlocked, it wouldn't be damaged. On a hunch, I tried the knob. It turned readily. The door swung open noiselessly, and I waited for the screech of security sirens. My estimation of Lester went down ten points for sloppy work.

Thanks to my visit with Clancey Vincouer, on the day I'd met Meg, I had a reasonably decent idea of the layout of the house. As I crept from the sunroom to the hallway, I recalled that the kitchen was across the hall, and there was an office halfway down to the door. You could have played tenpins in the hall. The ancient joists threatened to protest every step I took. However, Lester had spared no expense on the restoration, and I figured there were maybe ten finishing screws per square foot in the floor, to eliminate creaks. Lester picked up three points for being thorough.

I focused on the spear of light emanating from the office door, even as I caught my pulse accelerating from adrenalin. This was wrong, I reasoned. Something was out of kilter. If Vincouer was here, why didn't he answer the doorbell? It he was out, why was the door unlocked and the alarm system off?

Like in the comic book, all my Spidey-senses were tripping off like circuit breakers. For all I knew, Lester was a paranoid asshole with a fetish for twelve gauge pump guns, and he was waiting behind the door with a nasty surprise for the jolly Irish giant who had invaded his home. It was still legal in this state to shoot intruders, and that left me one weapon shy.

See, I don't like guns. They make otherwise smart men stupid. A man with a gun is going to use it first and reason later. I've pulled my fat fanny out of several potentially fatal scrapes by using my wits instead of a firearm. Guns are noisy, messy, and they draw attention. They're hell on the guy getting shot, to boot.

At just this moment, however, I'd have given my right ball for a .45 automatic.

The only reason I didn't make like the Cowardly Lion and dash out of this antebellum Oz was the thought of my cut of the money Lester owed Leduc. I'd have never gotten in this mess but for my own avarice. Now, that same weakness might turn out to be my downfall.

I reached the door, and drew in several deep, silent breaths before making a surprisingly graceful pirouette across it to the other side of the jamb, where the door was cracked open. As I slid my face across the jamb to peek inside, I wished for an instant that my nose wasn't so prominent, even as I realized I was taking the chance of having it summarily bobbed.

The light was from a desk light on the far side of the room. The high-backed desk chair was turned away from me, but I would scan the rest of the room from the door, which as it happened was in a corner. I listened intently, trying to hear any breathing over the rapid arrhythmic thump of my heart. There was nothing. Maybe Lester wasn't even in the room. Maybe he was upstairs taking a long leisurely dump while I stood terror-stricken outside his empty office.

Maybe I could take an extra day job to pay off Leduc.

It took me several long moments to step into the room. The door hinges had been well-lubricated, and the door swung open without resistance or sound.

This was no time for stealth. It was a purely quantum moment. Either Vincouer was in the chair or he wasn't—that was the rational argument. Until I looked, though, he was and he wasn't, like Schrodinger's cat. Only by looking could I discover the truth. I stepped across the room in two strides, and grabbed at the chair, even as I became aware of the stickiness beneath my feet. I knew what had happened before I saw it. My nostrils betrayed Vincouer's condition in the dim light and cupric aroma.

Vincouer was sitting in the chair, all right, but someone had beaten me to him. The stickiness beneath my feet was his blood, spilled from the gash that ran from ear to ear. My hand slipped a bit in it as I turned the chair to the light.

It had been done right, with a surgeon's skill. The cut was clean, deep, and lethal. Vincouer's eyes were glazed over in a terrified death stare, and his mouth curled in anger at the prospect that he had lost the big one.

And I had a problem. I was standing in the legal equivalent of a Bouncing Betty landmine. My hand was on the bloody chair. If I walked back out the room, I would leave a trail of blood in my own distinctive size thirteen footprint all the way out to the pool. I would have to ditch the bloody rubber gloves somewhere.

I still owed Leduc.

To make matters worse, I had to solve all these problems quickly, as I heard sirens off in the distance. There was no doubt in my mind at all where they were headed, and I sure as hell didn't want to be there when they arrived.

Fourteen

The problem was clear. Somehow, I had to get out of Vincouer's office without leaving either evidence of my direction of flight, or a sign that I had been there.

The first problem wasn't so hard. As my eyes became adjusted to the dim light in the room, I could see the dark umber outline of the pooled blood in the carpet beneath my feet. The human body contains a remarkable amount of the stuff, and I could thank my lucky stars that Vincouer had been sitting up when he was garroted. The blood flow to his brain was cut off rapidly, and his heart stopped long before he could pump out all of his supply. I figured he'd lost a quart, maybe more, and the pool was only a yard or so in diameter, soaked into the deep pile.

I gingerly eased one foot out of the jazz shoe I had worn, and stepped outside the sanguine border in which I stood. Then, leaning on the desk for balance, I reached down and slipped off the other shoe, grabbed both, and placed my other foot in the clear.

Okay, I was out of the blood, but even in the dusk I could see the outline of my shoes matted in the carpet. It wouldn't take a forensics expert to recognize that someone big had been in the room.

The sirens were getting nearer, and I dared to hope that there was a bank robbery or a high-speed chase somewhere in the area. I couldn't take the chance, though, and I had to act quickly. Reaching into my back pocket, I extracted a comb I kept there, and used it to delicately raise the pile in the carpet back into some resemblance of its original height. It sickened me a bit, but it beat the hell out of spending twenty years in Angola for a murder I didn't commit. By the time I was finished, it would have been difficult to determine with any assurance that anyone had stood in the spot. I dropped the comb into one of the shoes, and padded down the hall toward the sunroom.

I cursed myself for carelessness as I stepped outside into the pool deck. It had never occurred to me that Vincouer might have a redundant alarm system. For all I knew, I had set off a silent alert when I opened the sunroom door, summoning the cops. It was time to disappear.

I grabbed the briefcase and clipboard, and took off in my sock feet through the woods toward the strip shopping center three blocks away, where I had parked my Pinto. At least I hadn't done something really stupid, like park in Vincouer's driveway. In this case, I had only allowed myself the garden variety imbecility.

I was about a hundred yards into the weald when I saw the blue lights of the squad car pull up in front of Lester Vincouer's house. My dark clothing provided me virtual invisibility as I melded with the trees, and vanished into the night.

It was only when I got back to my car and on the road back to the Sleazy that I allowed myself a moment to panic. I punched the roof of the car several times in frustration, which slowly gave way to abject anger, and finally to outright rage.

I had been set up. Someone had intended for me to be caught standing over the exsanguinated body of Lester Vincouer, for me to take the fall for his murder. I had come within breaths of being framed, and it had been one beautiful job.

The possibilities were staggering. Leduc could have meant for Lester to die all along, and just tempted me with the prospect of liberty from him to get me on the scene. He had told me that he never killed people, but I knew what horseshit that was. If he was tied in with Lucho

Braga or the Anollis, there had to be corpses lying around sooner or later. I was expendable, though, just a poor schlub who owed the loathsome Cajun a few grand.

Leduc couldn't have known when I would be at the Vincouer house, though, I reasoned. I hadn't told him when I would make the collection, and Lester had only been dead for minutes when I came across him. The blood on the floor was only barely coagulated when I stepped in it. It was possible that the murderer had been bounding through the same woods by which I had made my escape even as I was discovering the body. Only Meg Coley knew the time period in which I had planned to make my visit. I had used her to get Clancey out of the house for three hours.

The thought that Meg might be involved only sickened me. She had the motive, after all. She hated Lester for raping her. She had opportunity, of a sort, as she knew when Clancey would be out of the house, and approximately when I would arrive.

That left method, which meant she would have to have an accomplice. Which also meant that she had set me up with the specific intent of killing Vincouer.

That didn't work, though. She couldn't know that I would ever visit Vincouer, or that I would ask her to have Clancey out of the house when I did. If she had hatched a plot to do away with him, it had to have been planned within the last three hours.

Then there was Sammy Cain. If he was still alive, if Vincouer hadn't done away with him, he could have been watching the house all the while, waiting for an opportunity to get Lester alone and whack him. His motivation was simple. With Lester out of the way, he could sweep back into Clancey's life as the consoling suitor, and whisk her away to La-La Land, even as he picked her pockets.

That didn't fit either. Cain was a slimeball and a weasel, but he hadn't ever killed anyone, so far as I could determine. He was into the big gigolo con. He liked fleecing the ladies, as much for the affection and attention they gave him as the money he received. He was a major league bad guy, but not an overtly dangerous one by history.

Which brought me back to Leduc, who had sent me to Vincouer in the first place. He was tied into the Bragas and the Anollis. If Lester had iced Cain, he had to have used the greaseball families to do the wetwork. So let's say that Lester really had held out on, say, Lucho Braga instead of Leduc. Cain's apartment had been stripped at the exact time I wasn't around to see it, which meant, as I had told Clancey Vincouer, that they knew I was watching the place. That meant they also knew I had been hired by her. Braga knows I work for Leduc, so he has Leduc cock up this story about a huge debt and send me to collect it. If they're watching me, they also know I'm sleeping with Meg, and wait for me to have Meg clear Clancey out of the house. They know I won't go there as long as Clancey is there, for fear of blowing her cover.

There were snags there, too. How could Braga, or Leduc for that matter, know that I would approach Vincouer at his home? What would keep me from putting the squeeze on him at his office?

Then I remembered that the card Leduc had given me had only had Lester's home address on it, not his business address. He'd even planted the idea, telling me to go to the house to talk with Lester.

I was getting paranoid. Bizarre persecutory fantasies were spawning right and left in my mind, and I had to pull over to get a grip. The shock of finding Lester with his neck opened had left me jittery and frightened, and I was reacting out of panic rather than reason.

Maybe, I considered, it was all a coincidence. It seems I never really escape death, that it seems to happen wherever I go. That night-garbed unwelcome visitor has been a frequent guest in my house, and has walked regularly at my side. I can't count on both hands and a foot the people I've watched die over the last five years, people who were not as quick or smart or lucky as I. I felt most alive as their mortality ebbed away and winked out in a cinematic iris of tragedy. It was always only later that the pangs of guilt seeped in to force away my exultation. It was at those times that I would swear to leave all my adventuresome forays into the darker venues of life behind me and seek out a portion of the dreaded permanence, to take a productive place in the world of men and go with the flow.

All of which would last until either I once again needed money, or someone needed a dangerous favor. It was then that I could almost hear the rustle of robes the color of pitch at my side, as Death would drop in for a quick snack, a bottle of Dixie, and maybe a pickup or two.

Sometimes I felt like the Typhoid Mary of sudden and unpleasant demise.

Lester Vincouer was dead, and there was nothing I could do about that. The matter of moment was to get rid of the evidence connecting me with him. I had two bloody shoes, a pair of bloody surgical gloves, and a bloody comb sitting on an old newspaper on the floor of the passenger side of the Pinto.

I stopped near the airport and pulled off the side of the road onto a dirt road leading back into the marshland. When I was far from the main road, I climbed out and dug through the trunk looking for something massive and weighty. All I could find was the tire iron. It would have to do. I folded the comb and gloves into the shoes and tied them to the tire iron with the laces, then tossed the whole works into the marsh. It sank like a stone, with a satisfying plopping noise. I set fire to the newspaper, and left it burning on the marsh bank. Off in the distance, I could hear the mournful screech of a peacock, and the lights of the distant city danced in the ripples of the thick greasy water. As soon as the paper was reduced to ashes, I returned to the car to make tracks.

It was still early. I had time to grab a beer and relax before I started work at ten. Somehow, though, I knew this episode wasn't over.

It didn't take long for me to be proven right.

I had a more difficult time than I expected working that night, struggling through four sets of the most mediocre drivel I had contrived out of the Conn band cornet in some time. Sockeye knew something was wrong, and he tried to take up the slack, but let's face it—he's ninety years old, and while his nimble fingers have forgotten more music than I shall ever know, he isn't what he once was.

Shorty was supportive, but also seemed relieved that the crowd was decent and ready to spend money. If it had been a slow money night, I'm sure he would have found a way to blame it on me.

I took a break around midnight and tried to call Meg Coley. The phone rang and rang, and for the next hour I was preoccupied by the image of her sitting with a sobbing, disconsolate Clancey Vincouer, as the police rummaged through her ruined house and life. I wondered if Meg had already begun to suspect that the dead man in the next room was my handiwork, and whether she was feeling the first twinges of alarm that she might have been suckered into being an accomplice.

Four in the morning came all too slowly, and I helped Shorty close up the smoky bar and put all the chairs up on tables. I thought I caught him looking at me suspiciously several times, cautious sidelong glances with accusatory overtones. Maybe I was just cracking up.

I went to bed just before five, but sleep was hesitant in coming. When I finally did drop off, just as morning birds started to chirp outside the window, my dreams were dominated by the image of Lester Vincouer's ravaged body sitting upright in his office chair, his eyes open and full of surprised rage. As I looked up, past the chair, I could see Meg and Clancey standing across the room, their mouths open in horror, their implicating fingers pointing in my direction. I even thought I could smell the bitter smoke from one of Leduc's Honduran cigars hovering in the air, and I knew that, somewhere else in my dream, hiding in the dark corners where I dared not look, he was sitting triumphantly, chortling over the ease with which he had tricked me.

The expected interruption came around nine, with an authoritative knock on my door. I knew who it was even before I pulled myself out of bed to answer it.

Farley Nuckolls is no stranger to my three rooms over Holliday's. He's a sallow scarecrow of a man who always seems to be wearing his father's castoff clothes. He has deep-set eyes, a sharp, curved, Evil-Eye Fleagle kind of nose, and almost no chin whatsoever. His lower lip just seems to sort of blend in with an extended turkey-wattle of loose skin at his neck. He looks very much like a cartoon turtle with a detective's gold shield.

He made a show of displaying the shield now, as I opened the door.

"Mind if I come in, Gallegher?" he asked.

"Got a warrant?" I mumbled. I'm no fool, even if I looked like one standing in the doorway in my boxer shorts.

"Do I need one?" he asked. "Something to hide, pal?"

Any time someone calls me 'pal', especially a detective with the parish sheriff's department, I get antsy. Images of Humphrey Bogart and Barton MacLane flash by my eyes. I don't like getting rousted, especially at nine in the morning. On the other hand, I wasn't so stupid as to believe that, if Farley wanted, something so simple as the lack of a warrant would keep him out. That sort of crap might play in Peoria, but in New Orleans the cops go pretty much wherever they want.

I scratched at my butt and turned away from him.

"Aw, screw it. Come on in, Farley. Want a beer?"

He didn't answer. Truth was, I didn't want one myself. I had a feeling I was going to need all my wits about me over the next little while. I told him to have a seat while I got dressed. I slipped on a pair of faded wide-butt jeans and a flannel shirt. It was a chilly morning, and I had no idea where I would be sleeping that night. As I slipped on my sneakers, Farley busied himself by perusing my library.

Farley Nuckolls isn't exactly a friend. It would be more appropriate to say that our paths cross all too frequently for either of our comforts. In the course of doing favors for friends (and, as I've stated, friends of friends), I have occasionally trod rather clumsily all over the outer edges of the legal envelope. Bend the rules long enough, and you are sure to attract the attention of nosy cops and ambitious detectives. Once in a while, I come across something that has more than incidental bearing on one of Farley's cases, and I've passed the information along.

Most times I keep it to myself.

Farley isn't exactly sure what I do. I don't think he knows about the favor thing, at least not the gory details. Sometimes I think he regards me as just another thread in the tattered fabric of Vieux Carre vagrants, ne'er-do-wells, and loose change. Maybe he's right. Sometimes I get the impression he knows more than he lets on, and allows me enough free rein to operate, as long as he benefits from it.

Farley Nuckolls, despite his benign appearance, can be a complicated man. He's also no slouch in the investigating department. He's smart, observant, and almost obsessively compulsive about tending to the details. Being a gold shield in New Orleans tends to carry a lot of baggage. The police department in Orleans Parish has a long and distinguished history of corruption. With the abundance of numbers rackets, illegal gambling, drug dealing, loansharking, prostitution, illicit cigarette distribution, and plain old garden variety code violations, the opportunity to skim is rampant. The best way to get away with something in this town is to assure that some cop with the right amount of juice is looking the other way even as he's digging in your pocket for payoff change. To my knowledge, and we have broken bread on numerous occasions, Farley is clean. He has expressed a keen disregard for bad cops. He's dangerous if you've done something bad, and at just this moment I had the notion that he suspected me of doing something downright malignant.

"Wanna tell me where you were last night?" he opened.

Did I mention he was direct?

"When?"

"Let's start around nightfall."

I took a cola out of my refrigerator and opened it as I sat on the couch. I pointed to it, offering him one, but he declined, shaking his head.

"Why?" I asked. "You think I've done something, Farley?"

"Have you?" he replied, taking the recliner for himself. After years of enduring my hulking frame, the chair seemed to swallow him up.

"Lots. Nothing up your alley, though, I'm afraid."

He sighed, and pulled out the ubiquitous pocket notebook. He flipped several pages, and settled on one that captured his attention.

"You know a guy named Lester Vincouer?"

I took a sip of the cola. "Never met the man."

"Know who he is?"

I thought about it a second. There was nothing criminal in what I was doing for Clancey.

"Sure. I know who he is. But I never met him."

He consulted the notebook again, though I hadn't the slightest doubt that he had memorized every fact he'd gleaned over the previous twelve hours.

"You know his wife?"

"Clancey? Yes, Farley, I do."

"How you know her? Clancey?"

"She hired me to find something."

"And what was that?"

"Her boyfriend."

Farley stood and walked around the room. He surveyed the bookcase again, and the diplomas hanging on the wall.

"I don't see any PI license up here, Gallegher. Have you hung out a shingle without telling the police?"

"C'mon, Farley. You and I both know that a PI license, like the vice-presidency, is worth about as much as a bucket of warm spit. I don't carry a weapon. You won't find a gun anywhere in this apartment. She just wanted me to do some legwork for her, without her husband finding out. There's nothing in that that's illegal, or requires a license."

"Yeah, okay," he said, with a tone that made it clear the matter was not finished. "And how'd she come across you?"

"Cully Tucker introduced her. They're old friends."

"Oh, Tucker," he said. He might as well have been saying '*cow flop*'. It didn't take Freud to recognize the disrespect in his voice.

"What's this all about? You come all the way up here to give me a hard time about looking for someone's boyfriend? I know a guy in Atlanta who runs a business just looking for long-lost lovers and class-mates and such. You don't need to be a PI to do that stuff."

"No, I guess not," he said, and returned to the chair. "Look, Gallegher, about eight last night, someone walked into Lester Vincouer's house in Lake Terrace and opened his throat for him. It was grisly. Also, about eight last night, someone called the Lake Terrace PD and said they saw some guy hanging around the front of Vincouer's house. Described him as a big guy, real wide, like a football player."

"You figuring on me in this, Farley?"

"I'm just asking questions. So, I'm asking this one again. Where were you about eight o'clock last night?"

"You know I don't have to answer that," I told him, then held up my hands as he started to protest. "But I will. I was out. I don't have any witnesses to support me, though. At nine, I was in Molly's next door having a Dixie. The bartender will vouch for me. At five yesterday I was here in my humble abode with a young lady. She will vouch for me, but I'd rather not bring her into it."

Farley consulted his notebook. "That would be Ms. Coley."

I nodded.

"Yes, it was. So I figure you've talked with both Meg and Clancey Vincouer, right?"

He didn't answer. Farley didn't like answering questions. He preferred to ask them. "You wanna tell me why you asked Ms. Coley to have Clancey out of the house last night between seven and ten o'clock?"

"Who called the Lake Terrace police, Farley? Did they leave a name?"

He ignored me.

"Ms. Coley says you asked her yesterday afternoon to see to it that Ms. Vincouer was out of her house. So she takes Ms. Vincouer out of the house, and Mr. Vincouer gets his throat cut. We got a call describing someone at the Vincouer house around the time of death that sounds suspiciously like you. So you wanna tell me what's up?"

"You trying to make me on the Vincouer killing, Farley? If so, I'm not saying anything else without a lawyer. You want to listen to the truth, and not some bullshit from an unidentified phone caller, then we have room to talk."

Farley Nuckolls closed his notebook, and placed it back in his jacket pocket.

"I always believed you were dirty, Gallegher. Every time you show up in my life, there's a body around. There was that Adam Kincaid mess…"

"Self-defense," I argued.

"I know. And Barry Saunders…"

"Also self-defense."

"Yeah, right. The former owner of a land-development company, presumed dead, gets whacked in your bar while presumably burglarizing the place. Self-defense my ass. Someday I'm going to get the real story behind that one."

"I doubt it."

"Don't test me, Gallegher. I'm tired of people dying in the process of trying to kill you. I know all about you and Leduc, which ties you in with the families and just about everything shady in this town."

"I'm not involved with the families." Which was, tangentially, correct.

He leaned forward, making him seem even smaller in the oversized recliner.

"I wanted to do this civilized, Gallegher. I have two uniforms downstairs in the bar talking with Shorty. Right now you look bad in this thing."

"Based on what? Who made this phone call, Farley?"

"Where were you at eight o'clock last night?"

"You want to make me for this?" I argued, a little louder than I intended. "Then arrest me right now. Take me downtown. You want to force this issue, you want me to lawyer up and tear your ponied case to shreds? You do it. Do it right now!" I held my hands out in front of me, pushing him to cuff me.

He couldn't do it, and he knew I had him cornered. There was nothing in his case but circumstance. Unless someone out there had a picture of me skulking out of Vincouer's sunroom, all he had was me working for Clancey, me asking Meg to have Clancey out of the house, and an unidentified caller describing some guy who could be any one of the Saints' front defensive line.

Farley was thorough, though, and it was just a matter of time before he pulled together enough threads to make a decent circumstantial case. If someone out there was trying to frame me, they'd find a way to get something incriminating in his hands. For the moment, though, he knew I'd have his ass on a bum arrest.

He stood and glared at me.

"I don't care for you, Gallegher. You bend every rule you run across, and you've shinnied out of every bust we've tried. If you hadn't helped me out on a couple of important cases, I'd have run your ass in years ago. I'm telling you here and now that you look dirty in this Vincouer thing, and I intend to see you in Angola before it's over. Don't leave town."

"Or what?" I said, "You arrest me right now, or get off my back. If I want to leave town, the Constitution says I have the right."

He'd used his last bullet, so rather than deal with me he turned his back and left the room, slamming my door on the way out.

I sat in the recliner and hyperventilated for almost a quarter hour. That had been close, and there was no doubt he would be back sooner or later. I needed help, lots of it, and I needed it yesterday. It was time to find out just who was trying to set me up, and get some advantage. I knew people who had been to Angola prison upstate, and I didn't like their travelogues.

Fifteen

"I shouldn't even be here," Cully Tucker told me as he grabbed his fried oyster po'boy at Mother's on Canal Street. "I don't like the direction you're headed in."

"How bad is it?" I asked. "Legally, I mean?"

"Man, you have really screwed the pooch this time, Pat. First thing, I don't want to know shit about where you were the other night. Don't bother trying to sell me some cocked-up story. I'm gonna presume you were in one of the pussy bars over on Bourbon."

"At least until nine o'clock. I have a witness from nine o'clock on."

"Okay, okay, so you got a witness. Just don't try to bullshit me. You got yourself in some deep shit here. You're up to your ass in circumstantial evidence. You were working for Ms. Vincouer, and you had been in the fuckin' house before. You were ballin' her best friend. You arranged for Clancey to be out of the house at the time of the killing. And then there's this phone call."

"An unidentified caller," I interrupted, "and the description could have been of anyone."

"Anyone who is your size and build. I won't even mention how you tried to pump me the other night on how to go about whacking someone."

"You just did."

"Don't fuck with me, Pat. I haven't decided yet whether I still want to know you."

"So what can you do?" I asked.

He took a huge bite out of the sandwich, and chewed vigorously, pausing only to wash it down with a gulp of the beer I'd bought him.

"It's a good sign that Nuckolls didn't run you in right away," he started. "It means he doesn't believe he has a firm case. Or, of course, it could mean that he's convinced you did it, and he's giving you just enough line to hang yourself. In any case, if he thought he could swing it he would have been up the D.A.'s ass twelve hours ago."

"I didn't do it, Cully."

"Like I care? I could retire with a nickel from every innocent guy I've defended. Most of them are in Angola."

"Oh, that's comforting."

"This is my point. So far as I'm concerned, you didn't do jack. I hope that's true. Nuckolls, on the other hand, is very annoyed with you. He doesn't like your lifestyle. The way he sees it, he's Wyatt Earp and you're the entire Clanton gang, and if he's gonna clean up Tombstone you gotta go. He doesn't care if you really did it or not, he believes you've done enough to deserve the green weenie. We gotta see to it that what evidence he has is all he gets."

"How do we do that?"

"First of all, you gotta drop this Sammy Cain business. The impression I get from Clancey is that she doesn't want to see your face. The way she sees it, your contract has been fulfilled. Next thing you gotta do is nothing."

"Nothing?"

"Nada, bupkiss, zippo. You get up in the morning, or afternoon in your case, you hang around your apartment, you play your sets at night. That's it. You gotta look clean, no extracurricular activities that make you stand out. You start making like Sam Spade, and Nuckolls is gonna have you eating state food so fast it'll make your head spin.

If he doesn't get any more than he already has, this thing is gonna die on the vine."

We ate for several moments. I had ordered the muffaletta, and it was hot and drippy. It went down just fine with the Jax brew I'd ordered.

"What I can't figure out," I said after several minutes, "was the method. This doesn't sound like a professional hit. Nuckolls said Vincouer's throat was cut."

"Yeah, I know," Cully said. "The dago mobs wouldn't mess with that shit. With them it's all clean and quick, one in the head, one in the ear, and three under the chin. You know what it takes to slit some dude's gullet when he's sitting in his chair?"

"I was thinking about that," I said. "It's one thing to sneak up on someone on the street or in a car. But throat-slitting is a very intimate crime. You either have to be real stealthy to get that close, or the victim has to let you near him."

"You're thinking Vincouer knew his killer," Cully stated. "I think you're right."

"So why set me up?"

"You're convenient. You've been playing a bad game for quite a while, doing stuff you aren't suited for. You didn't grow up on the streets like most of the made guys in this town. You don't know how to use that third eye in the back of your head. Setting you up would be a cinch for Braga or any of the other dudes."

He took a long satisfied pull on the beer, and said, "Look, Pat, you get popped, you call me, okay? Farley starts to lean on you, you call me. Don't talk to any more cops without me there. You're in way too deep to do this alone. Forget Sammy Cain, forget Clancey Vincouer. That's the best advice I can give you right now. Wait for this thing to shake down."

We finished the meal and separated at the door. I took off down the river walk, past the Natchez, toward Toulouse. Storm clouds were gathering to the west of the city, and the air was dense and tingly with electricity. The Mississippi was a milk chocolate brown, with frothy whipped cream barge wakes swirling in the current. My nose twitched at the scent of garlic and thyme from the Greek restaurant I passed, and I wondered if I would be deprived of these simple pleasures in the near future.

I still had an unpleasant visit to make.

I stopped at Holliday's and tried to call Meg Coley. The phone rang five times before the machine came on.

"It's me," I said after the tone, "Look, we need to talk. I don't know what you're thinking right now, but it wasn't me. I hope you don't think I set you up, because that's not the way it is. I'll call you again later this evening."

I hung up the phone and walked down the street to the garage where I had parked my Pinto.

It took twenty minutes to drive out to Leduc's house.

I didn't want to listen to jazz this time. At just that moment, I didn't need to be reminded that someone else did my job better than I could. I switched the radio to a classical station just in time to catch the opening strains of the Eroica symphony, and it carried me across the I-10 bayous, where I found the Cajun Cujos, Marcel and Rene waiting for me at the front steps of Leduc's house.

I stepped out of my car, the scent of bougainvillea and hyacinth filling my nostrils. Off in the distance, a cowbird called out forlornly. The sprinklers made a whishing noise and little artificial rainbows on each side as I stomped up the stone walk toward Leduc's front porch.

"Out of my way, guys," I told them. "I have to talk to your boss."

I might as well have been talking to the columns. Actually, the columns looked a little more intelligent. Marcel and Rene stood there. They did not seem impressed.

I pointed at the front door. "I'm going in there. You want to frisk me, that's fine. You know I don't carry a gun. I have to see Leduc, though."

I could tell they were terrified, by the way they froze in their tracks. This was going to turn into a Mexican standoff, if I couldn't find a way to get them out of the way.

"Wrestle you for it," I offered.

Marcel did seem to crack a grin. I was considering the old college try, a direct run up the middle, fourth and goal, when the front door opened, and Justin Leduc appeared. He was dressed immaculately, in a cream colored linen suit that betrayed not a single wrinkle, save for the razor sharp crease of his trousers. I had a momentary illusion that he had known I would come, and had stood by the door patiently, waiting for just this moment to make a dramatic entrance. The cravat knotted at his neck flowed down into the silk shirt like an obedient waterfall. Over it all, his eyes were darkly malevolent.

"It's all right," he said. "Let him in."

As if controlled by a single mind, which between them they might have possessed, Marcel and Rene stepped to one side, toward opposite columns. I felt like Moses walking between them. I could almost feel their hot breath as I strode by them toward Leduc. As I passed, they closed ranks and fell in behind me.

Leduc led me into the house, to the sitting room I had visited so many times before. He selected a cigar from the humidor, and I noticed he didn't offer me one.

"Where's my money?" he asked.

"I don't have it. You might have read about it in the papers. Somebody zagged Vincouer."

Leduc's face darkened, and his cheeks and ears became red. "You got some fucking nerve coming here, Gallegher. You fuck up the collection, Vincouer is dead, you have the gall the bring all this to my house?"

"I had nothing to do with it, Justin."

"Don't ever call me that!" he shouted. "You don't go be knowing me well enough to call me that, you."

He was enraged. It took a lot to make Leduc drop back into his Cajun patois.

"I'm sorry," I said. "It wasn't me, though. Someone got to Vincouer before I could make the collection."

Leduc did not seem assuaged. He took a long draw on the stogie and blew the smoke in my direction. I didn't get the impression that he meant it as a warm and sharing gesture.

"That cop, Nuckolls, he was here earlier."

"He visited me, too."

"I don't like cops in my house."

"I'm not crazy about them in mine, either."

He leaned forward, and his voice became a malignant hiss. "I don't give a flying fuck what you like and don't like. I have a business to run."

"I apologize," I said. "I'm just trying to make you understand that I had nothing to do with Vincouer's death."

"That cop says otherwise. You should have told me you knew the wife."

"I know. I figured you knew that already, though."

"Why you figured that, you, huh?"

I motioned toward the chair across from him, asking to sit. He waved his hand. I sat.

"I was under the impression that I had been watched. I'd like to ask several questions, if I might."

"Who did you think was watching you?"

"I wasn't sure, but I was hoping you might know. A couple of weeks ago, Ms. Vincouer asked me to help her find her boyfriend, a con man named Sammy Cain. She was afraid that her husband might have had him killed. You and I know this isn't an easy or cheap task."

"You didn't find this Sammy Cain guy?"

I shook my head.

"Not a hair. But a couple of days ago, his apartment was stripped clean. It looked like someone wanted to have all traces of Cain wiped away. Now maybe it was Cain himself, taking it on the road, but I also wondered if it was part of the hit."

"What would I know about all this?"

"You're in tight with the Braga and Anolli families. Lester knew you. I thought he might have gone through you to contract the hit, if Sammy was taken out."

"You thought this," he asked, his eyes narrowing.

"It occurred to me. Look, I don't care if Vincouer had Cain iced. On the other hand, Cain's apartment was stripped on the one day I wasn't watching it. That made me wonder if someone was watching me. When you asked me to pay a visit on Vincouer, I assumed you had been told I was working for Clancey Vincouer."

Leduc puffed on the cigar, and flicked an ember into the crystal ash-tray on the coffee table in front of him. "And what else do you think? That maybe I also arranged a whack on Lester Vincouer?"

"Someone did him. It wasn't me."

"Then all the cops asking questions must be making you very uncomfortable."

I waited. Leduc seemed to want to make a point. I had learned years before, as a therapist, that sometimes people told you more when you kept your own mouth shut. I had already made my point. It was time for Leduc to make his.

He placed the cigar in the ashtray, and reached into his inside jacket pocket, pulling out an envelope. He placed it on the table, and pushed it across to me.

"Your marker," he said as I picked it up. "I'm declaring your debt to me annulled."

"Thank you," I said cautiously.

"Don't thank me. I'm out two hundred thousand because of Vincouer dying, not to mention the twelve large you still owe me. You have become a liability to me, Gallegher. Maybe you really didn't kill Vincouer. I can't see any reason why you should have. But with the police crawling all over, I can't do business unimpeded. This is your buyout. I'm cutting you loose. In return, I will thank you to forget that I ever mentioned Vincouer to you. You were never told to collect from him. I don't need your problems in my house, or in my business."

He lowered his voice. "I don't like what you're thinking, though. If you have some idea I had Vincouer taken out, after sending you to collect from him, then you must also be thinking I set you up to take the fall. That's not smart thinking, Gallegher. That kind of thinking could get you hurt. I don't care what happened between you and Vincouer's wife. So far as I'm concerned, that's your business. I want this clear, though. I didn't help Vincouer arrange a hit on any guy named Cain. I didn't order a hit on Vincouer. You put that shit out of your head, you hear, you? Any shit you have come down, it isn't coming from me. Our relationship is terminated."

And just like that, I was fired. Leduc picked up the cigar and settled back into the sofa. He didn't seem interested in my presence. I stowed the envelope in my own jacket pocket, and pulled myself to my feet.

"See you around, boys," I said to Marcel and Rene as I walked past.

Eloquent as always, they watched me until I pulled the Pinto out of the drive.

Sixteen

Leduc's meaning hadn't been lost on me. I wasn't just unemployed, I was unknown. If I got myself in a bind, I couldn't turn to Leduc for help—not that I would have been likely to in any case. He didn't want to know I was alive.

Which, in the grand scheme, was fine with me. It was completely within the bounds of reason that he had arranged this mess for me, no matter what he said. A guy like Leduc would lie to God if he thought there was a buck in it.

As I drove back to the Quarter, I tried to arrange all the facts I had to this point. About the only thing that almost everyone agreed on was that Lester Vincouer had been a dislikable person who would be, by and large, unmissed. Everyone had reason to want some harm to come to him, but no two people had the same reason.

So, I asked myself, who profited most by Lester Vincouer's death? Obviously, that would be Clancey, who would inherit the house and business. On the other hand, she had been out of the house when Lester was killed, and I had a hard time seeing her consorting with the types that could arrange for a murder of this type. Of course, it was also apparent that Lester knew his killer, which didn't let Clancey off the hook entirely.

If anyone else might have gotten anything out of punching Lester's timecard, I had a hard time figuring out who it might be. Maybe he did have Cain killed, but didn't arrange it through Leduc. Maybe he got antsy and threatened to go to the cops, tell them it was a misunderstanding, much like that which led to the martyrdom of Thomas a' Becket. The families like to keep a low profile. They don't take kindly to threats. It was a reach, but I've seen people do worse things for lesser reasons.

I couldn't see what Leduc had to gain by zipping Vincouer, unless he had been lying all along about Vincouer being into him for two hundred thousand. Meg had told me that Lester was a big-time gambler, but that didn't mean he owed Leduc. For all I knew, Lester had won ridiculously, and Leduc was trying to get out of paying off. It wasn't exactly his style. He knew the risks of running a sports book, but it seemed that everyone in this situation was acting out of character.

Finally, who had made that telephone call? The front of the Vincouer house wasn't anywhere near the street. It would have been difficult for any of the locals to even see the front porch, let alone make out the physical characteristics of a person standing there. It was the kind of place where Clancey Vincouer could take her morning coffee stark naked without causing a stir among the neighbors. The phone call still smelled like a setup.

I parked the car and walked down Toulouse to Holliday's. Shorty hadn't gotten a call for me, so I called Meg again. There was no answer.

Who could blame her? At least the machine had kicked in. She hadn't taken off for parts unknown.

I hiked down Bourbon to a Chinese takeout joint and picked up some moo shu shrimp and a couple of egg rolls. It was getting dark when I got back to my apartment. I dropped the food on my table, and called Meg again. I was beginning to feel like a lovesick schoolboy, or maybe a stalker. It didn't matter, as all I got was the machine.

The Chinese pancakes were still warm, and I piled them with the moo shu and the hoisin sauce and rolled them up like burritos. It was sweet and salty and sour and I gobbled them up in minutes. The egg rolls I drenched in duck sauce and dragged through the Chinese mustard. I am, I surmised, a man of multiple tastes.

The telephone rang as I was chewing the last egg roll. I washed the food down with a swig of Dixie and picked up the receiver.

"Pat?" It was Meg.

"Boy am I glad you called," I said.

"I got your message. This has all been horrible. I got home with Clancey around ten, and there were all these police cars around. I didn't know what to think."

"Did you see Vincouer?"

"Yes. They wouldn't let me in the study, but I could see him from the doorway when Clancey identified him. It was so gruesome. The detective there said he hadn't seen anything that gory in years. The police said they had a call about a prowler. Was that you?"

I deferred the question. "I didn't have anything to do with the killing. The police were here today, and they told me what you said. It's okay. It was the truth. I can take care of myself in this thing. You have to believe me, though, someone else killed Lester."

"I… I want to, Pat."

"Can you come here tonight?"

There was a long pause. "No."

"I'll come there."

"Don't. I'm sorry, but I have other plans. The viewing, at the funeral home…"

I felt like eight varieties of cheap. It hadn't occurred to me that the visitation might be so soon. Here Lester was cooling in a casket somewhere, and all I could think about was my own primal urges. It came out in my voice, too. Even I could hear it.

"Of course," I said. "You should be there. For Clancey."

I could feel the waves of discomfort emanating off her over the phone. "You trust me?"

Again a long pause. "Pat, I don't even know you. I have to go. Give me a few days. I'll call. Or you call. I don't know."

"A few days," I repeated.

And the conversation was over.

All in all, it had been a day rich in rejection. Cully didn't want to be seen in public with me, Nuckolls was busy phoning in my reservation at the state prison, Leduc just wanted me gone anywhere, and now Meg was giving me the cold shoulder.

My life was made of a jillion moving parts, all of them smaller than my pinkie nail, and if I pulled the wrong lever or pushed the wrong button, it was all going to go *sproing* and blow bits across the room, and I was going to spend the next twenty years trying to piece it all together at Angola.

This was no time for aimless tinkering.

I was bothered by the recurrent intrusion of a story I'd heard a couple of years before, about a patsy named Arnold Freeman who allowed himself to be set up by Lucho Braga. Arnold was hungry, ambitious, and he liked the smell of fresh hundreds. He signed on to do some midnight bookkeeping for one of Braga's presumably legitimate enterprises, which was actually a conduit for laundering dirty gambling money. Braga would use the dirty money to prime the pump for the new business, and it was Freeman's job to disguise both the source and the destination of the company funds.

Braga had other ideas, though. He was taking the profits and salting them away in untraceable foreign bank accounts, after they were cleaned by Freeman. One day, Braga demanded an accounting, and the books Freeman produced didn't jibe with Braga's. Braga talked one of his made cops into opening an investigation into embezzlement, the theft of money Freeman could never account for, because Braga had hidden it so perfectly.

Lucho Braga does not take chances. There was always the chance that
Freeman, as unwitting as he had been to that point, might be just a shade
more intelligent. So, Lucho resorted to his own version of the final solution, and Freeman was found in the bayou a couple of weeks later done
up in the family way. No embezzler, no investigation. Lucho spent a
month in the Bahamas that winter, after liquidating the business.

At least, that's how the story went.

That wasn't going to happen to me. I was feeling brilliantly set up,
and if that was the case it was just a matter of time before some hotshot
stepped up from behind and drilled a twenty-two hollowpoint into my
ear. There was nothing I, by myself, could do to stop it. I am blessed
with excellent peripheral vision, but that still left nearly a hundred
eighty degrees of perspective I couldn't cover at any moment.

I needed help.

There were still a couple of hours left before my shift at Holliday's,
so I grabbed my Saints jacket and took a walk across Jackson Square
to a military surplus store on the far end of the Quarter, near Esplanade.
Like most establishments in this dreary, less-traveled section, Semper
Fi was a dark, shabby place with no front window. A hanging sign over
the front door, embellished with a sword embraced by a coiled viper,
was the only way to tell it from any of another dozen fringe businesses,
tattoo and scarification parlors, shooting galleries, whorehouses, and
porno shops in the area.

Semper Fi is run by a skinny, rat-faced, one-eyed vet named Sonny,
but I was there to see Scat Boudreaux.

The bayou country is full of strange and exotic characters, the kind
children see in their dreams staring in the window at them just before
they wake up screaming for momma and dry sheets. Some of them live
their entire lives in the salt marsh, surviving on the land by hunting, a
little dirt gardening, and fishing. They make what they must have, and
do without the rest. Others take what they learn in the backwoods and

parlay it into a sort of life in civilization. Of course, there isn't much that translates, save for shooting, 'wrasslin', and tracking.

Scat Boudreaux traded on shooting. The first time I met him was in a bar, where half the patrons were betting on him, and the rest against. His companion had bragged to the rest of the bar that Scat could put the eye out of a squirrel at a hundred yards and drop two more before the first one stumbled. Nobody could seem to come up with three squirrels, but one guy did have a boat and three empty beer bottles. After the wagering was done, he motored out in the river about three hundred feet, and placed the bottles on the bow. Had he been a little less intoxicated, the boater might have considered the wisdom in going below, but he didn't want to miss the show, and stayed topside. Scat drew a bead with an M-16 his partner had taken from his trunk, and in the space of a second shattered all three bottles, scattering shards of glass across the prow of the boat.

As it happened, I was on the winning edge of the betting, and I had occasion to talk more with Boudreaux's partner, Sonny, that evening.

Scat only came out of the bayou when he was drafted in 1968. He had made the mistake of signing a voter registration card during a vigorous Democratic Party drive in the out parishes, and then was called up on the carpet by the local draft board after not registering with them. He was the right age, the right socio-economic level, and had just the right lack of political pull to land his fanny in Southeast Asia.

In a singular moment of rare wisdom, the Marines recognized that a boy who had spent his entire life tracking and shooting one kind of creature or another in a feral, marshy, semi-tropical setting might just make a decent sniper.

Scat Boudreaux recorded over thirty kills, all one-shot wonders, in the deltas and jungles of Viet Nam. Then, in early 1970, some second lieutenant working on too much caffeine and too little sleep forgot to order the pickup chopper, and Scat got captured. He spent almost a year in a tiger cage before he escaped, and began an epic cross-country exodus to the South. It made the papers when he wandered into an ARVN camp just over the line, and then the hoopla faded, and Scat was mustered out.

The papers didn't report the whole story, though, including the little detail that Scat escaped his captors by killing them with bamboo knives he had made with painstaking slowness over the course of weeks, and that in his tortured, starved frenzy celebrated his victory by eating parts of each of them. They didn't report that he essentially cannibalized his way across the country, and later rationalized it as something he just had to do to survive. In retrospect, the Marines probably couldn't boot him out fast enough.

Sonny directed me to the back room of the shop, where I found Scat Boudreaux reclined on a bench, reading a copy of a mercenary rag. It was the type of radical right propaganda that purports to have conclusive proof that the Trilateral Commission and the Council on Foreign Relations have conspired with the Girl Scouts to fluoridate the flour used in their cookies in order to propagate a mass reduction in the collective IQ of all Americans, so that the enemies of freedom can destroy the republic.

Scat was wearing fatigue trousers and spit-polished boots, but he had foregone the olive green blouse in favor of a gray tee shirt that said "*Rugby Players Eat Their Dead*". On most people, it was intended as humor. On Scat, it was just scary.

"Look at this shit, Gallegher," he said as I walked through the door. "Says here that the fuckin' Illuminati have aligned with the Jewish Bund to control the European Economic Community. That's why they switched over to use just one currency, so they can corner the world markets and drive down the dollar. Couldn't you just see it coming?"

Perhaps I neglected to mention that Scat is certifiably psychotic.

Maybe it was the thirty kills, or the months of imprisonment, or the consumptive trek through the jungles of Southeast Asia. Maybe he was always this way. Whatever the case, it didn't take a genius to see that he was about a hundred twenty percent around the bend, with both diesels chugging.

"Go figure," I said, trying to find the most neutral approach. It didn't pay to set Scat off. "What next?"

"What indeed?" he said, shaking his head. "Whatcha got, Gallegher?"

He motioned toward a threadbare couch against the storeroom wall, and I sat carefully.

"I need help," I said. "I think I may have been set up, and someone might be getting ready to kill me."

"So what's new?" Scat replied. "Frigging IRS is up my ass trying to claim I owe them money. ATF wants a piece of me because I sold a couple of automatics to some guys going to fight in Nicaragua. The water ain't fit to drink, the air stinks, and the Illuminati have been aiming that damn microwave thing at the shop. Somebody out there wants all of us dead, Slick. Climb on the bus. Want a drink?"

He grabbed a Jax beer out of a cooler and handed it to me. As I screwed off the cap, he plopped a pistol down on the table in front of me, and field-stripped is as he spoke.

"Here's what you want, Slick. Browning nine millimeter automatic, thirteen round clip, gas activated, feels good, shoots good, a never-fail weapon. They don't come any more reliable, they'll blow a hole the size of a grapefruit in anything you aim at, and this particular baby has that added advantage of having the serial numbers welded off. Go ahead, try it on, see if it fits."

I stared at the handgun, and then back at Scat. His scattered sensorium aside, he made one spooky salesman. He might as well have been hawking a used '68 Chevy Nova.

"Ah, yeah," I said. "Actually, Scat, I was more in the market for professional services, someone to watch my six."

"You going in-country, son?"

"Sort of," I told him. I related the whole story, being careful to leave out the part about being at the Vincouer house on the night Lester was killed. Even a loony like Scat might be deemed credible on the stand, and I couldn't take any chances. I told him about Clancey's request to find Sammy Cain, the stripping of Cain's apartment, the assignment by Leduc to shake down Vincouer, the killing, and how the police were looking hard at me for it. I told him about being fired by Leduc, and about Leduc's connections with Lucho Braga and the Anollis. I reminded him about Arnold Freeman's untimely demise.

"The dagos," he said, shaking his head sadly. "You know, ol' son, you lie down with pigs, you come up stinking of shit. You're just begging for a dose of the ol' double deuce. The greaseball families have been aligned with the Trilateral Commission for decades, ever since Al Capone made an agreement with Meyer Lansky. That led to Kennedy being elected President, you know. It was all in the deal. It was the Illuminati what got to Kennedy, though, and that's why Sam Giancana and Lyndon Johnson had to have him killed. You know, it was right here, in this very city, that Oswald hooked up with Mark Lane and the Fair Play for Cuba Committee, and this is where they planned the assassination, right here on this very block. It's true, Slick, I saw it in a movie..."

I let him ramble for several minutes, get it out of his system, while I mused on how very desperate I must be to seek help from this unlikely a source. On the other hand, if he saw my involvement as an opportunity to engage in a paranoid war against subversive secret organizations, it was possible he would jump at the chance. He finally wound down, and popped open a beer to cool off.

"Here's what I had in mind," I told him. "I can't see everything, and I sure don't want to spend the next six months looking over my shoulder every fifteen seconds. You're an expert at being invisible. You can cover my ass while I go about trying to unravel this mess. If someone tries to take me out, you see to it they don't succeed."

He stroked his meticulously clean-shaven face. "What rules of engagement?"

"I just stated them. I don't care what you do. You know how to pull it off without being discovered. I don't want to know about it, unless there's no other way. I just don't want to get dusted before I can get myself cleared."

"I can't do it," he said, after taking a long draw from the beer. "Not alone. I have responsibilities, the shop here. It could get pricey. You're looking at four guys, rotating in shifts. Me, I'd do it just for a shot at sticking it to the bastards, but the guys I know are going to want some money."

I leaned back and put my hands behind my head, staring at the ceiling. I had never noticed that the ceiling was almost twenty feet up, with several storage lofts attached to the walls. Most of Semper Fi's business was in the typical surplus items, clothing, boots, some hardware. I had no doubt, though, that the room I was sitting in housed more than its fair share of lethal weapons. Most of it would eventually wind up in the hands of mercenary soldiers fighting in foreign countries. Some of it might be bought by terrorists posing as soldiers of fortune. It sickened me a bit to be dealing with someone like Scat, but what choice did I have?

"I don't have a lot," I said. "How much are we talking about?"

Boudreaux had silenced the voices in his head to do the mental arithmetic.

"If it takes a month, maybe fifteen thousand. That's five grand for each of the other three guys."

"What about you?"

He chuckled. "These guys, I'll get most of the money sooner or later. They get money, they spend it. They like toys."

"I don't know if I can raise fifteen thousand, not right away."

He stared at me for almost half a minute. I couldn't be sure what he was thinking. For all I knew, he might have been mentally redecorating his condo in the Twilight Zone.

"How much can you raise, Slick?" he said at last.

I had some money salted away from previous favors, hidden in various places in my apartment. I also had several thousand invested in mutual funds. It would take a week, maybe more, to access it.

"Let's say five grand."

He mulled this over for several seconds.

"Okay," he said, "Let's take a look here. You sleep for, what, six or eight hours a night?"

"From about four in the morning until noon, more or less."

"And you're in that bar playing your horn about six hours a day?"

I nodded.

"That leaves ten hours a day we have to keep an eye on you, noon to ten at night. The dago families, they're real particular about where they whack someone. They won't make a scene in the club, and if you take the proper precautions they won't be able to sneak up on you in your home. I can give you the five to ten shift. That means we only need one other guy for the daytime. Can you live with that, son?"

It wasn't the optimum arrangement, but I had operated with less protection in the past.

"It could work," I said. "I can have the apartment rigged with an alarm system…"

"Make it redundant. That way, if they take out one, the other will still alert you."

"I can do that. Shorty will keep an eye out in the bar while I'm working. The rest of the time you'll be around?"

"Count on it."

I was uneasy. I had depended on my damnable luck for years, like a guardian angel watching over my shoulder. Now I was putting my life in the hands of a guy who believed that bad guys were beaming microwaves at him.

"How will I know you're there?" I asked.

Something in what he heard struck him as being very funny, because he broke out in a disturbing chortle that grew into outright laughter. He took a long swig of the beer, and pushed the Browning toward me again.

"Take the gun, Gallegher. Consider it part of the service. Trust me, we'll be there. If someone's trying to kill you, you'll know we're there because you won't be dead. You get clipped, we'll give you your money back."

Seventeen

There are nights, rare and precious, when the music flows clean and deep. You get up on stage, maybe after a nap or a romp with a buxom enthusiastic hoyden, and it's like meditation. Your mind slows down, the rotation of the earth becomes a palpable thing, and the music flows effortlessly. Marathoners call it runner's high, basketball players refer to being 'in the zone'. Whatever it is, it's something to be treasured for it comes to us too few times in a life.

This was one of those nights. I had gone home and tossed a Chet Baker CD on the stereo, pulled down a bottle of Dixie and stuck my feet out the window. Chet and Paul Desmond made musical love while I drifted in and out of sentience up to the moment that my watch beeped and told me it was time to warm the chops for my shift downstairs. On a whim, I pulled out the cornet and jammed with the immortals on the stereo, Chet Baker conjuring heaven and earth from his trumpet, and long-gone Paul Desmond making sad smooth alto sax honey. It was presumptuous and damn near profane, but by God it worked, and when I presented myself on stage to my sparse but adoring public, I was brilliant.

The beautiful part of the deal was that it became effortless, like breathing, and it freed my mind to explore all the possibilities of my situation. I started with Miles Davis's "*All Blues*", and it set the tone for a night of low, slow mellowness that left lots of room for contemplation.

Part of my problem, I realized, was that I couldn't come up with a single suspect who had both motive and opportunity. This put me at a distinct disadvantage to the real killer who was trying to pin it on me. I had a lot of information, but none of if connected in a cohesive or productive way. It came to me, around two in the morning and in the middle of '*Concierto de Aranjuez*', that I was looking at this mystery from a hundred eighty degrees off plumb. I had been trying to figure out who had the most to gain by Lester's death, and it occurred to me that he might have been killed to hurt someone else. It was possible that whoever sliced through Lester's jugular was doing it to keep another person from profiting in some way.

A cognitive psychologist I once knew in a past life held that nothing we see or hear or experience is ever truly lost, but is just stored in priority of the level of arousal connected with it. It is for this reason that you can recall in winter-night clarity the first time you had sex, but the sixteenth time is considerably more fuzzy. This must be true, because in my reflective state as the muse swept over me I began to rerun my conversations with Clancey Vincouer and Meg Coley and Leduc, even with Cully Tucker. An idea began to form in the back of my mind, slowly emerging as piecework that is patiently sewn by a skilled tailor into a beautiful garment. I was aware of my growing excitement as I discovered each secret which had been hidden in plain sight.

I signaled for Sockeye Sam to take over, and took a break toward the end of the third set, so I could dash up the stairs to my telephone. It took several rings for Cully Tucker to answer.

"Who in hell is this?" he asked.

"It's me, Pat."

I could hear sheets rustling, as he reached over to check his alarm clock.

"Jesus, Pat, I have to be in court in six hours. What do you mean calling me this time of night?"

"I had some questions."

"They couldn't wait until morning?"

"No. Tell me, when a company goes public, how are the shares distributed?"

"Wait a minute," he said, "I gotta take a whiz and get something to drink. I'll be right back."

It took him several minutes to return to the phone. When he picked up again, he sounded more alert.

"Take my advice, Pat. Treat your prostate like your closest friend, or you'll never get a decent night's rest again. Now, what was this about a company?"

I had taken the opportunity to make some notes while he tended to his business, and I consulted the sheet in front of me.

"Okay, let's say you have a company, and you decide to go public and sell stock. How are the shares distributed?"

"You mean in an IPO?"

"*IPO?*"

"Initial Public Offering. The first day the stock goes on the market."

"That's it. Does everyone have an equal chance at buying the stock, or do some people get a jump?"

"Well, it depends. Since we're speculating, let's say you've been approached by someone who wants to play a major part in the company. There are ways to see to it that he gets first crack at a large chunk of the IPO. Why do you ask?"

"I was thinking about what Clancey told me the first time we met, about how Lester took the Vincouer Cannery public and made a wad of money overnight."

"Yeah?"

"Well, I was wondering who the first investor was, and who got the biggest piece of the pie."

Cully was quiet, and I thought I heard a sigh. He was sitting there thinking the pressure had gotten to me, and I was cracking up.

"Lester, of course, would have retained fifty-one percent," he began.

"To retain control of the company."

"That's right. He probably gave a certain percentage to Clancey."

"And the rest went on the block?"

"Probably. What's this all about, Pat? It's late."

"Stay with me for a moment. How could I go about getting hold of the list of stockholders, especially those who bought big in the IPO?"

"It's easy. That sort of thing is all public record. Before it went public, Vincouer Canning had to issue a prospectus, and include information about the financial status. Afterward, they had to issue an annual report, which should have listed the largest stockholders."

"Suppose someone bought a large block of stock, at the initial offering price, and then ditched it at the height of the initial stock rise?"

"You're presuming it did rise, of course. A lot of stocks go ballistic in the first several days, but some drop off the deep end as soon as they're issued. But, if you're right, that person would have made a great deal of money."

"Would he be listed in the annual report?"

"Not necessarily. Most annual reports only list the top stockholders at the end of the first fiscal year, and most often then it's only the Board members."

"But the company has to maintain a listing of all the stockholders, right? I mean, they have to know where to send dividend checks and copies of the report."

"Of course."

"And, in that case, there should be records available somewhere listing all the investors on any particular day?"

There was a longer silence this time, accented by a faint hum on the line.

"Yes, and it would be accessible. What's your point, here, Pat?"

"Clancey told me that Lester made a ton of money on the IPO, and that he used it to expand the canning business into Oklahoma and Texas *and to diversify into other businesses*."

"It's not unusual. Diversification provides security."

"But what businesses?"

Cully was becoming irritated. "I have no idea, Pat. Get to the point, please. I have court at nine, remember. Not all of us live like vampires."

"Are you my attorney?" I asked.

"Sure, I guess. Why?"

"I want you to follow up on this. I want you to track down the information on the early trades in Vincouer Canneries. Then I want you to get a copy of Vincouer's will, find out what stocks he's leaving to Clancey. Finally, I want you to find out who owns those companies. I'm willing to bet that the same name is going to come up over and over and over."

"And that name is?"

"Damned if I know. But you find it, and you'll find the most likely suspect in Vincouer's killing."

"And what do I do then? Make a citizen's arrest?"

"No, just hand the information over to Nuckolls. He's a sharp guy. He can figure out what to do. Maybe he'll give me a little breathing room."

I could hear Sockeye Sam's piano coming through the floorboards. It was sweet and viscous, like corn syrup. He was messing around with "*Apple Blossom Time*", and suddenly I yearned to be there with him, exploring that special language in which it was impossible for me to say a mean or hurtful thing.

"Will you do it?" I asked.

"Yeah, okay. I'll get on it after court tomorrow. Can I get some sleep now?"

"You go right ahead. I have to get back to work."

"Jesus, I wish you'd get a day job," Cully said, and hung up the phone.

Eighteen

I was in Kacoo's around five the next afternoon, sweating over a pile of steamed spicy mudbugs and a schooner of Jax. I had, judiciously, taken the corner booth, away from the window. Scat Boudreaux's assurances aside, I felt safer if I could see every soul who darkened the doorway.

I had slept until almost one, but my dreams had been tortured and convoluted, the kind I had known when wracked with a viral fever. There had been twisted shadows and spectral accusatory faces, and images of violence and sudden death. The intricate, almost diabolical scheme I had imagined while in my musical reverie ran through my head on an endless tape loop, until I awoke thrashing the pillow and swearing to dream of something else.

When I finally gave up after noon, I rose, showered, and tried to call Meg Coley. All I got was the answering machine again. She had probably stayed at Clancey Vincouer's overnight, to offer solace and consolation to the grieving widow. I liked the thought of that, that Meg would indulge in a selfless, altruistic act for the benefit of another person. It helped me rationalize away my decision to drop her from my short list of setup suspects. For a nickel, I would have called or gone to the Vincouer estate to see Ms. Coley, but I felt confident that I was not the most welcome visitor there at this exact moment.

The crawfish were succulent and drenched in Tabasco, and I tore them apart and gently pulled the sweet tail meat out and dabbed it with cocktail sauce before popping it in my mouth with a cracker to keep from incinerating my tongue. Just as the inferno became nearly unbearable, I would suck out the head and chase it with a swallow of beer. The effort of maintaining this ritual, and perhaps the chemical reaction taking place in my gullet, made beads of sweat stand out on my brow.

It was easier sitting in the corner, because the Browning stuck in the back of my pants was cold and hard and unyielding. I had a round chambered with the safety on, and I had practiced in my room for almost an hour until I got to the point where I could yank that sucker out and drop the safety in only slightly more time than it would take a skilled shooter to waste my sorry ass. I sincerely hoped I had something more stealthy and corporeal than a guardian angel watching out for me, somewhere out in the block.

I looked up just as Farley Nuckolls walked into the joint. He spied me in the corner, and sauntered over to my table, sitting himself down across from me without so much as a beg your pardon. He was dressed for comfort, in a short-sleeved cotton shirt and light colored khaki slacks. He took his Panama hat off and dropped it on the table. Catching the waitress' attention, he pointed at my meal. She nodded and hustled off to get him one.

"Your bartender told me you were here," he said just as I stuffed my mouth with some mudbug tail and a cracker. I chewed vigorously, reluctant to rush this sublime pleasure just for the sake of replying, and then sucked out the head, taking great pains to make it sound obscene.

After drowning the fire with the Jax, I sat back and eyed the detective.

"Who made the telephone call, Farley?"

"That's all you have to say?"

"You just ordered a beer. That means you're off duty. You made a point of looking me up, walked at least two streets over to find me. You aren't going to arrest me, and you aren't going to grill me again, so that means you must know something about the phone call."

The waitress placed a schooner of beer and a plate of crawfish on the table in front of him.

"You seem to know a lot for someone who wasn't in the vicinity of the killing, Gallegher."

"Who made the phone call, Farley?"

"We don't know. He didn't identify himself. I listened to the tape. There was lots of traffic sound in the background, trucks driving by, that sort of thing."

"If I were you," I told him, "I would have already driven out to look around for public phone booths near the Vincouer house."

"Which is what I did."

"And you didn't find any."

He picked up a crawfish and broke the tail off.

"It could have been a cellular phone," he said, as he dipped the tail meat in the sauce. "For all I know some upstanding citizen was driving by and saw you…"

"*A big guy*," I corrected.

"… okay, a big guy on the front porch."

"Now there's something you don't see every day."

"Could have been a neighbor, didn't want to get involved. Maybe he saw some big guy, like maybe a guy who knew that Vincouer would be alone in the house because he had gotten his punch to take Ms. Vincouer out on the town, saw this guy on the front porch and knew it wasn't Mr. Vincouer. So this civic-minded neighbor pulled out the car phone and called in a report."

He slurped the crawfish and chased it with a cracker and a swallow of beer. I could almost see the color rise in his neck.

"We are not going to get anywhere together," I told him as he suffered exquisitely, "if you are going to be so suspicious, Farley. And don't call Meg a punch. If you recall, I have been to the Vincouer home.

You can't see the front porch from Lakeshore Drive. The neighbors can't see the house either."

"Ms. Vincouer confirmed your story about looking for this Sammy Cain guy," he said. "Have you found him yet?"

"Haven't been looking. Between you and me, she suspected that her husband had done Cain a mischief. After Lester got killed, I just sort of lost interest in Sammy. If he's out there, he'll turn up."

"You know he's wanted in several states."

"He would appear to be an accomplished con man."

We sat and ate our shellfish for quite a long time after that, two men with vastly different problems, neither of whom had the slightest clue as to a solution. It was comforting, in a way, the kind of fellowship that probably brought hobos together in the Great Depression to congregate in railway yards. If misery loves company, Farley Nuckolls and I were just wallowing in mutual admiration.

"So," I said as I tossed the last mudbug head in the plastic basket, "am I still your favorite suspect?"

"You'll do," he said. "You could do yourself a favor if you could account for that missing time on the night of the murder."

"Would that I could. Of course, the Buffalo Bills were in town that night to play the Saints. Have you checked all their whereabouts?"

"You want to tell me why you had Ms. Coley take Ms. Vincouer out that night?"

I chugged down the rest of my Jax, burped as politely as I could, and motioned to the waitress for another.

"Clancey was getting weird. She probably told you about Sammy Cain's place getting cleaned out. She was becoming downright paranoid, seeing fiends behind every curtain. I figured she needed a night on the town."

"Your professional opinion?"

"Hey, when you're talking paranoia, you gotta go to the man that owns one. You know, I didn't have to tell you that just now. Cully

Tucker would take a bite out of my ass the size of Baton Rouge if he caught me talking to you like this. As I've said, I didn't have anything to do with killing Lester Vincouer, and I think you see it that way, too."

"Don't presume how I see things, Gallegher. If I can make you on this, I'd as soon ship you off to Angola as anyone else."

"You said '*if*'. That means you can't."

"Quit interpreting my words like some kind of political spin doctor," he said. "I can't make anyone yet. Doesn't mean I won't."

"Time will tell," I said.

He raised his glass. "Yes, indeed. Time will tell."

They interred Lester Vincouer the next day, in an ornate marble family mausoleum that would have comfortably housed eight or more of New Orleans' homeless, if it hadn't already been full of corpses. I didn't attend the funeral. I did pick up a copy of the Times-Picayune, and I read Vincouer's obit. It was flowery and laudatory, and was worth every penny Clancey paid for the expanded version. Its one fault was that it shed not the slightest ray of illumination on my current problem.

The funeral was at one in the afternoon. I waited a decent interval, long enough for the visitation at the Vincouer home, and called Meg Coley's number around four. I got the machine.

It was a sure thing that I wasn't going to make any progress on clearing myself if all I did was sit in my apartment blowing scales on the cornet. So I stowed the Browning in the small of my back and took a hike out to the river. When I got there, I hung a right and wandered over toward the Hilton, past the flashing lights and siren call of the Harrah's Casino. The casino had put up a wad of money to build a franchise at the corner of Canal and Poydras, across from the Aquarium of the Americas, and there was still the Flamingo, running its floating casino on a riverboat.

I was openly disturbed by gambling's apparent success in this bacchanal by the sea, as it added too many new temptations to indulge in my own addiction. On the other hand, I knew far too many decent people who had laid down their fortunes on the prosperity of the syndicates, and they would be terribly hurt if the casinos were to fail. One man's poison, I guess.

I was hoping, I suppose, that someone would take a potshot at me as I strolled past the Hilton. If Scat had kept his word, the odds of a successful hit were pretty long, and at least then I would know something tangible, rather than engage in flights of paranoid fancy. Like Jacob Marley, Vincouer was dead. There was no doubt of that. Someone had taken a blade and ripped the life right out of him the way you would slit open a mattress and yank out the stuffing, and I hadn't the slightest idea who had done it. I had fantasies, a dreamed-up conspiracy that made sense only if every piece of it fell into place. And I had a persistent police detective who regarded me the scornful way you would the first guy who screwed your kid sister, and who would love to see me chained to my seat on one of those yellow prison buses with the thick wire mesh over the windows.

No one took a shot at me. No one ran up behind me with a knife, or waited for me around a corner with a length of piano wire. I stepped on no land mines, and no safes or pianos fell out of twelfth story windows. I learned absolutely nothing more on this walk than I had in the last three days.

I did find a quarter on the sidewalk outside the Hilton, so the day wasn't a total loss.

Cully called me the next morning, around seven. He claimed he was trying to get me before he had to rush to court, but I was sure it was retribution for my late-night call to him.

"I checked your hunches," he said. "You know, for a guy who spends all his time over a bar, you're pretty sharp."

"What did you find out?"

"This was difficult. I had to contact Lester's attorney, ask for a courtesy. I'm gonna have to pay him back someday."

"I appreciate it, Cully. Now what did you find?"

"Okay, first the Vincouer Canneries IPO. As I suspected, Lester took fifty-one percent of the stock, and gave Clancey roughly three percent. At the opening bell, some hundred thousand shares were snapped up by a gentleman named Louis Antonio Braga."

"Lucho," I said.

"The very same. He bought the block at twelve dollars and change, sat on it for exactly three weeks and unloaded it at twenty-seven. He made a rough profit of one and a half very large, and it was a canny move, since the stock took a tumble several days later to settle at eighteen and a fraction."

There was a queasy lightness in my head, and I tried to pull all my thoughts together. I hadn't expected Lucho to be in the picture, and it complicated my theory.

"Okay, let's try this scenario. Lester takes Vincouer Canning public, but not before he lets a certain party in on the scheme. This certain party..."

"Give him a name. If you try to do the 'party of the first part' shit, I'm going to lose interest real quick."

"Well, it looks like we're talking about Lucho. So Lucho is into some nasty business, something illegal, and he needs to hide a shitload of money in something safe, but he doesn't want it just sitting around, because he's going to need it in the short term. An offshore bank is out of the question. He needs to launder the money in a hurry. He agrees to buy a bunch of stock, before the IPO, at twice the offering price, only the papers are written to reflect the actual price. The stock goes up, and Lucho dumps his shares after several days at about two and a half times the initial cost, or half again what he actually paid. According to you he bought a little over one million worth of stock which would mean he spent two million and change for it, and sold it for close to three million at the end of the week. He pockets the three million, making a million profit, and effectively hides a million in illegal proceeds."

"It's called collusion, Pat, and if the SEC found out both Lucho and Lester would spend years at Allenwood."

"I already figured that out, man. Remember what you told me three nights ago? You said that Clancey had confided in you that Lester had been salting away huge amounts of money in some offshore bank accounts. What did you call it? His 'retirement account'?"

"Yeah, I remember."

"So, let's say Lucho makes a deal with Lester, to take the million and make an investment in another business. Lester decides to pop it into some Bahamian bank to sit and gather interest, and tells Lucho to bite him, that if Lucho tries anything Lester is going to call the Feds and turn witness."

"Tell me more," Cully said, suddenly interested.

"Now remember what else you said that night? About what happened to Boom Boom, and how the worst thing you could do to the families is fuck with their women or their money?"

"Yeah, I said that."

"So, in our little fantasy we've established that Lucho is a very bad dude. Is it so hard to extrapolate that Lucho, being with one of the dago families, might want to exact a little revenge on Lester?"

"Makes sense to me. You forgot one thing, though. Lester took Vincouer Canneries public five years ago. They always say the families never forget, but it's also well-known that they are very impatient. If your story is real, why didn't they whack him five years ago?"

"Diversification, Cully. If the money is in some offshore bank, how would you get to it?"

"You couldn't, without the password. These banks, like in the Bahamas, or the Caymans, they're tighter than anything the Swiss have. You don't even have a name in these places, just some cocked-up number that only you and they know."

"My point exactly. So Lucho goes to Lester and threatens to take him out. Lester reminds him that not only does Lucho not know which bank the money is in, he also doesn't know the password number. They strike a deal. If Lester will invest in some of Lucho's legitimate businesses, say a half million, Lucho will let it go. He gets the money one way or another, what does he care?"

"It's a dangerous game, Pat."

"Lester liked dangerous games. Meg told me about his reputation, about how he wanted to win more than anything else. What could give him a bigger jolt than beating the families at their own game?"

"So why buzz him now?"

"You said it, remember? Once the families get their hooks into you, you're theirs for life, something like that?"

"It's true."

"So, now they have Lester by the eggs and they're squeezing. Before he knows it, Lester is in up to his eyes. He's being asked to invest more and more, and he can't see any way out. So he makes the threat one more time. Back off, or I'm going to the Feds. Only this time, he doesn't have a hand to play with, because Lucho has taken a hell of a lot more than the original half-million out of him. Lucho's in the black on this one, and it's time to give Lester one right up the old coal chute."

"Man," Cully said, "You got some kind of imagination, Pat. I want some of what you're drinking."

"And if he did buy the Vincouer stock at twice the going price, he got back the extra and a half million bonus. So far, it could work out just the way I thought. What else did you find? What did Lester's attorney tell you?"

"I asked him about the will, and who gets what. You see, I had to find out what companies Lester had diversified into. Then, I had to find out who owned the companies."

"Okay."

"The first company was Fairfax Industries in Dallas. They produce sorghum and corn syrup. The owner is a guy named Orum Cordette."

"Not Lucho Braga."

"No."

"Lucho isn't on the board of directors?"

"No. At least, he wasn't at the time of the last annual report."

"Damn."

"Next Lester bought a hefty chunk of Consolidated Timepiece, a watch manufacturer in Chicago. The owner still isn't Lucho Braga, but a fellow named Brian Semple."

"Give me the short version, okay Cully? Lester invested in a number of firms, and none of them were owned by Braga, right?"

"That's the thrust of it, my man. Hey, don't feel so bad. You can't score a homer every time you get up to bat."

"Wait a minute," I said, flashing on an idea. "Can you check to see if Braga owned stock in these companies at the time Lester bought in?"

"That's a tall order, Pat. There are some eight or nine companies here."

"I could help."

"No offense, Pat, but I think I should handle this. In the time it would take to show you how to do this thing, I could have it done myself. Give me several hours, maybe tomorrow, okay?"

It seemed like the only logical thing to do, so I agreed. I rolled over and when back to bed, but restful sleep was a furtive and stealthy quarry after the disappointment Cully had brought.

I got up at noon and went out for breakfast. When I got back, I called Meg again. There was still no answer, so I gave in and called Clancey Vincouer's house.

She was cool and distant when she came to the telephone.

"Mr. Gallegher," she greeted.

"Ms. Vincouer, I'm sorry to disturb you at this time. Please accept my condolences on the loss of your husband. I've been trying to locate Meg Coley, without much success."

"Is it true that you had her take me out the night my husband was killed?"

"Yes, I've already spoken with Detective Nuckolls about that."

"Do you know who killed Lester, Mr. Gallegher?"

It was a monumentally stupid question. If I did know, I'd have been in Nuckolls' office two days earlier. You couldn't have kept me quiet.

"No, ma'am, I'm sorry. I have no idea."

Which wasn't exactly correct, but voicing my suspicions would have served no good purpose.

"I haven't seen Meg since the funeral," she said. "She was here for the visitation after the service, but she left that evening."

"I've called several times, but all I get is her answering machine."

"Perhaps she's been working," Clancey observed.

"I've mostly called at night. I don't know many banks that are open that late."

"Banks?" She sounded confused.

My little alarms started to go off.

"Yes, she told me that she worked in banking, on a sort of on-call basis."

I heard her laugh sadly at the other end of the line.

"Mr. Gallegher, she works for a bank, all right, but it's the bank at the Flamingo. She's a blackjack dealer there, part time. I suppose she didn't want you to know."

It had to be blackjack, of course. The confluence of active and passive principles in my life wouldn't have had it any other way.

"Please," Clancey said, "don't tell her you heard this from me. She works unusual hours. That might explain why you haven't been able to reach her. Can I ask you something personal?"

"Sure," I said, still trying to recover from the shock.

"If you had killed my husband, would you tell me?"

This brought me back to the moment. Clancey was just as much in shock as I was. She was so caught up in the horror that had invaded her life that she believed that anyone would answer such a question in the affirmative.

"Ms. Vincouer, please believe me, I had nothing to do with it. No, ma'am, I didn't kill your husband."

"No," she said, "I never believed that you did. Even when Meg told that police detective that you had told her to get me out of the house. I believe that you are an honorable man. I'm sorry that I involved you in my personal tragedy."

I again offered my condolences, and hung up.

Meg had lied to me about her work. Maybe it was a little lie, borne of embarrassment or shame, or maybe it was part of an elaborate cover to hide some motive more nefarious. I wasn't sure how to respond, or even how I should feel. She had made me promise that there would be no commitments, and she had asked me not to look for her. On the other hand, I had never promised I wouldn't seek her out. 'No promises' had been our agreement.

How would she respond, though, if I showed up at the Flamingo? It could queer everything, and I had rediscovered through her a vital part of myself I had neglected for too long, since Claire's death. Was it worth risking all that just to satisfy my own curiosity?

It was all too much to deal with, heaped as it was on top of all the other cataclysms in my life. I handed it off to my Higher Power, and spent the balance of the afternoon at a meeting. I didn't speak this time. I had no idea how to express the melange of thoughts, fears, and feelings I was experiencing. Instead, I sat and listened to other members pour out their triumphs and failures, and the entire time my mind was occupied with a single notion.

It had to be blackjack.

Nineteen

I got back to Holliday's around five, with a seafood po'boy and a six-pack of Dixie, intent on throwing on a first-class buzz before I went on stage that night.

The telephone rang midway through my second bottle.

"Hey, sport," Cully said, "We got a score here."

"Talk to me."

"I tracked down each of the companies Lester Vincouer invested in after he took the cannery public. There were fourteen in all, and none of his stakes came in under a million. In ten of the companies, Lucho Braga had invested between seventy-five and a hundred large just the day before."

"Were any of these companies Fortune 500 concerns?"

"You're sharp, boy. Not a one. They were all young, struggling businesses which had already gone through their initial bump."

"I know you're not an investment counselor, Mr. Tucker," I said, "but what would happen to such a company's stock if someone were to suddenly drop in, say, a million dollars?"

"People would take notice, Pat. They would start to ask why someone would risk that much money on such an obscure issue. They'd say shit like 'What does that guy know that I don't'. Then, just to cover their asses, they would push a little into the pot themselves."

"Thereby raising the price of the stock?"

"Thereby raising the price of the stock."

"Let me guess," I ventured. "Braga got out of each company within a week after Lester got in."

"You are a suspicious and distrustful person, Gallegher. You are also correct."

"So, how much did Braga make on these adventures?"

"I haven't figured it all out, but it came to well over two million. Actually, even though Lester left his money in, he also made a pretty penny. Of course, he also risked about ten times Lucho's stake. So far, Gallegher, it looks like you're batting a thousand on your conspiracy theory. Lester and Lucho Braga were in cahoots, working to drive up the price of stocks to make Lucho a tidy fortune, all of it legal."

"Legal?"

"Well, not exactly legal, but who's gonna gripe? With Lester dead, who's going to testify against Braga? We have some tidy coincidences here, but if you prosecuted every guy who made some lucky guesses in the market, you'd have half of Wall Street in the pen at Allenwood. This is shady as hell, and it lends credence to your theory of who killed Lester, but I'd just as soon put my dick in a blender as walk into court with this sort of evidence. Mind if I ask you a question?"

"Shoot."

"What you gonna do now, Pat?"

Outside my window, I could see a couple of street musicians setting up under the ghostly blue neon outside the voodoo shop. One was emaciated, with a pitiful little goatee, and he was dressed in fatigue pants and a checkered flannel shirt left open over a Coors tee shirt. The other was a young girl, maybe nineteen, and even from twenty yards away I could read her needle tracks like an interstate road map. Her eyes were sunken and angry, and her mouth set in a determined, protective fuck-you kind of straight line. She was too young and too strung out to know she had already lost her fight with life.

"I haven't the foggiest idea," I told him. "I suppose, though, that I'm going to have to have a talk with Lucho Braga."

I found Dag D'Agostino in his office, in much the same posture as I had left him, hunched over his desk staring at bills.

"Did you knock them dead with the sermon, Dag?" I asked.

He seemed genuinely happy to see me, but terribly tired. I stopped him from standing and coming around the table, for fear that he would be overcome by the effort.

He sat back down and gestured for me to do the same.

"Well, my adventurous friend, what can I do for you?"

I winced at the undertone in his voice. It did seem that I only turned up at his church when I needed something. It was of little comfort to me that Dag was the codependent type who believed that it was his calling to forever be doing something for someone. It felt unseemly to enable his own delicate, altruistic addiction.

"I could use a favor."

"Okay," he said, hesitantly. Many of the things I do traipse clumsily around the line between good and evil, and I think he was worried about aiding and abetting some delinquency.

"Lucho Braga attends your church, doesn't he?"

"Yes," he said cautiously. "He's a regular attendee at Mass. He takes communion here."

"You don't like him, do you?" I asked, sensing his discomfiture.

"A shepherd loves all his flock, Pat. I'm not allowed to play favorites among my congregation. Mr. Braga may engage in businesses that I find personally distasteful, but that makes it even more important to serve him, to attempt to bring him to the truth. Christ didn't spend much time among the cultural elite, you know."

"Of course," I said, chagrined.

"None of which changes the fact that Mr. Braga is a slimeball. He's also a very old slimeball, which means I have very little time left to work on him. Why do you ask?"

I grinned at his shared insight. As always, Dag had managed to disarm me with little more than a verbal parlor trick.

"I need your help to set up a meeting with him," I said.

"With Lucho Braga?"

"I think he's trying to kill me."

Dag settled back in his seat. "Perhaps you had better tell me all about it."

"I'm not sure you want to know all about this one, Dag."

"We could move to the confessional, if you'd like."

I was being silly. Anything I told Dag would be held in the strictest confidence, whether in the confessional or in one of the pussy bars on Bourbon Street. It was sort of a code with him, partly an expression of his devotion to his parishioners, a way of justifying their faith and trust in him, and perhaps also similar to my own peculiar version of *bushido*. It was a matter of honor, of assuring that whatever we did, we would be able to look back on it and believe that we acted according to the strictest of principles.

Of course, our ultimate goals were more often than not at opposite ends of the moral spectrum. Perhaps it was a poor analogy.

I told him everything, this time including how I discovered Lester's body. Because of the sanctity of the confessional, I didn't need to worry that Dag might be compelled to testify against me should it come to that.

"And you want to meet with Mr. Braga?" he asked. "It would seem to me that you would be wiser to be on the first bus out of New Orleans."

"And Farley Nuckolls would be right behind with lights flashing and his siren wailing. Lucho won't dare refuse a priest's request for a meeting, and he won't dare whack me during a meeting set up by a priest. It's the only way I can guarantee my safety."

He stared at me quizzically as he ran through his own internal debate. It was a risk. He knew it. I knew it. On the one hand he didn't care to live with the guilt of setting up a meet that ended with Irish blood on the walls. On the other, there was the possibility that, by not setting up talks between Lucho and me, he might feel responsible if I wound up being splattered when it could have been avoided. Sins of commission, sins of omission—it was the eternal tightrope walk of the earnest cleric.

"I'll see what I can do," he said at last. "I don't suppose, when this is all over, you'd consider sticking to music? Is that too much to hope?"

"Dag," I told him, "When this is over, I may join a monastery."

"That will be the day. Let's settle for a little more than one Sunday a month at Mass."

I added it to the expanding list of commitments I was acquiring in the course of digging myself out of this mess.

I got back to the bar an hour before my first set. I went to my apartment and put in another call to Meg Coley. The telephone rang five times before the machine picked up. I left another message, and spent the next thirty minutes warming up on the Conn band cornet.

The telephone rang, and I grabbed at it.

"Meg?" I asked expectantly.

"No," Dag said. "Sorry, Pat. It's me. I called Mr. Braga and explained that you wanted to meet with him. I even offered to let you use my office. He said that you could see him at a restaurant at the corner of Chartres and Saint Louis, tomorrow at eight-thirty."

"I know the place. He eats breakfast there every day."

"I also asked him to keep it clean, no violence, that you wanted to straighten things out. He assured me that you wouldn't be harmed, as a favor to me."

"I appreciate it, Dag."

"Pat, be careful. I can't escape the impression that you are in way over your head here."

"I'll be very careful, Dag. It wouldn't hurt, I suppose, if you were to say a prayer for me."

"Every day, my friend. I do it every day."

I replaced the receiver and telephoned Cully Tucker. He had turned his number over to a pager service, and I punched in my number. He called back in less than five minutes. I could tell by the background noise and the poor quality that he was on the cell phone in his car.

"I meant to ask you earlier," I said.

"Yeah, Pat."

"Did you know that Meg Coley was a blackjack dealer at the Flamingo?"

There was a short pause, before he said, "Sorry, man, I had to make a right turn. No shit, really? I had no idea."

"I just figured, since you were so tight with Clancey, that she might have mentioned something."

"No, not a word. We haven't seen each other in a lot of years, though, up until the last month."

"Did you tell her I was a gambling addict?"

"Shit no, why?"

I shifted the receiver to my other hand. "Meg didn't tell me she was working there. She lied, said she was working at some bank. I thought maybe she was afraid of telling me about the casino because of my problem."

"Well, if she does know about it, it didn't come from me. What are you gonna do?"

"I don't know," I told him. "I was thinking about going over there."

"You're serious? You want to confront her right there in the casino?"

"The thought had occurred to me."

"Not wise, dude. In the first place, you got a blackjack jones. You get within fifteen feet of a five dollar table, and it's like pissing on a spark plug. In the second place, the Flamingo is not going to take kindly to some guy hassling one of their dealers. That's the kind of thing that might make them want to give you a nice long ride under the riverboat, you know what I mean?"

"I wasn't going to hassle her, just make her aware that I know where she works. If she's keeping it a secret for my sake, maybe that will take care of it."

"And what if she has some other reason? I gotta tell you, big fella, you're acting awful hinky about this twist. I mean, I've seen her and all, and she's got a lot I could go for, but the way you talk it sounds like you're carrying around a lot more than the standard six inches for her."

"Don't call her a twist, Cully. She could be special."

"She could be murder. Don't forget how she handed you over to Farley Nuckolls."

"What's your point?"

"So tell me again how many people knew you had asked her to get Clancey out of the house that night. You got such a hard-on for this girl, maybe you've lost your perspective. I am your attorney, Gallegher. Listen to what I'm telling you. If you get pinned on this thing, it's twenty minimum at Angola. Maybe they're gonna make you ride the bolt on Old Sparky. This is no time to be thinking with your dick."

I conveniently neglected telling him about my meet the next morning with Lucho Braga. I was afraid he might wrap his Seville around a light pole.

"Okay, Cully. I'm sorry to bother you. I was just wondering."

"I understand. Look, Gallegher, I've known you a lot of years. If I hear or think of something that can help you get out of this jam, I'll let you know. I don't know squat about this Coley chick, though. I do not need the kind of problems she could bring to my life. You hang in there, Pat, it's gonna be all right. Hey, I'm losing my cell here. You need anything, you page me, okay?"

I started to say goodbye, but his phone cut off, just after some annoying static. I had the feeling he was tired of listening to my nonstop existential angst anyway. I entertained a fleeting fantasy that he had installed some kind of static generator just so he could claim he was going out of cell any time he wanted to end a conversation.

Cully was right about so many things. Despite my feelings for Meg, I really needed to be spending a lot more time thinking about my own ass than hers. She was mysterious, and she hinted at a fuzzy past. She had insinuated that she could disappear at the drop of a hat, which indicated an uncertain future. All that and the image of strapping in to the hot seat at Angola did more for my ardor than a cold shower.

Still, the nagging question of why she lied to me gnawed away like heartburn. I slipped on my Saints jacket and stowed the Browning in the small of my back. Even as I stepped down the back stairs of my apartment, I told myself I was making a stupid mistake, one that I could regret for a long time.

Twenty

It was a crisp night, the kind of early autumn evening that initiated thoughts of a fireplace, a bottle of wine, and a mirthful winsome romp with some new love. Even in the intrusive lights of the Quarter, I could make out stars in the cold night sky, with my old friends the Pleiades beckoning me onward through the darkness. I crossed Decatur Street and made my way upriver toward the junction of Canal and Poydras Streets, where they kept the Flamingo.

Riverboat gambling had been legalized several years earlier, even before the parish agreed to consider allowing the big casinos in New Orleans. The riverboats had to dock somewhere, to take on provisions and a new flock of pigeons. The Flamingo sailed out of the pier attached to the Spanish Plaza, across the street from the World Trade Center at the Riverwalk.

I was in luck, I suppose. The Flamingo had just issued its last call horn when I shambled on board. Shortly, it edged away from the dock, and I was committed for the duration. I could feel the faint roar in my ears as my pulse sped up and my blood pressure kicked ahead a couple of dozen points.

There is something flashy and alluring about a gambling vessel, or any casino for that matter. The visceral response to the bright oscillating lights and the incessant ringing noise of the slots had to be reflexively conditioned in some way to our earliest memories of carnivals and arcades, and tugged at our need for unbridled salacious enjoyment. There was nothing in the pit that did not give me a thrill, from the scantily clad waitresses handing out free drinks like Halloween treats, to the steady 'Make your bets' call from the croupiers and dealers from the roulette tables to baccarat.

I passed by a baccarat table filled with eager and enthusiastic oriental gentlemen, keeping meticulous records of every card played from the multiple deck boot, each of them hoping and praying for the elusive natural nine to fall their way.

In an isolated corner of the gaming area, reserved for high rollers, a single man, unshaven and reeking of cigarette smoke, wearing a yellow sport coat over an open-collared shirt, sat at the roulette table placing bet after bet. A small, enchanted crowd had gathered around the boundary ropes circling the table, some of them murmuring softly each time the gambler laid down a thousand dollar chip on a numbered space, never bothering with playing all red or all black. To his right, a somber uniformed casino banker sat next to a telephone, watching intently as the sad-faced man placed thousands of dollars of wagers on each roll of the wheel, and the assembled spectators gasped as each time the wheel stopped the croupier racked in their average yearly salaries.

Most people, I suppose, have some sort of mental fantasy of the professional gambler as being part Rhett Butler, part James Bond, dressed immaculately with carefully trimmed and buffed nails, grinning courageously as he watches fate and lousy luck eat away at his life's blood. I have spent far more time in the pits than is either healthy or wise, and it is my fervent belief that most, if not all, professional bettors look exactly like the sallow, grim-visaged burnout at the roulette table. He had divested himself of his soul long ago, and all that was left was the money running through his nicotine-yellowed fingers like the sands of his rapidly shortening time.

Unlike the spellbound group of ghouls standing around the table, I had no stomach for the spectacle. It was all too reminiscent of my own fall from grace, the very descent that had led, indirectly, to my present desperate circumstance.

I spied her finally at a dollar twenty-one table. She was dealing to one person, a nattily dressed tourist with a fanny pack. Her fingers were nimble and quick as she flashed the cards from the boot, gliding them across the felt with the dexterity of a stage magician. The tourist watched helplessly as she busted him twice, and then he stood to search for better luck elsewhere.

She assumed the traditional position as he left, her hands clasped behind her, back erect, eyes forward. I circled from behind her to slide into the far right chair, and I dropped a twenty on the felt.

"Fives and ones," I said.

She glanced around, as if hoping for reinforcements, as she shelled out the chips and tamped the money through the deposit slot to her left. I flipped two dollar chips onto the betting circle in front of my chair.

"What in hell are you doing here?" she rasped with a phony grin as she dealt first my cards and then hers. I was showing nine, seven and deuce. She had twelve, both sixes. So far, I was ahead. She had to stand at seventeen.

"Imagine my surprise," I whispered, motioning for her to hit me. She dealt a five for me, and a seven for herself. I still only had fourteen.

"You can't stay here," she said.

I tapped my cards, and she slipped a seven on top of them.

"What do you know?" I said as she doubled my chips. I let them ride. "First hand in five years, and it's a winner. Why did you lie to me?"

"I can't talk here." She dealt out a nine and an eight for me, and a total of fifteen for herself. "I'm being watched. You're going to get me into trouble."

I motioned to be hit, and she dropped a three on my pile. I waved to stand.

"You couldn't possibly be in as much trouble as I am, dear," I told her as she dealt herself bust with an eight. "I know we said no promises, but I at least hoped you would answer my telephone calls."

A waitress appeared at my side with a tray and a Pepsodent smile.

"Drink, sir?" she asked.

"Yeah, iced tea, extra lemon." The casinos give away liquor because it loosens the inhibitions and causes gamblers to make sucker bets. They hate it when a pigeon orders soft drinks or tea.

My two dollar stake had grown to eight, and I was beginning to feel that ol' black magic creeping down my spine. I was in the zone, and if I wasn't careful I was in deep danger of falling back into my wicked, wicked ways. I let it ride, all the while promising myself I'd go to meetings every day for the next week.

"I've been very busy," she said, dealing me a thirteen, jack high. "The casino called the day after the killing. Will you please leave?" She drew eleven, three and eight.

"Not until you tell me why you lied," I said. She dropped another three on my deal, and six on hers, forcing her to stand.

"I can't explain right now," she said, dealing me four. I was up to sixteen dollars. "I get off at midnight. Can I come to see you tonight? At the bar?"

"By all means," I said, clearing my chips. I dropped two on the felt for her tip, feeling just a little dirty about it, and stashed the rest in my jacket pocket. The waitress brought my iced tea, and I toasted Meg with it silently before moving on.

On a whim, I dropped all thirty two dollars in chips on red at the roulette table nearest the exit, and won. I was up forty-four dollars over my stake.

Why did I feel so poor?

The boat docked an hour later. I had spent the rest of the trip topside, taking in the lights of the city, and gazing at the Crescent City Bridge across the river to Algiers, lit up like a Christmassy span reflected dully in the muddy waters of the river.

I was late for my shift, but I really didn't give a good goddamn. I had left the bar knowing I was making a mistake, and now I was reaping the poisoned fruit of that tainted decision. If there was any chance that I had misjudged Meg's trust in me, it had been blown the moment I sidled up to her blackjack table and made like Sam Spade putting it to Bridget O'Shaughnessy. Even if she did show up at the bar later that evening, it was certain to be a cool and anticlimactic meeting. More likely, she would dash to her apartment, grab whatever precious goods she owned, and hightail it down the I-10 to a new life somewhere west of the Rockies.

She and I were so alike, in so many different ways. Our reserves of faith in goodness and truth from our fellows had been exhausted long before we fell into each others' lives and arms. We each had a difficult time believing in ourselves, let alone anyone else. The only verity was in the moment, the fleeting pleasure of the desperate coupling, the grasping and moaning that felt like reality and tapped into our meager resources of light and joy. The emptiness we both carried in the balance of our waking lives were the price we paid for our worldliness and all-too-salient awareness of our own mortality. I could read her like the book of my own life, and I knew precisely how she felt.

I had won forty-four dollars, and was certain that I had lost the war. Not only that, I had blown my recovery, and had to start over at Step One. I had a problem with my gambling behavior, and it had once again taken control of my life.

The fog was creeping in from the river as I passed Woldenberg Park and decided to take a shortcut past the Jax Brewery. My thoughts were so concentrated on my monumentally stupid fuckup with Meg that I almost missed the baseball bat whistling through the air toward my head.

I saw the shadow of an attacker to my rear, as the bat came around, and I instinctively raised my hand to ward off the assault as I dropped to roll away. My right elbow took the glancing blow, and it numbed me all the way up to my shoulder. I raised to my knees just as the bat came around again, and fumbled with my clumsy left hand for the Browning stowed in my belt.

This time the bat missed entirely, and banged into the pavement to my right. I jumped up inside the arc of the swing, and head-butted the mugger in the solar plexus.

His wind popped out with an emphatic and satisfying '*ooph*', and I circled his chest with my arms, dragging him down to the ground. The Louisville Slugger clattered across the sidewalk.

He was a big one, almost my height, but with the telltale signs of a much more rigorous training program. I could feel his chest expand as I grasped him, and the muscles rippled frenetically as he fought for freedom.

The Browning was still in my belt, as I hadn't been able to get to it southpaw. If I let go of this gorilla, he'd coldcock me before I even got to my feet.

Suddenly, he wrapped his legs around me and twisted violently, and I lost my grip on him as he rolled away. He gained his feet almost before I could reach my knees, and his booted foot swung around in a roundhouse karate kick. I leaned back just in time to feel the breeze as it whisked by my face. He was off balance, so I jumped up and tried to get inside his defensive zone again. He rewarded me with a quick left-right combination that snapped my head back and rocked my world. My ears went deaf suddenly. It seemed as if the available oxygen was depleted to the point of starvation, and my vision started to crinkle and dim at the edges.

I took a deep gasp, tried to clear my head. He was circling to make another stab, the way a trained boxer does when he knows you're about eight seconds to midnight, and unleashed a right that I deflected with my left arm. I brought my right up to his gut, with a follow-through that would have made Jack Nicklaus proud, and it doubled the guy over at the waist.

He wasn't finished though, and when I tried to bring my elbow down on his neck, he dropped and rolled away to my left.

I had him really pissed off, and I could see in his eyes that if he had the opportunity he was going to take me off at the neck. I had been lucky up to this point. I was no match for him, so I reached back and grabbed the Browning, bringing it up in front of me in the standing shooter's posture, and flicking off the safety just as he started to lunge at me.

I don't know if I would have squeezed off a round at him then or not. It was an academic question, as at that second another figure dashed out of the fog and slapped the attacker over the head with a billy club. He crumpled into a heap at my feet, as Scat Boudreaux stood over him triumphantly.

"What took you so long?" I asked.

"You were doing all right. I just didn't want you to do something stupid with that piece."

The attacker was starting to snore a bit. Scat had hit him pretty hard. He was likely to be out for a while. I sat on the concrete, against a dumpster. My nose was bleeding, and I could feel the pulpy torn tissue in my mouth where the guy had smashed it against my front teeth. My tongue was bleeding, and I supposed I had bitten it sometime during the brief fight.

Scat was dressed in camouflage fatigues, and his face was darkened with greasepaint. I wondered where he had been all evening, and whether he had managed to get on the riverboat with me.

"Well, it looks like you earned your money." I told him. "You'd better take off. The cops are sure to be here any minute."

"Sure, sure. Gimme the piece, first. I'll leave it at your bar. The cops find it on you, there's gonna be hell to pay. Hey, you know this guy?"

I handed him the Browning and looked down at the prostrate figure sprawled on the pavement. He was lying face up and the glare of the mercury vapor light from the overhead street lamps played across the lines and shadows of his face, dancing off the high cheekbones and losing itself in the full beard.

"Never met him," I said, "but I know who he is. You just brained Sammy Cain."

The police did come, just as I said they would. Some tourist heard the commotion while Sammy was kicking my fat ass, and called 911 from a pay phone outside the Jax Brewery complex. The motorcycle cops arrived only seconds after Scat faded back into the night to resume his protective surveillance.

Sammy Cain was still out cold when the officers arrived, so naturally I was the bad guy, even if I did have about a quart of blood all over my shirt from my nose and split lip. Cain started to stir while I was being cuffed, and as soon as they were confident that he wasn't going to die the cops piled us both into a squad car for the ride over to the Rampart Street Station.

It took Cain several seconds to get his bearings, and when he did he had this surprised, curious expression on his face.

"What the fuck you hit me with?" he asked sluggishly.

"Never screw around with the forces of goodness," I said.

"Shut up back there," one of the cops said. "This is a short ride."

I was in no mood to cross him. It took about ten minutes to get to the station the long way, and once there Cain and I were booked and given our phone calls. Interestingly, Cain had nobody to call. I called Cully, who was at home for a change, and he showed up about a half hour later to go my bail for public affray. I dearly wanted a few minutes with Cain, but he didn't seem likely to go anywhere, and I had work to do.

"What the hell happened?" Cully asked as he drove me around the city side of the Quarter. After dark you can't drive on the inner streets, Bourbon specifically, and all the cross streets were blocked.

"Damned if I know. I was just walking back from the Flamingo, and he came out of the shadows with a baseball bat."

"The Flamingo, huh? I shoulda known you couldn't stay away from that dump. I suppose you played some twenty-one, too."

"Won forty-four dollars."

"Ah, the heady aroma of victory. Did you find your girl there?"

"Yes I did."

"How about that? You found two people in one night."

"Doesn't count. Cain found me."

"I don't suppose you find anything suspicious about that."

"You mean I find Meg Coley, who's been avoiding me for almost a week, and less than an hour later Cain takes a swing at me? Yeah, I find that very suspicious, Cully. It was eating at me all the time I was in the lockup. What do I owe you for the bail?"

"I'll add it to your bill. Do me a favor, okay? Take my advice for once in your life. If I tell you to sit tight, and don't do anything, sit tight and don't do anything. Don't think for a second that Nuckolls isn't going to hear about this fight of yours tonight."

"Nuckolls," I said, thinking about the detective for the first time. "Listen, Cully, I need you to get in touch with him and let him know that Cain's in the lockup. Farley might want to talk over the Vincouer killing with him."

Cully let me out at Holliday's, and I went in to talk with Shorty. He noted my split, swelling lip almost immediately.

"I suppose you'd like the night off," he said.

"I can't play with this lip," I told him. "If you'd like I can find someone to take my place."

"Don't bother. I'll just let Sockeye go on solo. You look like shit, man. Why don't you just go to bed?"

I considered it good advice, but I was still expecting a visitor. I went upstairs and showered, after tossing my shirt into the sink with some bleach to take out the blood stains. After dressing in a Tulane University sweatsuit, I opened a Dixie and settled into my recliner with the new Umberto Eco novel. It was already midnight. I figured it would take Meg an hour to get to Holliday's after getting off at the Flamingo.

One o'clock came and went, and my eyes started to feel gritty from the reading. I tried to get out of the recliner to get another beer, and felt the all-too-familiar stiffness that comes from having the crap kicked out of you. All of the major joints felt just slightly out of alignment, grinding against each other in a painfully disagreeable manner. It reminded me just how far past forty I was. I limped across the living room to the refrigerator for the Dixie, and used the beer to wash down three ibuprofen. I know, I know, you're not supposed to take them with alcohol, but if I didn't do something I was going to feel a hundred years old in the morning.

Eco was taking more effort to slog through than I was willing to muster, so I flipped on the television to catch a baseball game between the Braves and the Giants, which took far less concentration to follow.

Chipper had just knocked one damned near into the San Francisco Bay when I heard the knock at my door. I struggled out of my recliner and keyed the alarm code into the keypad next to the door, after hitting the one in the kitchen. It was a major hassle, but I figured Scat's advice about redundant systems might save my life.

Meg had gone home to change clothes, and stood in the doorway in a tight pair of designer jeans and another in her alluring series of sheer silk blouses, through which I could see the outline of her bra, which itself defined her ample cleavage. It was an outfit clearly chosen to distract, which only heightened my suspicion. Of course, I reasoned, it could also have been a blatant attempt at reconciliation.

"What happened to you?" she asked, touching my swollen face with cool, slim fingers.

"I was attacked on the way home tonight, by Sammy Cain."

She seemed genuinely shocked. "Sammy! He showed up?"

"With a baseball bat. He's in the tank over in the Rampart Station. Cully bailed me out." I sat on the sofa, and she plopped down beside me.

"Did you call Clancey to tell her?"

And, of course, I hadn't. Clancey Vincouer had not fired me yet, and I supposed I should have contacted her once I had Cain tackled. The fact was, I had completely forgotten.

"No, I'll call her tomorrow. Do you want anything?" I gestured toward my beer.

"Don't get back up. I'll get it." She walked into the kitchen and returned with a bottle of beer.

"I suppose I owe you an explanation," she said.

"If you want. I don't have any hold on you."

"You could have gotten me into a lot of trouble at the casino tonight. Each of the tables is watched by a security camera. When you sat down, I nearly lost it. They look for that sort of thing."

"Good thing they don't use microphones."

"Yes. I'm sorry I lied to you."

"Okay."

"I didn't mean it maliciously. We... we had a nice thing going, and I didn't want to scare you away."

"I'm a trumpet player in a bar, Meg. What would I find frightening about a blackjack dealer? A prostitute or contract killer, maybe..."

"It wasn't that. I didn't want you to be uncomfortable, to feel—I don't know—like there was a part of my life you couldn't share."

"You're referring to my addiction." I ventured.

"Yes, that's it."

I nodded and took a long sip of the beer. "That was considerate of you, but totally unnecessary. As you saw tonight, I can play a few hands and walk away. It's not the kind of thing I'd want to do every day, but I can handle it in very small doses, especially if I'm winning. The recovery process isn't written in stone. People backslide all the time.

Failure is expected. It just means you have to start all over again. How did you know about my problem?"

She placed the beer down on the coffee table and slid her hand along my knee. "Oh, come on, Pat. Do you think I would go to bed with someone I hadn't checked out first? After you left Clancey's house the day we met, she and I had a long talk about you."

"She told you I had a gambling addiction?"

"Not in so many words, I suppose. She said that Cully Tucker had told her about you doing favors for people, and how you sometimes collected debts for some loan shark in town, because you owed him a lot of money. That's why she asked you to help her, darling."

"Strange how Cully doesn't recall that conversation. I spoke with him earlier this evening. He claims he didn't know you were working in a casino, and that he said he never told Clancey about my addiction. You see, I had already considered that you might be embarrassed because of that. I wanted to put your mind at ease."

She blushed slightly, but maintained her composure. I had to hand it to her. She was a cool one.

"Oh, he probably forgot, dear. It's a small matter. Everybody's hooked on something. You can't swing a dead cat anymore without hitting one kind of recovery program or another. I was in one myself."

It was an interesting diversion, but I decided to follow it out.

"You?"

"Oh, yes. I already told you I was married young. It was a disaster. My husband was a drug addict, cocaine. He went through tons of money, just plugging it up his nose. I threatened to leave him, and he went into a treatment program. I had to go, too."

"He didn't stop, though?"

"He stopped, finally. Of course, I'd left by then. I hear he's remarried, living in Texas, working in the family business. It's all terribly boring, not at all the life I saw for myself. In a way, he did me a favor. What is it, darling? Are you suspicious of me?"

I drained the beer, and set the bottle down.

"Yes, as a matter of fact, I am. You were the only person who knew that Clancey would be out of the house the night Lester was killed. You turned me over all too quickly, and then I found out you had lied to me about your occupation. You've been avoiding me ever since the killing. Tonight, I was attacked soon after I found you at the Flamingo. Why wouldn't I be suspicious?"

She had been looking directly into my eyes as I voiced my concerns, and tears had formed in hers. One escaped furtively, and coursed down her cheek.

"I can't believe you'd say that," she protested, "after what we've shared. Have you stopped to consider that Cully might be lying, or simply forgot telling Clancey about your gambling addiction? I already told you why I haven't called—I've been working night and day. I can't explain why Cain attacked you tonight. Maybe he's been aware of you watching for him all along, and simply wanted to get you out of the way. I told the police the truth because I ..."

She stopped, the tears flowing freely now. If she was faking it, she was good. She dabbed at the cascade with her fingers, and then fell across my chest, sobbing uncontrollably, wetting the front of my sweatsuit. I reflexively pulled her to me, feeling the warmth emanate off her body.

"I'm so sorry, darling." she choked between racking sobs. "I'm ashamed to admit this. You asked me to take Clancey out, and while we were gone Lester was murdered. I told that detective about it because, at that moment, I was afraid that you had killed Lester. I was hurt. I thought you had used me to get to Lester, to murder him. Please forgive me, Pat. I wasn't thinking. I panicked."

And the torrent started again.

I held her for several more seconds, as much for myself as to comfort her, and then pushed her away.

"Cut it out," I commanded. She stared at me, her face registering something like shock.

"Don't look at me that way," I said, "I was a psychologist for years. I developed an immunity to women's tears in the Nixon administration. This isn't you, Meg. I know enough about you to know you wouldn't crack at the drop of a hat this way. This is a manipulative bullshit performance, and a bravura one at that. You are a hard, cold woman who uses other people to get what she wants. This is just part of the act, and a damn well-practiced one, but what are you in danger of losing here? If you really cared, you'd have returned my calls. Everyone I've talked to over the last several days has referred to you as my punch, my twist, and I took up for you. I was blinded by pussy, pure and simple, and I thought it meant something..."

"It did mean something..." she started.

"Get real. I meant about as much to you as Clancey did to Sammy Cain. You said it, baby, you're two of a kind, feeding off the weaknesses and affections of others to achieve your own desires without having to put in the sweat or the hours."

She dropped the supplicative stance and went ballistic.

"What do you know about it?" she shouted. "No sweat? No hours? It isn't work to put up with the bullshit cares and worries of these pampered assholes? They don't know what stress is, they wouldn't recognize genuine hunger if it bit them on the ass. Yes, I admit it. I use Clancey Vincouer. She's grateful for it. I'm her friend, her companion. I go shopping with her, have dinner with her, spend time at her home even when she isn't in the mood to be with me, just in case she has an urge to talk. I'm her human version of a lapdog. I am her sole connection to what's real and human and tactile, and I think she should reward me generously for that. What do you know of that? What gives you the right to criticize me?"

"I don't know anything about it," I told her. "But you tried to manipulate me the way you do Clancey, and I resented that. I'm not her. I'm not that gullible. Don't try to lull me with crocodile tears."

She slugged down the rest of the beer and stared at me the way a rat would when cornered by the exterminator, with a mixture of fear and contempt. It was a sad look I had seen in adolescents who thought I was trying to talk them out of a delinquency they not only enjoyed but had incorporated into their personality. Meg was certain that she had stumbled onto the perfect scam, and resented not only my discovery of it, but the fact that I did not approve. She was proud of her wheedling into the upper crust, and wanted sanction from me, which would not be forthcoming.

"I have to go," she said, standing and turning to the door.

It wasn't enough for her to just leave, though. That didn't give her enough of an advantage in the situation. She stopped at the door and looked back at me, the resentment and scorn clearly etched on her face.

"And to think I was planning to sleep with you tonight."

"Wait a minute," I said.

She stopped, halfway out the door. As soon as I tried to stop her, her face changed from disdain to expectation. The promise of her charms, she thought, had once again turned the battle to her control. She was pathetically wrong.

"What made you decide I didn't kill Vincouer?" I asked. "We haven't passed five words since the day he was killed, and yet you've suddenly decided I didn't do it. You thought I had set you up, and now you don't. Why did you change your mind?"

The disappointment radiated from her eyes, which shot their arrows into my chest. She was a woman who hated to fail, and despised losing. I had just sacked her for a mighty loss.

She didn't answer me. She simply stepped into the stairway and closed the door. I listened to her footsteps as she headed downstairs, counting my regrets with each one. Then I opened a new bottle of Dixie and sat in my window, watching the late-nighters stroll along Toulouse, so unaware of my despair.

Twenty-one

Eight-thirty in the morning was a lousy time to meet the Reaper, so I approached the tiny restaurant at the corner of St. Louis with some degree of trepidation. I didn't dare stow the Browning in my belt going to meet Lucho Braga. It might be taken as a sign of antisocial tendencies, and could result in my summary ventilation. I did call Scat Boudreaux, but he wasn't going to be a hell of a lot of good for me if he wasn't actually in the joint.

I stepped in off the street, which seemed strangely unoccupied this early in the morning. I wasn't usually awake at this hour, and it was like looking at your room in a mirror, everything there, but weirdly juxtaposed.

Braga was there, at a table in the back. He was six days older than baseball, with a wiry thatch of shock-white hair and a sharp aquiline nose. His lips were puckered by the multitude of lines around them. He was dressed casually, in a red leather Saints jacket that cost at least a couple hundred more than my nylon version. His pants were khakis, the really good kind with great pleats. Under the jacket he wore a pima cotton print shirt, and a tie with lots of crawfish and Tabasco bottles on it. He was eating breakfast, as I had suspected he might, the table full of small dishes filled with bacon, sausage, eggs, home fries, and french toast, Braga's own little all-you-can-eat breakfast bar.

I wasn't certain how to proceed. There were, maybe, fifteen other people in the restaurant, a respectable number given the size of the place. I could count without effort at least six shoulder holsters. Braga was surrounded by soldiers, any one of which would have been delighted to paint the ceiling with me.

One of the troops noted me standing in the doorway, and sidled over from the bar, where he had been enjoying his morning OJ.

"Can I help you?" he asked. "You look like a man could use some help."

I didn't doubt it.

"I'm Gallegher," I told him. "I was supposed to meet with Mr. Braga this morning."

The fellow seemed dubious, but nodded and walked over to Braga's table and leaned over solicitously to announce my arrival. Braga glanced over in my direction without breaking stride in his eating, and said something I couldn't hear, then turned his attention back to his eggs. The man from the bar walked back to me.

"Mr. Braga invites you to have a seat over here…" he gestured toward a table against the wall near the door, "…and have some breakfast. Mr. Braga says it's on him."

I sat at the table, wondering whether the condemned man was to enjoy a hearty meal. The waiter was at my side almost instantaneously, and I ordered the Hungry Man's Special from the menu, a bounty by any standard, but nothing compared to Braga's spread.

The food arrived presently, three eggs over easy with country ham, grits, and home fries with a small basket of biscuits on the side. I ate quickly, never taking my eyes off the old man in the back of the room. Braga was a messy eater, who often forgot to close his mouth when he chewed. I chalked it up to his age, without trying to discount the fact that he was essentially a cheap thug who had managed to hit it big two thousand miles from Chicago, and had probably never really acquired the basic social graces. He glanced over in my direction once, and I forced a smile and a nod of acknowledgment at his largesse in providing what might be my last meal.

Two men appeared in the doorway, dressed in business suits worn just a bit threadbare at the joints, with soft-soled black leather shoes. The one on the right was about forty pounds overweight. His vanity led him to try to squeeze into a suit which no longer favored him, and which clearly betrayed the shoulder holster he was wearing. That made seven guns I had found. I wasn't encouraged by the way this hidden objects puzzle was going.

The two men were greeted by the same fellow from the bar that had met me, only this time he allowed them access to the Great Man. As the man with the shoulder holster stood watch, the other one pulled an envelope from his jacket pocket and laid it on Braga's table. Braga picked it up and slid it into the inner pocket of his leather Saints jacket. The two men turned and left without a word, and I sipped my coffee wondering what kind of payoff I had just witnessed.

The orange juice guy walked over to my table.

"Mr. Braga will see you now," he said. "I would appreciate it, Mr. Gallegher, if you would stand and assume the position."

I'd done this one before. I took to my feet, and turned to face the wall, which was made of brick, molded and fired long before my grandfather was born. I placed my hands against the cool, rough bricks while I was frisked. Finally satisfied, he told me to turn around.

"Sorry about that. Can't be too careful."

I crossed the dining room to Lucho Braga's table, and he motioned toward the chair across from him, telling me to sit down.

"So, Mr... um, Gallegher?" he said. His voice was creaky and breathy, and his eyes had taken on the near-translucent cast of extreme seniority. "Father Alphonse tells me you would like to talk."

"Thank you for seeing me," I said. "I'm not sure why I'm here. I worked for Justin Leduc until a few days ago, as a collector."

He nodded sagely.

"He sent me to collect some money from a man with whom I believe you have had some business dealings, as you have with Mr. Leduc."

Braga's rheumy eyes narrowed perceptibly.

"You should be careful," he said. "It's a nasty business you're involved in."

"I'm not sure I'm doing this very well," I said. "I'd thank you to jump in and correct me when I go over the line. The man Leduc sent me to collect from was Lester Vincouer. He was murdered before I could collect, and now the police are trying to make me for it."

"That's a shame," the old man said.

"You should see it from my end. Mr. Braga, I had been hired by Ms. Vincouer to find a man with whom she had been having an affair, so I was around a lot. You and Mr. Leduc have been associates before. Mr. Leduc sent me on this collection. You and Mr. Vincouer have been associates, he's invested a lot of money in companies that you had also invested in, but I also believe he has a considerable amount of your money stashed away in a foreign bank account…"

He held up his hand.

"Mr. Gallegher, you are about to cross the line. You got some fuckin' nerve coming into my place, when I'm eating my breakfast, the most important meal of my day, and telling me about my business with a dead guy. But I can see that you are in a jam, and I've been in a few of those in my life. So let me set the record straight. Your questions are obvious, and I will settle this thing right now. I did not kill Lester Vincouer. I did not have him killed. I am not trying to set you up to take the fall for him being killed."

"I'm trying to find some answers," I told him.

"You won't find them here," he said. "I don't know you, Mr. Gallegher."

"What is that?" I challenged. "Some kind of mob talk? I don't know you, like 'you never existed, you're nothing'?"

"Like in, *I don't know you*," he repeated. "Until Father Alphonse called me last night, I had never heard your name. I didn't know that you worked for that asshole Leduc. I didn't know you were working for Lester Vincouer's wife. There are some seventy trillion people in this world that I never heard of, don't even know they exist, and until exactly five minutes ago you were one of them. Can I make it any plainer than that?"

I settled back in my seat, more puzzled than ever.

"I'm sorry, Mr. Braga. I meant no offense. I'm in a great deal of trouble, and I had hoped... well, I don't know what I hoped. Maybe that you and I could come to an arrangement."

"There is nothing to arrange," he said, after taking a sip of his coffee. "You are a young man in a lot of trouble, and you are scared, so I will forgive your angry words. Please understand, though, that what you are dealing with has nothing to do with me. Since you know so much about my affairs, let me tell you that my business with Mr. Vincouer was over several years ago. It's over, Mr. Gallegher. Done. I don't give a rat's ass about the money in Vincouer's foreign accounts. I made much more off him, and then we ended our business together. That's it. There is a deal I will make with you, though."

I swallowed hard, with an uneasy feeling about what was coming.

"What's that?"

"You are going to forget everything you have told me today. You will not tell anyone about the foreign accounts, the investments, any of it. This is a simple thing to do. You just forget you ever knew about any of it. In return, I will forget that you were rude to me at my breakfast. It will be as if this conversation never happened, okay?"

"I understand," I said.

"And if you can't keep this deal," he said, without changing expression, "then my friend at the bar is going to find you, and he's going to shoot you a lot, and then he's gonna bury you out in the bayou somewhere, and then maybe he's gonna dig you up and shoot you again. I saw you today as a favor to Father Alphonse, and as a favor to him I promised that you would not be harmed. I will keep that promise. On the other hand, I cannot be held responsible for what might happen should we need to meet again. Do we have an understanding?"

I nodded, vaguely aware of the sticky wetness that made my shirt cling to my back.

"Thank you for your time, Mr. Braga."

"Think nothing of it, Mr. Gallegher. Now, if you don't mind, I would like to finish my breakfast."

There was nothing for it. I had tried and come up empty with Braga, my grand conspiracy theory shot down in a brilliant Technicolor blaze, like one of those fireballs that occasionally streak across the sky on a spine-tingling clear night.

Braga could have been jerking me off, of course. He could have been playing me the way a cat does with a captive rat, sure of the kill but savoring the torturous buildup. I didn't think that was the case, though. Even as I had sat at his table, I noted the feeling that I was in the wrong place, asking the wrong questions of the wrong person. It was that left-over sensitivity to the feelings and intuitions of others, held out from my days as a therapist, the empathy that told me instinctively that I was headed up a blind alley. Braga had tried not to show it, but he was almost as wary of me as I had been of him. A priest called him in the middle of the night asking for a meeting with holy sanction. I had, inadvertently, rattled his cage.

He had, of course, heard about Lester Vincouer's death. He had, almost as assuredly, absolutely no awareness of my existence. I just dropped out of the blue and disturbed his digestion with my pleas for clemency.

I was lucky he hadn't had me shot on the spot.

It occurred to me as I traversed Jackson Square, and absently watched a juggler plying his trade among a gaggle of tourists, that I was looking for answers that were much too large for the problem. I was violating Occam's Razor, looking for the elegant and complex when the parsimonious would have sufficed.

The juggler was tossing knives in the air now, rapt and intent on the whirling blades even as he carried on his patter, committed so dearly to memory that he could replay it without thinking.

"This is my job, ladies and gentlemen," he called out over the *whish* of the blades cutting the humid air, *"Please do not hesitate to pay me the full value of the entertainment I have provided for you today. Remember, the sweat is real..."*

Damned right it was. This case was making me sweat more than any I'd taken over the last five years, more than any in my fifteen year history as a therapist. The sweat was, indeed, real. It was time to take the heat off me and direct it toward someone else.

I knew what I was going to do long before I reached the Rampart Street Police Station, which served the French Quarter. It was in a tidy stucco building surrounded by a knee-high stone wall and a wrought-iron fence. Inside, sleeping off the effects of Scat Boudreaux's billy, was Sammy Cain.

I met with the watch officer. He told me Cain's fine had been set at a hundred dollars. I dropped it on the counter, signed the papers waiving the hearing on public affray, and then left the building while they went to rouse him.

I watched from across the street as he sauntered out of the Station and hung a sharp left toward Bourbon Street. He seemed to know where he was going. I crossed Rampart and shadowed him from one street over, trying to match his pace.

I lost him at Bourbon, as I expected. He hadn't turned right there, or I would have seen him walking toward me, so I made a left and dashed one street down, and started looking into the various shops, strip joints, and bars on the west side of the street.

I caught up with Cain in a squalid tavern called Octi's. He was sitting at the bar, holding his head delicately between his hands as he worked to focus on his reflection in the mirror. I saw the bartender place a schooner of beer in front of him, and I wandered into the bar and sat to his left, between him and the door.

He didn't notice me at first, as he concentrated on self-medicating his aching head with the brewski. The bartender approached me and asked what I wanted. I wanted a beer, badly. I ordered a Coke.

When he heard my voice, Cain turned to me, made a grimacing face, and then turned away again. I was relieved. I had thought he might faint dead away. I have that effect on people.

"What the fuck you doing here?" he asked, after taking a swig of the beer.

"You don't sound very appreciative. Maybe you like stewing in the lockup?"

"That was you bailed me out?"

"Who did you think did it?"

He shook his head, with a wan grin on his face.

"Damned if I knew. You think I don't have friends?"

"I haven't run into any so far. You're a hard fellow to find."

He gulped at the schooner, which I noted pessimistically was already half empty, and said, "Maybe you don't look hard enough."

He pulled a small cigar from his jacket pocket and, after tearing off the wrapper, lighted it. He tossed the multicolored matches on the bar top, and took a long leisurely draw on the stogie.

"You could be right. Of course, just because I couldn't find you, in the corporeal sense, doesn't mean I didn't find out all about you. Mind answering a few questions?"

He didn't say anything, so I launched in anyway.

"Who cleaned out your apartment?"

"I did. It was time to move on."

"So soon? You hadn't made the big score yet."

He turned to face me, and I thought he blew smoke my way on purpose. He was lucky I didn't take it personally.

"What big score?"

"The one on Clancey Vincouer. See, that's one of the inconsistencies I've noted over the last week. All of the other women you fleeced were spinsters or widows, and the occasional divorcee. Clancey was married. What were you planning to do, blackmail her?"

He turned back to his beer. "Maybe. It would have been a good idea, at that. Fact is, Gallegher, I was just sucking off some of the fumes from her money. A present here, a present there. She tell you about the Rolex?"

"No."

"She gave me a Rolex Oyster, one of the nice gold alloy ones. About twelve carat. I sold it for over a thousand, all legit. Sucking off the fumes, Gallegher. Maybe I never planned to hit her big, go after an expensive score. Maybe I never planned it that far ahead."

"And maybe you killed Lester so you could have a clear playing field."

"Go fuck yourself," he said, reaching for his beer glass.

"So why'd you jump me last night? Was I getting that close?"

"You were a bother. I saw you watching my place day and night. I don't need that shit, man. I decided to cosh you, put you off your feet for a few days while I decided what to do. You got lucky. What in hell did you hit me with, anyway? I never saw it coming."

"I am good and true and fighting for the forces of purity," I told him. "You never had a chance."

"Bullshit."

"You could be right. So, what do you plan to do now, what with Lester dead? Thinking about moving in on the widow? Maybe suck off a few more fumes?"

"Get real," he said. "You say you know all about me. You probably already told Clancey all about it. I couldn't get close now."

"Don't sell yourself short, my man," I said, and pounded down several ounces of Coke, savoring the sudden burning, tingling sensation. "Did you know that Clancey still asked me about finding you the day you cleaned your place out?"

He twisted in his seat, but kept his eyes on my reflection in the mirror. "No shit?"

"You are some ladykiller," I said. "So, what should I tell Clancey?"

"What do you mean?"

"She hired me to find you, Cain. So here you are. I've done my job. I can't drag you back to her kicking and screaming. She's going to want to know something. Should she expect to hear from you?"

He finished off the schooner and waved at the bartender for another.

"I don't think so," he said at last. "It's tempting, but she wouldn't ever really trust me. It would be nice to latch onto all that stuff, but it would be like living in jail all the time, someone watching and waiting for you to make a move."

"Could be a regular mink-lined mousetrap," I offered.

"Damn right. So tell her it's over. Tell her I've left town. Tell her anything you want."

I drained the Coke, and set the glass down on the bar.

"You are a cowardly dickhead," I said.

He flared suddenly.

"What the fuck?"

"You heard me. You don't even have the balls to face Clancey and tell her you're leaving. She's not one of your usual twists, Cain. You haven't shaken all that much out of her. There's no reason to cut and run in the night the way you usually do. All she wants is to know that you're safe, and you can't even muster enough backbone to set her mind at ease. This could be the sweetest score of your life, trading some freedom of movement for all the bennies, the house, the pool, a piece of Lester's companies. Fact is, when I think of it, you stood to gain the most from Lester's death."

"You better watch your ass, Gallegher," he said lowly. "Maybe next time you won't see me coming."

"Let me tell you something," I said, pulling my face closer to his. "I didn't bash your head last night. I have a guy out there, a fellow who was a sniper in Viet Nam. This guy can shoot the nuts off a hamster from a block away, and he's covering my six all the time. He turned out your lights because I was a half-second away from blowing you away. You attack me again, and he has carte blanche to shag your sorry ass clear into the ozone. One minute you're standing there, and the next there will just be this oozy pink fog where you used to be. Understand?"

He glared at me, but didn't say a word.

"Let me clarify. Stay away from me. Stay away from Clancey Vincouer. If you did kill Lester, and you're trying to set me up for it, you better hope I don't find out about it. Do not screw around with me. Are we clear?"

I didn't wait for a response. I dropped a dollar and a half on the bar, for the Coke, turned, and walked out into the sunlight of Bourbon Street. I had scored a small moral victory, but still hadn't the slightest idea who killed Lester Vincouer, or how to convince Farley Nuckolls that it wasn't me.

Twenty-two

There was a mint set of Beiderbecke 78's in my apartment that said I was obligated to pay Clancey Vincouer a visit, and I couldn't think of a single decent reason to put it off. I walked around the block from Holliday's to the rental garage where I kept my Pinto, in back of Irene's restaurant. It was a clear, clean autumn day, with a rare lack of humidity for the Quarter. The sky was dotted with wispy, high clouds, and there was the hint of impending winter in the air. I cranked down the windows and enjoyed the steady blast of crisp dry air as I cruised up the I-10 toward Lake Terrace. My nose crinkled and the aridity made my sinuses ache exquisitely. It was my time of year, the fall. It was a time, when I was a student, and later a professor, that always heralded a new love affair, the shedding of past failure, a renewal of effort. It was hayrides and dorm parties and frat keggers. Later in my life it meant faculty dinners and football tailgate soirees, and the occasional devoted coed siren with a cute little erotic crush, but never, never one of my actual students. God, I love the fall of the year, even in this semitropical locale where the trees seem to lose their verdance but never their leaves and where a flaming red maple is about as common as beri-beri. It was a hell of a time to be worried about riding the bolt at Angola for a killing I didn't commit.

Every homeowner in the parish seemed to have installed in-ground sprinklers that year, and as I walked up the flat stone path to Clancey Vincouer's ten acre front porch I savored the cool mist vaporized by the streams of water soaking the lawn.

I had expected her to be in widow's weeds, but when she opened the door Clancey was dressed in a paisley pool cover, her arms and legs unclothed, and she was barefooted. She didn't say a word, but her flashing eyes regarded me with all the suspicion afforded a cat by any self-respecting mouse. I scared her, I suppose. She waited for me to reveal why I was there. Maybe she thought I had come to finish the job.

"I found Cain," I told her.

Her expression changed instantly to one of deference.

"Do come in, Mr. Gallegher."

I followed her through the door, past the entry to the study where I had found Lester with his throat slit less than a week earlier, toward the sunroom at the back of the house, next to the pool. She didn't offer me anything to drink this time. In fact, I got the distinct impression that she wanted to be rid of me as quickly as possible.

"I'm sorry about your husband, Ms. Vincouer," I offered. "I never met him, but it was tragic. Please accept my condolences over your loss."

"Thank you. It's been very difficult. As you know, Lester and I weren't very close over the last several years. In a way, it's a lot like losing a roommate more than a husband. Still, I deeply loved him, once."

She gestured toward the sofa, and I sat, and glanced briefly out toward the pool. Meg Coley was there, lying on a chaise near the diving board, naked as a jaybird, on an oversized beach towel. She hadn't been lying about that, after all. Her skin glistened with tropical tanning oil and a fine sheen of perspiration. She didn't look in my direction, despite my telepathic urgings that she do so. I felt a primal longing for her rangy, slender form.

Clancey noted my gaze, and cleared her throat.

"I considered telling her you were here, so she might cover up. But I figured, you've already seen all there is to see, and she's not the type to hide. What happened to your face?"

I turned my attention to her. She was sitting in a wicker and flowered print lounge chair across from the sofa, with her feet on a matching ottoman, crossed at the ankles. Even in the transition from bright light to the dim interior, I could make out the start of fine spidery veins at her knees and thighs, the ornamenture of maturity that led right up to where I would have expected her to be wearing a swimsuit bottom. When she sat, her coverup rode up her thighs, and from my vantage, even with an instant's glimpse, I could tell that under the sheath she was as naked as Meg. While my arousal on viewing Meg was based on my shared intimacy with her, I found the barely hidden charms on Clancey Vincouer a more forbidding, covert provocation. It was the difference between living in a nudist enclave, and peeking into the girls' shower at the gym. The one was natural, the other damned near illicit.

"Cain tried to flatten my head with a baseball bat last night. I didn't want to let him. We fought about it. He lost."

"I have a hard time imagining Sammy losing a fight with you," she said.

"I cheated. He and I were taken to the Rampart Street Police Station, and Cully Tucker bailed me out. I went back this morning and paid Cain's fine. We had a long talk in a bar on Bourbon Street."

She pulled herself forward on the arms of the lounge, and the bottom of her coverup bunched open. I worked hard to ignore the view. Real hard.

Not hard enough.

"What did he say?"

"He's leaving. He doesn't want to see you again. He's afraid that now you know what a sleazebag he is, you'd never trust him. He likes the idea of getting to all your money and your stuff, but he doesn't want to live under the constant suspicion and scrutiny. And there's something else."

"What is it?"

"He didn't say it in so many words, but I got the impression he thinks it's too easy. I heard a report on the radio the other day about hunting clubs in the Northwest, where wild game animals are kept in pens, and you can drive through with your gun, and when you see something you'd like to shoot you just stop the car and blow it away. There's nothing sporting about it, but it's easy, and it beats hell out of tramping through some rainy cold forest for a day and a half. I think that's the way Cain sees living with you, or even marrying you. He would get all the goodies, but without the stalk. He likes the stalking part."

"Yes," she said, absently.

"I'm sorry," I said. "I know this isn't what you wanted to hear. But I did find him, like I said I would."

"Yes," she said, slipping on her sunglasses. I couldn't tell if she was bothered by the glare from the pool, or if she was trying to hide the luster of tears in her eyes. "You did promise that. What will you do now? To Sammy?"

"Probably nothing, unless he gets frisky again. If that happens, he's going to die very quickly. I've hired someone to protect me. He doesn't mind dropping the hammer on people."

"This protector sounds like a bad man."

"In many ways he's extremely honorable. He just has a different way of resolving problems. You... you know I'm a suspect in Mr. Vincouer's killing."

"Yes."

"I didn't kill him, Ms. Vincouer. The police will figure that out sooner or later. In the meantime, I'm working on it myself. May I ask you several questions?"

She stared straight ahead, but I couldn't see through her sunglasses where her eyes were tracking. They could have been on me, or Meg, or an ax murderer poised behind me ready to strike. It was eerie, in a way, so I just focused on my own reflection in her lenses, to maintain something resembling eye contact.

"I suppose."

"Did you know your husband was laundering money for a man named Lucho Braga?"

"No, but it doesn't surprise me."

"Did you know he owed over two hundred thousand to a man named Justin Leduc?"

"No. That wouldn't surprise me either."

"Did you know that he has an offshore bank account, and that it might have several million dollars in it?"

"Yes. He called it his 'retirement fund'."

"Did you know it was dirty money?"

"It wouldn't surprise me."

"You don't seem to surprise easily."

"When it comes… came to Lester, no. He liked risk and danger, Mr. Gallegher. He would lie awake at night and hatch schemes and wake me up and tell me about them. He was obsessed with planning the perfect crime, not that I ever thought he would be capable of going through with it. The offshore account doesn't matter anymore."

"Why's that?"

"I can't access it. Lester never gave me the account code."

"Surely he left it somewhere. In a letter, in your safe deposit box, with his attorney…"

"Nowhere, I'm afraid. He kept it in his head, as far as I can tell. Somewhere in the Caribbean is a numbered bank account with a king's ransom, and nobody will ever claim it. It's a romantic notion, don't you think?"

"You're being very cavalier about it," I said.

"Mr. Gallegher, when I sell off all of Lester's holdings, I'm going to be an extremely rich woman. Lester's attorney tells me it should bring in over a hundred million, on top of what I already have. I couldn't spend that much in two lifetimes, let alone what I have left in this one. I can afford to be cavalier about a million or two moldering away in a bank somewhere."

"Who do you think killed your husband, Ms. Vincouer?"

She turned her head away, toward the pool, and emitted a nearly silent sigh. Outside, Meg stretched and rolled over to her stomach, so she wouldn't burn. Far down the hall I could hear the insistent ticking of the grandfather clock, and the quiet whoosh of the air conditioning ducts.

"Honestly, Mr. Gallegher, I haven't any idea. You say he was involved with gangsters. Maybe they killed him. I don't know. I wonder if I ever will."

I had nothing left to ask. Braga's denial had left me a long way down a dead end alley, and before I could start on a new trail, I was going to have to retrace my steps.

"If I learn anything, I'll be certain to let you know," I said.

I stood to leave, and she also rose to let me out. She thanked me for my concern, but I heard nothing in her voice that indicated any significant regard for my efforts or my welfare.

"If there's anything else I can do," I offered, as she stood at the door, "please don't hesitate to call me."

"I don't think that will be necessary," she said, coolly. "I believe our business is concluded. Thank you for finding Sammy. I'm glad he's alive."

And she closed the door. I was dismissed, apparently, fired for the second time in the last several days. I stepped down to the flagstone walk and started down the driveway to where I had parked my car. On either side, the sprinklers squirted and refracted light. The moss hung heavy on the overhead tree limbs. In the distance I could hear a mockingbird imitating a nutria, at the wrong time of day and far from the nearest salt marsh.

As I reached for the door handle on the Pinto, I suddenly remembered another question I had wanted to ask. I cursed myself for not keeping some kind of notebook, the way real investigators did.

Several seconds later I was back on Clancey's front porch, and I knocked on the door. There was no answer. I knew she was home, so I just trundled around the house to the back fence.

I saw them long before they could see me. Clancey had joined Meg at the poolside, and had removed her coverup. I could tell, even from a hundred feet away, that I had underestimated her previously. Clancey had kept herself well for her age. Her stomach was flat, devoid of the parous bulge that childbirth would have left her, and her breasts betrayed only the slightest effects of gravity. She was bending over Meg, rubbing oil on her back.

I felt uncomfortable, practically perverted, watching the tableau revealed to me as I stood secluded in the shadow of the rhododendrons. I should have retreated, out of respect for the women, but I couldn't. My curiosity overwhelmed my judgment, and I was still infatuated with Meg. Perhaps I was a bit envious of Clancey's access to her. Whatever the case, I stood in the arbor and watched, only distantly aware that I should be ashamed.

Meg rolled over and grabbed Clancey's hand, and pulled her down to the chaise. I could tell, even from my far vantage, that Clancey had been weeping softly as she massaged Meg's back. Meg sat and gathered Clancey into her arms. At first I thought it was an innocent attempt to comfort her, but then the embrace turned torrid. Meg drew Clancey's face to her own, and they kissed hungrily for several moments until Clancey pulled away and reached down to caress Meg.

I turned and left when Meg eased Clancey down to the chaise, and hunched down to begin kissing the inside of the widow's thighs. I knew what was coming, and I had no more appetite to play the voyeur.

All the way back to the Quarter, I struggled with my confusion. My first reaction, perhaps an unreasonable one, was to feel betrayed. I had rationalized my feelings for Meg to be more than they now appeared, partly out of my own yearning and loneliness, but more because it made me feel good about myself to believe that she wanted me.

I ran down the mental checklist of all the emotions I would have expected to feel—anger, rage, sadness, remorse, disappointment—and was mildly surprised to discover that they were all absent. I was only aware of a vague emptiness, situated somewhere between my head and heart, as if a vital organ had been ripped from me as I was conscious but anesthetized. It was the converse of the phantom limb phenomenon experienced by amputees, where they can feel an arm or leg long gone. It was torturously elusive, this feeling of loss where nothing was actually missing.

My consciousness was compartmentalized into layers, operating on myriad levels at one time. At the base was my raw-nerved emotional response to what I had observed, dominated not by some straight-laced sense of moral outrage, but rather by my own inadequacies and insecurities. I had romanticized my affair with Meg, despite her cautions that I shouldn't, and now blamed her for doing the nibble and stroke with Clancey Vincouer. I had known all along, in that rational, realistic self that I kept compartmentalized for solving problems, that she survived by using people like ladder rungs. Still, I had hoped that she would make an exception in my case.

On the next level was the awareness of a tangled system of relations. Even as I wrestled with my inadequate emotional response, I was trying to unravel the twisted series of sexual liaisons I had encountered since the day Cully Tucker brought Clancey to the bar. Clancey had slept with Lester, of course. Sammy Cain had screwed Clancey. Lester had raped, and later made love to, Meg. I had seen Meg fondling Clancey.

Meg had sex with me. Repeatedly.

Who was using whom? And for what purposes?

Finally, there was the outer crust of consciousness, the one which had consumed me for days. Who killed Lester Vincouer? How did they decide to frame me for it? How had the killer gotten so close to Lester without alarming him?

I had gone too long without sleep. Heat shimmers rose on the I-10 as I drove back toward the city, slyly lulling me into indifference. I fought to stay awake, and not only because I was driving. I couldn't escape the intuition that time was running out for me to save my skin. If I was frustrated, I could only imagine the bafflement Farley Nuckolls must have been feeling. It was getting to the point where he was likely to lock me up just to show the brass that he was still on the case. I couldn't find out much from jail.

I felt much the same as I did in the months just before I finally got it on with my first lover, Sally Mierscynski. It was a time of desperation and longing, and not the faintest idea how I would finally manage to cross over into that promised land which had been—supposedly—trod by so many of my peers. It was the sense of seeing, and perhaps even being able to smell, the ripest, sweetest, most luscious bunch of grapes on earth, just slightly out of reach. The temptation to drop the quest was balanced by the assurance that, once attained, the object of desire would yield rewards beyond measure. The anticipation was heightened by the maddening resolve of the killer not to be found.

I only hoped that, when I finally did find Lester's murderer, I would be able to convince Farley.

Twenty-three

I didn't have to wait long for Farley. He was at the bar when I got back there. I saw him sitting at a table on the far side, near the bandstand, nursing a Dixie Shorty had comped him. Cops always drink free at Holliday's.

I started to ignore him, run up to my room and throw myself at the first available mattress, but then thought better of it. Nuckolls wasn't a regular at my bar, or any other for that matter, so being here meant he wanted to talk. Drinking a beer meant it wasn't official. I drew up a chair and sat with him.

"I don't go on until ten tonight," I told him. "You're about nine hours early."

"Good," he said. "From what I hear, it would just ruin a cheap beer. You worry me, Gallegher."

"Gotta take a number for that these days."

"Off the record, you want to tell me why you were with Lucho Braga this morning?"

"You have a tail on me, Farley?"

"You always answer a question with a question?"

"Who made the telephone call?"

"Is that all you can ask? You're all anal retentive about that fucking phone call."

"You still don't know, then. See, Farley, if you can't figure out who called, and where they called from, then you've got no case against me. It's a classic frame."

"We know where the call came from, smartass. A pay phone."

"In which state?"

"It was in Kenner. At a strip shopping center. There's a bank of three phones, and the telephone company records told us it was the middle one."

"Jesus, Farley, Kenner's a good twenty minutes away from Lake Terrace. You're telling me some guy's going to see me at Lester Vincouer's home, and then drive clear across the bayou to call the cops? Get real."

He grasped the beer bottle ferociously, his knuckles white from the exertion.

"Why were you with Braga this morning?"

"Why are you asking this stuff off the record? Are you investigating this murder or not?"

"Will you answer the fucking question?" he yelled, slamming his fist onto the table. "For Christ's sake, Gallegher, I'm trying to keep your sorry ass out of Angola here, and you keep avoiding the questions."

"What in hell are you talking about, man? What do you care whether I go to Angola? I thought you couldn't wait to see them knock the fire out of my ass in Old Sparky."

He was becoming really agitated, and I had bought enough time to come up with an answer. It was a fine line I was trying to walk, between becoming a human fuse box and waiting for one of Braga's gunsels to aerate my skull.

"Okay, okay," I said, "You know all about Leduc. He fired me several days ago. My debt to him is paid off. I thought maybe Braga might be hiring. Man cannot live by cornet alone."

Farley eyed me warily, and then said, "Bullshit. I had a visit from your friend Cully Tucker this morning. He showed me some interesting investment records dating back almost five years. He seems to believe that Braga and Vincouer had some kind of ponzie scheme going, where Braga would buy low and Vincouer would drive up the price. So now Vincouer's dead, and you spend the morning noshing with Braga. I don't like the look of it. You do not travel in a savory crowd, Gallegher."

"What else did Cully tell you?"

"He mentioned that you were a guest at the Rampart lockup last night, after a run-in with this guy Sammy Cain that Ms. Vincouer asked you to find. I checked, and you paid Cain's fine this morning. I was not pleased. I would have enjoyed an opportunity to talk to him."

"I talked to him for you. He went after me because I was getting close to him. He wanted to lay me up for a few days so he could disappear. He won't be bothering me again."

"He bothers me, though. This guy was sleeping with Clancey Vincouer, and then he disappears days before Lester Vincouer is killed. Just to tie up all the loose ends, I would like to know where he was the night Vincouer died."

"Wait a minute," I said. "You knew I met with Braga, but you didn't know I saw Cain. There was no tail on me. You had someone at the restaurant. You've infiltrated Braga's program, haven't you?"

"You know I'm not going to answer that."

"So what are you saying? I'm off the hook? You're looking at Cain on this thing now?"

"Again with the questions. I don't know what you got yourself knotted up in, Gallegher, but I get the idea it involves more than just Vincouer's death. All I care about is clearing the books on the killing. You're a big guy, Cain's a big guy. All I have to go on is a phone call claiming there was a *big guy* at the Lakeshore Drive house near the time of the murder. You I've talked to. Now I want to talk to Cain. You got him out of jail. You want to tell me where he is?"

"This is beginning to sound more like an interrogation, and less like a friendly conversation," I said. "Listen, Braga doesn't want me talking about his business. Cully already told you everything I know about that.

It was a dead end, in regards to Vincouer. I don't want to go to prison, Farley, but you have to believe me when I tell you that I have no more idea who killed Vincouer than you do. I don't know where Cain is. I haven't seen him since this morning, and he didn't tell me where he was going. The fact is, I don't know shit. I'm back at square one."

"That puts you one step ahead of me," Nuckolls said. "For the record, if I had anything solid, you'd be back in lockup right now. You look dirty in this thing, but so does Cain, and Braga, and maybe even Leduc. Hell, maybe even Shorty was in on it." He lifted his bottle and saluted Shorty at the bar. Shorty glanced up, his face registering not a single known emotion.

"You call me if you find out anything I need to know," Nuckolls said. "I know your sense of civic duty isn't the best, but this is your ass riding on the line. I want to hear from you the minute you think of anything related to the murder. Got it?"

"Detective, I will make it my number one priority. Right now, though, I am about to drop from exhaustion. If you don't mind, I'm going to hand the investigation over to you, and go catch eight hours."

I left him sitting in the bar, and half-stumbled up the mildewed stairs to my quarters. It was a relief to know that I wasn't Nuckolls' only suspect, but sleep was still elusive and fitful. I kept flashing on the image of Clancey Vincouer, recumbent on her deck lounge chair, being serviced by the woman I hadn't been able to get out of my mind for days.

Clancey with Lester, Clancey with Cain, Lester with Meg, Meg with Clancey, Meg with me.

Meg with Cain?

I shook that one off. The implications of that pairing were simply too monstrous to contemplate.

Still, was it so outlandish? Meg had demonstrated beyond doubt her ability to adapt. If the situation required, she could just as easily have done the slap and tickle with Cain as with me.

I didn't like the directions my inquiries were taking me. I worried that I was conveniently ignoring something fundamental, some motive hidden in plain sight, so unmistakably obvious that it eluded discovery. I had to simplify, to slice more finely with Occam's Razor, look for the trees instead of the forest.

But first I had to sleep.

The dreams insinuated themselves slowly, but with an undeniable urgency. As my body rested, my unconscious mind began to work on the problems that had bedeviled me in sentience. All the players were lined up, with lists written on a wall over their heads. Each one, Clancey, Meg, Cain, Leduc, Braga, every person involved in Lester's life and death, was marked with a number, which I later supposed was a ranking of some kind. The lists contained names, times, motives, opportunities, possible rewards. Clancey hadn't been at the house when Lester was killed, but she had the most to gain by his death, money she claimed ran into the tens of millions of dollars. Cain could win, too, simply by returning to Clancey after a decent interval, but he had claimed that he wasn't planning to do this. Meg seemed to have nothing to gain, up to the point that I spied her going down on Clancey. At that moment, her stock went up tenfold. Was she merely consoling a close friend in an ultimately intimate manner, or was her sexual conquest of the grieving widow an overture to some kind of calculated grab for some of the loot?

Leduc seemed to gain the least. He had sent me to collect almost a quarter million, and as a result of the murder had not seen so much as a penny. On the other hand, he was the only person, besides the gooney Cajun brothers, Marcel and Rene, who knew for certain that I would be visiting Lester. Leduc's opportunity was occulted by his motive.

The dreams went on through the night, permutations of conspiracy unending and relentless. The Buddhists say that there are many ways to God. In my slumber, my alpha-driven mind constructed a hundred different paths that could have led to Lester's murder. Each one crumbled ultimately under its own weight, unsupported by either motive, opportunity, or means.

Finally, the mind surrendered to the inevitable conclusion that I simply still didn't know enough. I was trying to build a nuclear reactor with stone knives and bearskins, and succeeding only in driving myself nuts. Rather than overload and crash like some kind of primitive computer, my fevered brain abandoned the task of solving the unsolvable, and I drifted away into a dark, yielding softness, where nothing was more threatening than the temptation never to wake up.

Twenty-four

The telephone awakened me shortly after six that evening. The shadows were stretching across the library wall, and outside I could hear the Quarter cranking up for another night of debauchery. My head was full of mush and my mouth offended me as I reached for the receiver.

"Yeah," I said.

"I'm offended," Meg told me.

"Just a minute."

I sat upright in the bed, and rubbed my swollen eyes. I reached for the glass of water on the bedside table, and took a swallow, letting it swish around my mouth for a moment to clear out the dragons and give me time to think.

"Sorry," I said. "Offended?"

"You were at Clancey's house today, and you didn't take the time to say hello. Did you get an eyeful?"

Boy, did I, I wanted to say, but decided to keep it to myself.

"It was tempting. I had business with Clancey, though, and after our last conversation I wasn't sure you wanted to see me."

"Don't be silly. A lovers' spat. You violated our agreement. You tracked me down, and then accused me of the vilest crimes. What did you expect? I'm sorry I blew up at you that way, though. I guess I overreacted."

"So when did you decide I didn't kill Lester?"

There was pause on the line.

"That again?"

"It's an important question."

"It came to me slowly. Maybe it was your voice on my answering machine. You sounded so desperate. You really wanted me to believe you. Then, you were attacked by Sammy Cain. Why would he do something like that, if you weren't a threat to him? Thank God you had your sniper friend to protect you. Clancey told me all about it. How are you feeling?"

"My face hurts, my ribs hurt, I have trouble getting out of a chair, and there's this incidental ache in the middle of my chest that just won't seem to go away. I think I'm getting better, though."

"Can I make it up to you?"

"What did you have in mind?"

"I was thinking it would be nice to get away for a day. Take a trip somewhere."

"The Caribbean, maybe."

"Don't be silly. Neither of us can afford a trip like that right now."

"Yeah, and Farley Nuckolls told me not to leave town."

"Does that include boating on the lake?"

"I think we're a boat short."

"That's what you think. Clancey has a cabin cruiser, one of Lester's little indulgences. It's called the *Mariposa*. That's Spanish, for *Butterfly*. It's moored at the City Yacht Harbor. We would pack a lunch, take a day cruise out on the lake. Maybe catch some rays."

"The gentle lap of waves against the hull, the cry of seabirds..."

"I was thinking of another kind of lap and another kind of cry."

"Clancey would let you take this boat?"

"She already said I could. I have the keys in my hand, here."

I took another long swig of water. My mouth was parched and sticky.

"It does sound inviting."

"Well, don't get your hopes up. It's not a really big boat, only thirty feet, about. But it does have all the bells and whistles, and the sleeping cabin is nicely decorated."

"I don't know much about navigation."

"It's just Lake Pontchartrain, darling. All we need is a compass to find our way back. We could leave in the morning, and get back in time for dinner. I've been dying for you to take me to the Court of Two Sisters."

"Well, why not?" I said. "Maybe I've been too wrapped up in this Vincouer thing, after all. When were you planning to take this sail?"

"Are you free tomorrow?" she asked, with only the slightest breathiness.

"I don't work tonight. My lip is still too sore to blow the cornet. What say I get some more sleep, and I'll pick you up in the morning?"

"Is eight too early? I'm at Clancey's house."

"Eight's fine. I'll see you there, if you don't mind riding in a Pinto without air conditioning."

"We could take one of Clancey's cars, once you get here."

"Tell you what. Let's figure all that out when I get there in the morning."

We said our goodbyes, and I hung up the telephone. There was a hollow cold nodule resting in the pit of my stomach, a pang that had nothing to do with hunger. Little red flags were popping off all over my head, and my hearing was muffled and echoed at the same time. I was in way over my head, now, and there was nothing left but to play the game out and see where it led.

After a shower that left me feeling no less grimy than I had been before going to sleep, I picked up the telephone and dialed Stanley Porch's number.

It rang six or seven times at his end before he picked up. I could hear merry voices and music in the background. Stanley was having some sort of party.

"This is Gallegher," I told him.

"Hey, man, how in hell are you? This can't be a business call. I don't owe Leduc a cent right now."

"I don't work for Leduc anymore. I need a favor."

There was a pause, and suddenly the party noise was muffled, as if Porch had stepped into another room.

"Gallegher, I got guests here. Can't it wait?"

"No," I said, trying to sound menacing. "I seem to recall keeping you from getting smoked about two weeks ago, and in my memory you showed a lot of gratitude. I also recall that you agreed to come when I called."

"Yeah, but this is business, man. I got clients here."

"I don't doubt it. I also would hazard to guess you got three or four whores up there to entertain them. Maybe I'll just call the precinct house and let them know you're pandering these days."

"No! Don't do that. These guys are important marks. I land this deal, and it could make my whole year, you know what I mean."

"Listen to me, Porch. That leg-breaking I spared you wasn't canceled, it was just delayed, and I own it now. You don't want to fuck with me when I'm calling in your marker, no more than you would Leduc. I need help now, and you're the guy can put it together."

I could almost hear the sweat running down his face over the telephone. He had his ass in a crack, and I was pulling from the other side.

"What do you want?" he asked finally.

And I told him.

"You're nuts," he protested. "How in hell am I gonna get that done tonight?"

"I don't care how. I just want it done. You make the arrangements. You call me when it's done, with the details, and I'll set up all the rest. Got it?"

"I got it. This is gonna cost me big, you know."

"Have you checked out the day rates at the orthopedic hospital lately? You're getting off cheap. You get this done for me, and your debt is written off."

He agreed, and then hung up to do my bidding. It was a powerful feeling. I could see why Leduc and Braga and the Anollis liked it so much.

There was a fire in my belly now, and it wasn't enthusiasm. I could see that it was going to be long night, so I gobbled a couple of antacids and a glass of milk before grabbing my Saints jacket. I locked my door after setting the burglar alarm, and took the outside steps three at a time to Toulouse Street.

I had a lot of errands to make before daybreak.

Twenty-five

It had been months since I had seen the sun rise over the bayou.

Frankly, the sight was more romantic in concept than execution. Still, it was a novelty, as the sky streaked with the first false dawn, then deepened into a royal blue horizon again before the first pink rays arced over the salt marsh flats. The early morning humidity acted as a prism, staining the heavens with all the colors of the rainbow, and painting the few wispy clouds with a watercolor melange of violets and sapphires. It did the heart good to behold the natural wonder of a new day's birth.

I only hoped I would live to see it end.

There was a scant ground fog clinging to the earth as I turned into the Vincouer driveway, and parked in the turnaround at the front walk. Meg was waiting for me on the porch, rocking in one of the straight-back rockers with the plain round finials. She was wearing a mid-thigh length sleeveless sundress, cut daringly at the bosom, and she was holding an actual picnic basket in her lap, authentic right down to the checked cloth covering all the goodies. Her hair had been meticulously done, poofed out to *here* like a model in a high fashion magazine. I was sure I saw her eyes sparkle, and I felt conspicuously underdressed.

She rose and stepped lithely down to the driveway.

"Do you want to take one of the Mercedes?" she asked. "Clancey said it was okay."

"Let's take my car," I told her. "It's going to be nice day, we can ride with the windows open."

"Good thing I brought a scarf."

She pulled a silk scarf from the picnic basket, and started to tie it around her head after she sat in the passenger seat.

"Should have brought a sweater," I told her. "It might get chilly out on the salt today."

"We can always go below if it gets uncomfortable."

"City Yacht Harbor?"

"Yes. You know where it is?"

I knew. It hadn't been all that long since Trent Kirby had tried to feed me to the sharks out in the Gulf, because he was afraid I was going to turn him over to the cops for dognapping a champion purebred teacup poodle. It had been a nasty scene. I was still here, but the sharks hadn't gone hungry that day.

We took Lakeshore Drive out across Bayou St. John and the Outfall Canal to the Marina, which we curved around to the Yacht Harbor. We parked in the shell lot near the north end, off Breakwater Drive. Meg got out of the car first, and pointed toward the second pier down.

"It's Slip B-12, the *Mariposa*."

She was an impressive craft, all thirty feet of her, bobbing sedately in the swell, with the twin teal and purple chevrons decorating her gleaming white hull. The pilot house towered over the deck, and there was a line of portholes midway between the gunwale and the waterline, through which I could glimpse the fine teak woodwork in the cabin.

"You know how to drive this thing?" I asked.

"My father was a Navy man, headed up the Power Squadron when I was a lass. I grew up on the water."

"Hold on," I said, and walked to the back of the Pinto. I opened the trunk lid, and pulled out a broken-down rod and tackle box.

"What's that?"

"It may be a long day on the water. I could eat that whole basket in about five minutes. I thought we might get in a little deepwater fishing."

She surveyed me with a look somewhere between coquettish and quandary.

"I had thought we might find something else to do."

"Sounds great to me. We do have to remember, though, that forty is a distant memory for me. I may not be as good as I once was, but I'm as good, once, as I ever was, if you get my drift. There will be time to drop the line a few times. Come on, now, let's get aboard."

We walked out to Slip B-12, and boarded the *Mariposa*. She looked even bigger from the deck than she had from the parking lot. I stowed the fishing tackle at the stern, while Meg ducked into the cabin to put the food in the refrigerator. I met her at the pilot house.

She put the key in the ignition, and flipped the switch for the bilge blowers.

"It will take a couple of minutes to clear the tanks of fumes," she said, throwing her arms around my neck. "Bet I can make it pass more quickly. I'm sorry about our fight, darling."

She pulled her face up to my own, and pressed her lips against mine. I found that, despite myself, I responded to her ardor, and the time did pass quickly indeed.

She pulled away, breathing heavily, and reached out to touch my bruised lips.

"I'm sorry. Does it still hurt much?"

"Other things hurt worse. I'll live."

She turned back to the control panel. It only took a couple of seconds for the diesels to catch, with an oily insecticide smell and a deep inboard rumble. The water to the stern boiled from the exhaust, and Meg pushed the telegraph to quarter back.

We had cast off lines before boarding, and the *Mariposa* slowly eased out of the slip into the channel between piers. Meg massaged the wheel, and the boat turned effortlessly. In minutes we were headed out into Lake Pontchartrain at half speed ahead. As soon as we cleared the marina channel, she shoved the telegraph full ahead and the craft began planing across the swells and troughs. The sun was several degrees over the horizon, and the atmosphere had taken on a transparent layered blueness that was like a prize shooting marble, with swirls of lacy clouds streaking the azure skyscape. It was a fine day to be at sail, with the mist and spray in the air, and gulls screeching desperately as they tried to keep pace with the standard where clear sailing flags fluttered in time with the widening wake. We passed small sailing vessels and fishing trawlers, and finally broke out of the blue water into deep green brine, and the wake began to foam from the cavitation in the brack. The city receded in the distance, and finally it winked out altogether, and there was nothing in all directions but verdant water and the brilliantly clear sky above. Meg reached out and pulled the stick to all stop. The diesels spun down to idle, and she turned the key to *off*.

"Damned nice of Clancey to let you use the boat," I said.

"She likes me."

"I know."

She stepped down from the pilot house, and gazed at me curiously.

"What's that supposed to mean?"

I rested my haunches on the stern transom, and crossed my arms, never taking my eyes off hers.

"Let's just say I know Clancey's closet has a revolving door, and you have the key."

She shook her head, her fluffed-out hair bouncing in the breeze.

"I haven't any idea what you mean. Are you hungry yet?"

"I saw you, Meg. Yesterday, when I came to see Clancey. I forgot to ask her a question, and I walked around the house to the pool area. She has a striking figure for a woman her age. You two looked good together."

"You watched us?"

"Up to the point that you began to engage in a certain unnatural act. After that, I felt a little dirty, so I split."

"Like you've never gone down on a woman…"

"I went down on you, as I recall, but that's not the point. I wasn't after your millions at the time."

She broke eye contact first, as she shrugged her shoulders and stared out over the waves.

"You still don't understand, Pat. Clancey is a woman in need. I can satisfy those needs. Besides, I never said my own closet had a one-way door. I also never promised to be faithful. Neither of us did. Are you jealous, all of a sudden, because you saw me making it with a woman?"

"No," I said. "I'm pissed off because you're trying to frame me for killing Lester Vincouer."

Her eyes snapped back on mine, with a feral, angry light that made my balls draw up a centimeter or two.

"Fuck you," she said, "Fuck you twice."

"You gave it away yourself," I continued. "When you called me last night to ask me on this little one-way sailing jaunt. You said that you were thankful that I had my '*sniper friend*' to protect me when Sammy Cain tried to take me out behind the Jax Brewery. I never told you I had hired a sniper."

"Clancey told me about it."

"I didn't tell her, either. All I told Clancey was that I had someone protecting me. I never mentioned a sniper. In fact, I only told one person about that, and it was Sammy Cain, when we met in Octi's bar on Bourbon Street yesterday morning. The only way you could know that I had hired a sniper was if you had talked with Cain."

"That's ridiculous."

"Is it? It seems pretty logical to me. Lester made a sweetheart deal with Lucho Braga, in which Braga would buy into a company cheap, and then Lester would punch up the share price by purchasing large blocks of stock. You knew all about the 'retirement account' in the Bahamas, because Clancey seems to have told everyone about it. When Sammy Cain leeched onto Clancey, he came around, and you saw in him a kindred spirit. Don't deny it. You said so yourself the first night you came to Holliday's. You described him right down to his toenails, and said later that you were no different. You people could spot each other a mile away in a pea soup fog.

"So you and Cain struck up a deal. You saw a chance at a really big score. The only problem was that you didn't know which bank the money was in, or what the password was. You slept with Lester to get the password, but he wouldn't give it up. He didn't even tell Clancey what it was.

"So, you went to Plan B. If you couldn't screw the password out of Lester, you would beat it out of him. This is where the story takes a strange twist, though. You needed a fall guy to take the heat for Lester's murder, to draw suspicion away while you and Cain disappeared with the money. I just happened along at the right time, when Cully introduced Clancey to me and she hired me to find Cain. You said, on the night Cain attacked me, that you hadn't told me about your job dealing blackjack because of my gambling addiction. I never told you about that. Cully told me he didn't tell you or Clancey. The only other person who did know was Leduc. You knew I worked for Leduc, because Cully did tell Clancey about that, and you two had no secrets, supposedly. The way I see it, you and Cain approached Leduc with an elegant plan for getting Lester's money. Leduc called me in with an enticing offer. I was to shake a quarter million out of Lester for a gambling debt, and in return my debt to him would be settled. I was sure to jump at a chance like that.

"The fact was, though, that Lester never owed Leduc a dime. It was all a ruse to get me to make a visit to Lester, after Cain killed him, so that the police could catch me there and make me for the murder. In return for setting me up, Leduc was promised a percentage of the take from the Bahamian account.

"The plan blew up in your face, though, when I didn't get caught there. Oh, I was there, all right, but I got out and covered my trail before the cops arrived. Leduc panicked and cut me loose, you wouldn't return my calls, and I started sticking my nose into everyone's business.

"What finally tipped me off was Sammy Cain, when we were talking in Octi's yesterday. He had no real reason to attack me the way he did. I was nowhere near finding him, no matter what he said. I could smell that lie from Poydras Street. What really scared him was that I had found you, and the two of you were afraid that I'd add everything up. He decided to kill me, make it look like a robbery, and disappear. This would have taken me off the trail, and left Farley Nuckolls without a suspect. Eventually, you figured, the whole thing would be written off as an unsolved case. Anyway, when I was talking to Cain yesterday, he lit a cigar with a pack of matches from the Paradise Beach Holiday Inn."

I pulled the pack of matches I had palmed from the bar at Octi's from my shirt pocket.

"This pack of matches, as it happens. Paradise Beach is in Nassau, the Bahamas. Bahamian banks are famous for their numbered secret accounts. You let Cain into the Vincouer house the night Lester was killed, before you and Clancey went out. Cain snuck up on Lester and looped a piano wire around his neck, and threatened to kill him if Lester didn't tell him all about the 'retirement account'. Lester gave him the information, but Cain was smart enough to know that Lester could have the money wire-transferred long before Cain could lay a hand on it. So Cain garroted Lester, and took off for Paradise Beach. Cain made the telephone call to the police from Kenner—he lived there, remember. Once he accessed the account and confirmed that the money was there, he was supposed to transfer Leduc's take into another account. Meanwhile, you stayed behind and saw to it that Nuckolls was put on my trail as the prime suspect. "

"You're fantasizing," Meg told me. "You're delirious. Nobody would believe that story."

"No? I called Clancey Vincouer last night, after I spoke with you. It was a gamble, but if you had answered the phone I could have covered with some cocked-up reason, maybe to change the time for our date today. I asked her the question I had intended to ask yesterday. She told me that you and she left her house at seven o'clock on the night Lester was killed. You had told me earlier that you would leave at seven-thirty. That gave Cain a half-hour lead time to kill Lester, get back to Kenner, and call the police before I arrived at the house."

"It still doesn't prove anything."

"That's what Leduc said last night, too. After you asked me on this little excursion, I drove out to his home and laid the story out for him. He laughed at first, but then I urged him to check his numbered account. Imagine his surprise when he discovered that Cain had neglected to make the transfer. He confirmed all my guesses. That's proof."

Her face darkened, and her eyes betrayed her with a trapped, desperate emptiness. He voice dropped and became low and guttural.

"You think you're so goddamned smart. You don't have a thing. Nobody will believe you. Leduc won't testify against us, because he'd have to admit he was an accomplice. The money can't be found. You put in a lot of work for nothing. When Sammy gets finished with you, even the sharks won't want what's left."

I had, once more, underestimated her. She wasn't going to break down just because I uncovered all her secrets. Of course, I wasn't finished yet.

"The hell with it," I said. "The hell with everything."

I made my way back to the transom, grabbed the broken down fishing rod, and began to assemble it.

"It was a good plan, all things considered," I told her. "You made only one major mistake."

"What was that?" she asked sullenly.

"Your reach exceeded your grasp." I fitted the ocean reel on the rod, and ran the hundred pound test line through the ferrules. "You and Cain were small-time con artists, pulling the small game against helpless women who only needed a little affection to open their purses and homes. Neither of you had ever committed a murder before. You couldn't know that there were a million ways to screw up, or that I might not be caught in the house with Lester's corpse, or that I might be as good at asking the right questions as I am."

I tied a ten ounce lead weight to the line, and then a spinner lure attached to a two inch barbed hook. "You were just out of your element. You blew it, and you're caught."

"What are you going to do?" she asked.

"Damned if I know. It depends on how generous you are. I'm a simple man, and I have simple needs." I cast the line out, twenty yards or so, and sat on the fisherman's chair just forward of the transom. "What do you think's fair?"

She didn't answer. Instead, a metallic *ka-chung* rang out across the water, a dead, hard sound without echo. I didn't turn around. It wouldn't have mattered. I knew who it was.

"Mr. Cain," I greeted. "It's about time you showed yourself. Been lounging in one of the closets down below?"

"Don't move, Gallegher," Cain said.

"Oh, yeah, right. Like I'm going to get up and run away. Come on, have a seat over here. You can stay out of my reach."

I gestured toward the bench seats on the gunwales, and kept my eyes on the line bobbing in the waves. Out of the corner of my eye, I saw Cain edge around to the seats, and slide down, all the time training the automatic toward the middle of my chest.

"Pompano are supposed to be running today," I said. "Meg told me last night that she couldn't wait for me to take her to the Court of Two Sisters. Ever eaten there, Sammy?"

"Yeah," he said.

"Their *pompano en papillote* is to die for. Tried it?"

"No."

"Too bad. There's nothing to match it up at Angola, so I hear. Do me a favor, Sammy, and take that envelope out of the tackle box."

I pushed the box toward him with my foot, taking care that I never took my hands off the fishing rod. He kept the pistol on me, and reached down to grab the envelope I had stashed in the top compartment.

"What the fuck is this?" he asked.

"Read it."

He handed it to Meg, who tore the envelope open. She pulled out a single sheet of typed paper and a smaller envelope. She unfolded the sheet.

"You should look at this," she told Cain.

"Read it to me."

She read out loud the paper I had typed.

Scat: I am going to be leaving the City Yacht Harbor at eight-thirty tomorrow morning on the Mariposa, Slip B-12. Also on the boat will be Meg Coley and Sammy Cain. I suspect that they are going to try to kill me out on the lake. I would appreciate it very much if you would watch for the Mariposa to come back in. If I am not on the boat, I would consider it a very great favor if you would kill everyone who is. Make it messy. Enjoy the money I gave you, and happy hunting.

Pat

"My friend does not miss," I said. "If I say kill you, you will die. It's that simple."

"Well, Gallegher," Cain said, "You're royally fucked. You see, I transferred all of the money from Vincouer's account into one I set up in Nassau when I was there, and the boat's tanks are full. We can take this little floating brothel of Lester's all the way to Galveston or Key West if we want. There's no need to go back to New Orleans. Your boy is in for a long wait."

"Open the other envelope."

Meg tore into the envelope.

"It's a copy of a letter I sent to Farley Nuckolls this morning before I picked up Meg. I'll save you the time. It outlines the whole plan to kill Lester, from motive to opportunity to method. I also told him about this boat trip today, and suggested that you might not want to go back to

New Orleans. I also figured that you might be able to make either Texas or Florida. That letter asks him to alert the Coast Guard. With any luck, they'll be painting this craft with their radar within an hour."

Cain jumped up, but had the presence of mind to keep his pistol on me.

"Let me see that," he said, and grabbed the letter from Meg. It took him all of a minute to scan the note to Nuckolls.

"Fuck me!" he exclaimed. "Fuck it all!"

And he turned back to face me. His mouth dropped open, as he stared down the barrel of the Browning nine I had stowed under my ample ass when I sat down to fish.

"Round chambered and safety off," I told him. "What we have here is a standoff, Cain. How many people have you killed in your sterling career as a con man? I have five to my credit. That gives me an edge on experience."

"What in hell..."

"You think I'm so stupid that I'm going to get on a boat on the open water without a piece? Sammy, you are so green at this thing that it boggles the imagination you got this far. I would have figured it out days ago, except I was hampered by my innate sense of economy. I was looking for one person who killed Lester Vincouer. How was I to know that everyone did it?"

"What now?" he asked.

"I see two options. We can shoot it out, winner take all. Or we stand here drawing down on each other until either the Coast Guard shows up, or Leduc gets here."

"Leduc!"

"Yeah. When he figured out that you were going to stiff him, he decided to meet us out here on the lake. He wasn't about to let you get away with all the money. Tell me, Cain, how much is there in all?"

Sammy kept the gun leveled, but he was getting shaky. It isn't all that heavy, holding a pistol on someone, unless you do it for a long time. After several minutes, twenty-five ounces starts to drag on the arm muscles.

"A little over four million."

"How little over?"

"Six hundred thousand."

"What was Leduc's take?"

"A fifth."

"So you take forty, and Meg gets forty, and Leduc gets twenty. Leduc does not like to get shafted out of almost a million dollars. It's worth his time to make the trip. If Leduc gets here first, he splits the money right down the middle with you. If the Coast Guard gets here first, nobody gets a thing, except you and Meg, who get the 'E' ticket ride in the electric chair at Angola."

Meg grabbed at Cain's shoulder.

"Jesus, Sammy. You said it would be all right."

I held my Browning steady, with my elbow braced against my thigh, while his gun became shakier, and I let him think it over for a few minutes.

"Sammy," Meg said, pointing to the south. A fast boat had just crested the horizon, and was speeding toward us.

"Coming like a bat out of hell," I said. "I'd say it's Leduc. A cutter can't make that kind of time."

"What do you get out of this, Gallegher?" Cain asked.

"My name gets cleared. Leduc has a lot of pull at the NOPD. In his gratitude to me for turning him on to your double-cross, he's going to grease the right palms and have the Vincouer investigation go away. You can keep your dirty money. I just don't want to go to prison."

A speck appeared about a thousand feet over the water, three or four miles downwind, and slowly grew larger as it approached the *Mariposa*. Scat Boudreaux and his pilot circled twice in the seaplane I'd ordered Stanley Porch to find, before putting down fifty yards from the boat.

"What in hell?" Cain exclaimed.

"I lied. The guy who was supposed to be at the dock in New Orleans is actually on that plane. He's here to see to it that nothing bad happens to me. I had to find some way to keep you here."

"You okay, Slick?" Scat yelled across the water.

"Not a scratch," I yelled back. "Is that as close as you can get?"

"Can't risk taking off a wing. You're going to have to swim for it."

Cain glanced over at Meg, and then back at me.

"Swim?"

"Scat's my ride home. Once this game plays out, I'm not about to go back in with either you or Leduc. After the way I've been set up, and considering what I know, it wouldn't be a good idea to trust any of you."

Scat sat in the open door of the seaplane, a high-powered automatic rifle braced loosely against his shoulder.

It took several minutes for the *Joker Poker* to pull alongside. Leduc was piloting. The Cajuns were carrying Tec-9 submachine pistols, but I had a bad feeling that they had been modified to full-fire capability.

"We've got a face-off," I yelled to Leduc. "He got the drop on me before I could cover him."

"It's okay," Leduc said. "Stand back. The boys will take it from here."

I sat back in the fishing seat, my Browning resting against my thigh, but ready.

Leduc walked to the gunwale of the *Joker Poker* and stared Sammy Cain down.

"Did you forget something, Cain?"

"What do you mean?" Sammy asked.

"We had a deal, us. You were supposed to transfer some money into my account. I just checked it again, and it's not there."

"It's in my account," Cain said. "I took it out of Lester's account and put it where nobody could find it but me. You think I trusted you? I wanted to make sure I would be safe before I transferred your share."

"It's too late for that," Leduc said. "We're going to do the transfer here, right now, on the ship-to-shore."

"I don't think so," Cain said.

Leduc turned to Marcel.

"Kill the woman."

"No!" I shouted. "Meg walks on this one, Leduc."

Leduc turned to me, his dark Arcadian eyes narrowed to irritated slits.

"You're calling shots here, Gallegher?"

"My friend in the floatplane has instructions. No matter what, Meg and I are out of it."

"Are you stupid, Gallegher?" Leduc said, his face twisted with contempt. "This bitch set you up to take the ride for Vincouer's murder. Just which head are you thinking with, you?"

"Call me sentimental. Call me a fool. I don't care. Cain's the one who tried to stiff you, Leduc. Your beef's with Cain."

Leduc looked like a three card monte dealer whose whole shuck had been rearranged while he wasn't looking. It took him several seconds to reshuffle.

"Okay," he said. "It's getting late. Cain, I want your account number now. If you don't give it up, I'm going to have Rene shoot you up and call it a wash. It's occurred to me that dealing with you has become more troublesome than it's worth."

I swiveled the seat to face Cain.

"I'd give it up if I were you. You can do the transfer, settle for whatever you can get out of the deal, and disappear. It beats dying."

Cain shifted his weight from one foot to the other, as his eyes moved from me to Leduc. His head was still working overtime measuring all the angles, and they all came up obtuse. He was, simply put, not the brightest crook I had ever run across.

"We do the deal, just the way we said, right?"

"No," Leduc replied. "We do it my way. I have to come out on the lake to do this thing, it raises my end. I want half."

"Half!" Cain shouted. "That means Meg and I only get a quarter each."

"Can't spend a penny if you're dead," I offered.

"You shut up!" Cain shouted, swinging the gun toward me. Out of the corner of my eye I could see Scat stiffen and draw a bead on him.

"Watch it, Cain. My cover's getting nervous."

He glanced over toward the plane and took the pistol off me.

Leduc leaned forward, his hands resting on the gunwale of the *Joker Poker*.

"I'm getting impatient, Cain!"

As if on cue, both Rene and Marcel raised their automatic pistols, ready to finish it.

"Okay!" Cain yelled. "We'll do it. The account is with the Bank of Nova Scotia. Number 4387602. The password is BUZZSAW."

"Gallegher will do the transfer," Leduc announced. "I'm not taking my eyes off you, Cain, until I'm over the horizon, you got that? Come on over, Gallegher."

I stepped over the gunwales of both boats, and was directed to the ship-to-shore radio at the helm. Leduc had set up a laptop computer to make the arrangements, and he gave me the directions. He had pre-loaded all the electronic service numbers for the Bahamian banks, and it took me all of ten minutes to shift two and a half very large into Leduc's account.

Leduc instructed me to step back onto the *Mariposa*. It occurred to me that the situation was about to get very dangerous.

"You're one stupid fuck, you know that?" Leduc said to Cain. "We had a deal, Cain, a generous one for you. You had to get greedy, you and your whore there. Well, it's gonna cost you, big."

I'm not sure to this day what Leduc meant by that, but Cain apparently saw it as a threat. He raised his automatic and shot Marcel twice, high in the chest. Little scarlet florets erupted on his white shirt, and he staggered back before his brain shut down, then he simply collapsed to the deck, striking his head against the gunwale. Rene swung the Tec-9 around in a spastic reaction to his brother's death. As the arc passed me, he instinctively squeezed the trigger, and splinters of teak and mahogany blew out of the deck a half meter from my feet.

Two biting cracks echoed across the salt, and I knew that Scat had opened up on the second bodyguard. I heard Meg issue a muffled, sickeningly truncated scream as Scat kicked off two shots into Rene, and the second Cajun was taken off his feet by the impact of the rifle rounds. Leduc was just pulling his automatic from a shoulder holster under his left arm. He had been so certain that the Cajuns would protect him that I doubted he had even taken the safety off.

Cain drilled him through the chest twice before Leduc's gun was all the way out of his holster. Leduc crumpled to the deck of the *Joker Poker*, dead before his head came to rest.

I had hoped Cain would stop there, but in his puny, greedy little brain he probably saw an opportunity to walk off with the whole prize. Maybe I had known all along that he would make a try for me. In any case, I was ready. He turned his pistol on me. I was faster and better. He hadn't even gotten the automatic all the way up before I blew a hole in his chest the size of a grapefruit, just the way Scat described it. His eyes took on that glazed, fish market look I'd seen all too many times before, and he dropped the .45 to the *Mariposa's* deck.

"You fucked up," I told him as he fell to his knees. "You thought I wouldn't be ready. I never trusted you."

I couldn't tell you to this day whether he heard it all. I tossed the Browning over the gunwale, and it disappeared into the water.

Meg was lying on the deck at the base of the ladder to the pilot house. There was a neat row of crimson flowers laced diagonally across her chest from right to left, and it didn't take a surgeon to see that Rene hadn't left a decent organ untouched. Her eyes were open, and her mouth was moving a little as I knelt to give her what help I could.

I leaned down to try to make out what she was saying. She drew in as large a breath as she was able to manage, and whispered.

"You are one lucky son of a bitch."

With the last word, blood bubbled from her mouth and nose, filling the air with the acrid stink of a ruined body, which mixed nauseatingly with the odor of burned cordite smoke that hung in the air like a deadly fog. She tried to take two more breaths, racking failures at respiration, and her body stiffened spastically before going limp.

I closed her eyes. It was the least I could do. The others didn't matter.

Crossing the deck, I jumped from the *Mariposa* to the *Joker Poker*, and made some notes from the computer Leduc had neglected to shut off before drawing down on Cain. After stepping back onto the Mariposa, I ditched the fishing tackle and the letters I had given Meg and Cain, and dove over the side. The entire time I swam toward the seaplane, all I could think of was how ironic it would be to survive the blood bath on the *Mariposa*, only to be eaten by sharks on the last leg home.

After what seemed like three lifetimes, I pulled myself onto the pontoon of the seaplane, and Scat helped me up into the cabin. The pilot started the engine immediately, and seconds later we were airborne. We circled the boats one more time, and Scat let out a low whistle.

"Man, they got chewed up something horrible, them. You are one lucky son of a bitch."

"Yeah," I said, with one last regretful glance at Meg, sprawled out on the fine wood deck. "Everyone seems to think so."

Epilogue

The bad ones come back to get you. It doesn't matter if your rational, logical self knows they're deader than dirt and have been for months, they still find a way to sneak into your bedroom at night and dance around on your face until you lurch upright with lemur eyes and wet rolling off your back. Sam Spade, Mike Hammer, and Philip Marlowe notwithstanding, you don't ship one off to that undiscovered land from whose bourne no traveler returns without paying the freight in sleepless nights.

It's two months gone now, that bloody day on Lake Pontchartrain, and I still can't seem to hang eight hours of sleep together without a little horror break. I'm sitting in my recliner, my feet hanging out the window of my humble quarters over Holliday's, and I'm fingering some interesting vignettes on the Conn band cornet, even though I can't seem to muster the energy to pucker up and blow. At my side is a frosty bottle of Dixie, the beer that makes better musicians of us all.

It's my sixth this fine evening.

Farley got my letter, courtesy of Stanley Porch, just about the same time I was drawing down on Cain. The Coast Guard found the boats sometime that afternoon. I had lied, of course. There was nothing in the real letter to Farley that indicated I would be on the Mariposa, and you know now that Scat Boudreaux wasn't waiting at the Marina. When they found the boats, it confirmed everything I had told him, and he decided the case was closed.

I visited him the next day, and provided a statement. He was cordial and appreciative, but his face made it clear that he still thought I had something to do with the violent way this whole thing ended. He was satisfied that the money was forever consigned to a couple of anonymous accounts in the Caribbean, especially after Clancey confirmed that Lester had been salting his illicit proceeds there. I still don't think he trusts me, but I was cleared, and I knew I didn't kill Lester Vincouer, so at least that turned out the way it should have.

I don't feel so bad about Cain and Leduc. Their avarice led them to hatch a plan to kill Lester Vincouer, and if they had been caught they would have taken turns soiling Old Sparky at Angola, so in a way I just saved the State of Louisiana a bundle of money in legal fees.

I'm still bothered about Meg, though. I suppose I knew, going in, that Cain was going to have to be fragged. He was too volatile, too prone to rash, stupid acts to be trusted.

Somehow, up to the moment that Rene laced up her lush, voluptuous torso, though, I had thought I had found a way to spare Meg. In that I failed, and I haven't slept all that well since.

Looking back on it, I guess I should have gone to Farley as soon as I figured out how and by whom Lester was murdered. On the other hand, if I had done that, I never would have had a chance at all that money.

Nassau was sunny and warm, and the waters in the cruise ship harbor were as clear as fine crystal. I took a couple of hours out of my vacation to open a numbered account in a Costa Rican bank branch there. The Bank of Nova Scotia was only too happy to honor my claim to the funds in account number 4387602, as soon as I produced Cain's password. Likewise, Leduc's bank was delighted to help me transfer the two and half million I had placed there the week before.

I didn't keep all of it, of course. Scat got his five grand, and I gave some to Dag to renovate the plumbing in the parish and stock the soup kitchen for a while. He was grateful, and he didn't ask questions. He knows it all comes up even in the bottom of the ninth. Cully Tucker wanted to write off his end, since he felt so bad about getting me into this sorry gig in the first place, but when it came down to brass tacks he took ten grand for his legal work.

I gave most of the money to Clancey Vincouer, and told her that Meg had given it to me for safekeeping before she and Cain went out to meet Leduc on the lake. She bought the story, I think, and in my version Meg wasn't totally vilified. It made Clancey feel better, though I believe that she will be a lonely woman for a very long time.

I kept about a million. It was far and away the smaller portion of Lester's retirement account, and I figured that twenty percent was a pretty decent commission for what was essentially found money. I couldn't invest it stateside, you realize, because of the tax thing, so I just left it in my Costa Rican numbered account. It earns a fairly decent rate of interest, considering the current prime, and by the time my chops give out it will constitute the principle for a reasonable pension.

I still do favors for friends, and friends of friends, though nothing since has achieved quite the level of danger I found in the Clancey Vincouer incident. That's fine with me. It worries me, the thought that I might get my fat fanny shot out from under me with all that money sitting in the bank unclaimed.

So, I grab what sleep I can, jam the night away with Sockeye, shoot the breeze with Shorty, and try to keep a low profile with the law. You could say that life is back to normal, after a fashion. The world keeps turning as ever before, and my favorite stars keep returning at night to assure me that my personal tragedies are the temporal stuff of dust and smoke, which will dissipate in the passage of days and months, and for that I am thankful.

For I am, after all, one lucky son of a bitch.

About the Author

Richard Helms has worn many hats in his four and a half decades. He has been an entertainer, actor, radio announcer, university instructor, racing driver, and is presently a forensic psychologist working for the courts in his home state, where he specializes in the management and treatment of sex offenders. When he isn't writing, he indulges his other hobbies, including reading, gourmet cooking, building guitars and violins, and pulling for his beloved Charlotte Hornets.

Mr. Helms lives with his spouse, Elaine, their two children, and four cats, in Weddington, North Carolina.